Far South

Far South

David Enrique Spellman

SERPENT'S TAIL

Partially funded by an Arts Council of Wales Creative Wales Award.

A complete catalogue record for this book can be obtained from the British Library on request

First published in 2011 by Serpent's Tail,
an imprint of Profile Books Ltd
3A Exmouth House
Pine Street
London EC1R 0JH
www.serpentstail.com

ISBN 978 1 84668 810 2
eISBN 978 1 84765 772 5

Designed and typeset by sue@lambledesign.demon.co.uk
Printed by Clays, Bungay, Suffolk

10 9 8 7 6 5 4 3 2 1

Mixed Sources
Product group from well-managed forests and other controlled sources
www.fsc.org Cert no. TT-COC-002227
© 1996 Forest Stewardship Council
FSC

You have in your hands extracts from the casebook of Juan Manuel Pérez, a private investigator, who was contracted to search for Gerardo Fischer, the founder and director of the Real and Present Theater Company. Fischer disappeared on January 9th 2006 from the Temenos artists' colony in the hills near the town of Ciudad Azul, a lakeside resort on the western shore of the Lago Gran Paraíso, in the Sierras of Córdoba. Transcripts of witness statements, some written down later, have been interspersed with the casebook narrative, along with a thirty-page section of a graphic novel/diary that belongs to Damien Kennedy, the company's set designer. More responses to Gerardo's disappearance are available on the Far South Project website in text, film and image. The url-addresses or keywords are found in this book.

Gerardo Fischer left South America, as did many others under political threat, in the early seventies and spent much of his life traveling the world, with longer stays in Rome, Sydney and New York. In 2004, he returned to Argentina to put on new theater productions including his adaptation of Fernando Pessoa's *Book of Disquiet*.

Our deepest thanks go to Juan Manuel Pérez for the materials from his casebook. This is his personal response to Gerardo's disappearance and, as such, is as much his story as Gerardo's.

Clara Luz Weissman,
Far South Project Coordinator.[1]

1 http://bit.ly/farsouth1

Extract from the casebook of Juan Manuel Pérez
January 10th 2006
Hours: 16:00 to 17:30

I first heard of the disappearance of the Uruguayan theater director, Gerardo Fischer, not long after four p.m. on January 10th 2006. I was stuck in a traffic jam in the town of Ciudad Azul. Ciudad Azul is beautiful lakeside resort about seven hundred kilometers west of Buenos Aires, in the Sierras of Córdoba. The hotels fill up in the summer with people trying to escape the heat of the city. No chance of that today, the temperature must have been around thirty-five degrees. The sun on the black metal of my Ford Executive had heated it up like an oven.

My cell phone rang.

A woman's voice: 'Is this Juan Manuel Pérez?'

'What can I do for you?'

'Are you the Juan Manuel Pérez who used to work for the federal police?'

'That's right.'

'This is Ana Valenzuela from the Temenos Artists Colony.'

I knew this woman. A few years previously, I'd been the investigating officer on two brutal robberies they'd had up there. And I'd put away a certain Pablo Arenas, and his nephew. Three bent local cops had sold Arenas the guns to do the robberies and had taken quiet money from him. They got jailed too.

And that was the end of my police career.

My car got trashed. I got death threats. Somebody – friend or friends to the cops we'd jailed – had decided to make life impossible for me. I kept getting assigned jobs that nobody else could be bothered to investigate. It was frustrating. Or I was paranoid. And I got a big mouth. Maybe I mouthed off once too often to the head of my division. I got fired. So these days, instead of robbery and homicide, I investigate cases that involve alimony and child support. Ana Valenzuela must have gotten my number from the ad I run in the local newspaper.

'How can I help you?' I said.

'Gerardo Fischer, our theater director, is missing. You have to help us. Would you please come to the colony?'

'How long has he been missing?'

'Since yesterday afternoon.'

'That's not very long.'

'His house... It was open... everything open... He'd never do that... He was due in rehearsal yesterday... and today... and nobody has seen him for... I don't know... he's gone.'

She was distressed. This much was clear.

'Have you called the local police?'

'I have. But they said they'd pass it on to the missing persons office.'

Of course they would. The department has some decent guys in the locality now, who genuinely protect people. But no way were they going to mobilize a search on a missing person case only just twenty-four hours after it was reported. This Gerardo Fischer might be in some local farmhouse with a mistress of his and might show up for dinner tonight.

But Ana Valenzuela was panicked. She obviously thought that this was a kidnapping. We do have them from time to time but not like in the big cities. Ana wanted something done now. Immediately. I could understand that.

'Please, you have to come.'

'Okay. I'll be there as soon as I can.'

'You know Sara Suarez's house? Come there, okay?'

'Okay.' I rang off. I saved Ana's number on my cell phone.

My first thought was that this was going to be a paying job. My second thought was that it was going to be better than snooping around motel rooms trying to snap pictures of couples having sex. And the third, my gut instinct was that something was radically wrong up at the colony.

Could there be some connection between this Gerardo Fischer's disappearance and the fact that Pablo Arenas, the man who had robbed the residents of the artists' colony at gunpoint, had been released from jail not three weeks previously? It was possible. And I don't like Arenas. Why should I? He got me kicked off the force.

But my car was at a standstill at the road works. The municipality was building a major new overpass along the edge of the town, close to Gran Paraíso Lake. A tractor-trailer was parked in the middle of the roadway. A huge concrete bridge strut hung in mid-air dangling from the arm of a crane.

I took off my shades and reached up to the rearview mirror to see how presentable I might be to a prospective client. A goatee in need of a trim, dark green shadows under my eyes, two days of stubble on my face and the stubble on my otherwise bald scalp made me look dingy. I guess I hadn't been sleeping too well recently. I put the wraparound shades back on as if they might mask me. They didn't. It was still me in the mirror, Juan Manuel Pérez. The not-cop.

Out beside the tractor-trailer, a construction foreman barked into a radio handset. The crane arm swung the concrete bridge strut over the construction site. The air conditioning fan whirred. The red stop sign didn't change to green at the head of the line of cars. I had a copy of the local newspaper on the passenger seat, *La Voz del Interior*. I lit a cigarette and cast an eye over the front page. The newspaper was still full of the international fallout over President Kirchner's canceling of Argentina's debt to the IMF.

It made him popular with me at any rate. Lower down the page was a report on a robbery from the military airport in Córdoba. Some cases of weapons had gone missing and an investigation was underway into the major security breach. Now that was something that the cops would have to move on fast. They'd commit a lot of manpower to that: far more than on a missing person case. I read as far as the third paragraph about some bogus catering service that had got a truck onto the base.

The tractor-trailer moved off. The crane began to lower the strut into place on the bridge site, the traffic sign turned to green, and the cars ahead of me inched forward through clouds of dust kicked up by the earth-moving machinery.

I got the Ford Executive in gear. I eased through the construction site. The road out of town was clear. I accelerated up the hill, going west, passed the cookie factories and the roadside barbecue restaurants. I turned down Route 60 toward the village of El Naranjo Campanil.

Open country, foothills of the Sierras, rolling hills with grass and rocks and scrubby trees, a roadside shrine to the Madonna. After ten kilometers, I turned off Route 60 and onto a dirt road. After six kilometers of washboard rises and washed-out cambers, dry streambeds and stands of trees, and easing around recently exposed rocks, I pulled in through the gate of the artists' colony.

It was called Temenos. They called it that because Temenos in Greek means 'sacred space.' In Spanish, it's an order, an imperative: it means 'Fear us.' You wouldn't think many people would fear this bunch of artists. That had proved to be a serious mistake for two of the people who had tried to rob them. One of the would-be robbers was dead. Pablo Arenas had lost a finger and the piece of an ear. But now the son of a bitch had just been released from jail.

I let the cloud of dust settle behind my big black car. I took another look in the rearview mirror but I didn't see any improvement in the way I looked. My mouth was stale. I got out of the car.

A furious barking of dogs came from inside Sara Suarez's

house. The house curtains twitched for a second and then the door opened. Sara came out onto the terrace. She was a stocky woman, about fifty-five years old, dressed in shorts and a kind of cotton smock. The young woman who'd called me, Ana Valenzuela, was behind her: dreadlocks piled up on top of her head; a cotton slip and surfer shorts. I lit a cigarette. Sara looked like I was bringing her the worst news she'd ever heard in her life. Ana was pale. And the dogs made me nervous.

'Hi,' I said when I reached the terrace.

'Come in,' Sara said.

The dogs barked behind a door to the living room.

'We've talked to everybody on the property,' Ana said. 'Nobody's seen him. Gerardo was due at rehearsal yesterday evening... and again this morning... and he never misses a rehearsal, ever. The least he would do is to let us know.'

'What about friends of his off-site?'

'We've called everyone we know,' Sara said. 'And we called the hospitals as well in case he'd been involved in some kind of accident.'

'His house was left open,' Ana said, 'and when I went in there was no sign of him or his computer and we haven't heard anything from him since yesterday morning.'

'Any sign of a break in, robbery, anything like that?'

'No,' Ana said. 'Just his laptop was missing, nothing else.'

'He owned the house?'

'No, he was just staying there while we developed a new play based on Pessoa's *Book of Disquiet*,' Ana said.

I like to read. I've got a good library at home. I know that book. I didn't see how they could ever adapt anything from it. But that wasn't my business.

'His car?'

'Still in the parking lot,' Sara said.

That wasn't a good sign.

'Let's hope a friend came by to pick him up. Maybe they've gone for a ride somewhere and he'll just turn up.'

'Ana and Sara exchanged a glance of panic.

'Don't worry. We'll go down to his house, now... take a look around.'

'You go with him, Ana,' Sara said. 'I'll stay here by the phone.'

'Look. I hate to bring this up but... I'm not a cop anymore. I work privately now. Do you understand?'

'Don't worry,' Sara said. 'We can cover your fees, I'm sure.'

I nodded.

'I'm a little expensive. I'll need a retainer fee of one thousand US dollars up front to cover my time and expenses.'

'That's fine,' Sara said.

'In cash, if that's not inconvenient.'

Sara and Ana exchanged another glance.

'It will take a couple of days,' Sara said.

'That's okay.'

It might take time to raise a thousand dollars in cash and this Gerardo Fischer might have turned up by then. If he did turn up, I needn't charge them the full amount. But I didn't want to say that.

'We can deal with the details tomorrow,' I said.

'Shall we go to the house?' Ana said.

'Yeah, let's go.'

A red dirt trail led downhill from the terrace behind Sara's house. Ana Valenzuela led me through Temenos. She was small, about a meter and a half, no more, but her tight white t-shirt clung to the curves of her body. She had a colored sarong tied around her waist. Her skin was a golden brown and her natural blonde hair caught the light so it showed up on her arms, a little downy around her upper lip, but not unattractive. On her left forearm she had some kind of oriental letters tattooed in blue.

It was still hot to be walking under the late afternoon sun despite the breeze in the hills. The Artists Colony was made up of small houses built on little plots of land among rocky outcrops and small areas of pine and eucalyptus. A large meeting hall or theater stood on a piece of flat land near the center of the property. We kept going downhill until we reached Gerardo Fischer's house. It was a low one-story affair with steel grills on the door, shutters on the windows, and a low, stone wall around the perimeter of the plot. Ana unlocked the padlocks and the mortise locks and we went into the kitchen. It was cooler in here. There was no living room as such. I saw no obvious signs of any break-in or violence. Why would I? She said on the phone that she'd found the place wide open.

'What time did you say it was, when you found out he was missing?'

'About two-thirty,' Ana said. 'I'd just been to the river. I was still in a swimsuit and a sarong...'

I could imagine her in a swimsuit, her dreadlocks all wet.

'I was just passing by,' she said, 'when I saw that the steel grid over the kitchen door was wide open. That was unusual. Gerardo should have been taking his siesta... but why hadn't he locked up first? I came in through the gate. I just knew that something was wrong.'

http://bit.ly/farsouth2
Witness Deposition:
Ana Valenzuela (Extract 1)

The kitchen was empty. The windows were wide open. I went along the corridor to the bedroom. The bed was unmade. The upper sheet was all twisted. The pillows had fallen off. I went over to the window. Down below in the orchard, the hammock was empty. It was hanging between two plum trees. A gray pampas fox was eating the fruit that had fallen into the dry grass between the roots of the trees.

A fox eating fruit, I thought, how come?

I called out: 'Gerardo!'

The fox raised its head. It looked straight at me. I felt this crawling-like static across my skin and my shoulders. My mouth was dry. Everything felt wrong. I saw that Gerardo's laptop wasn't on the desk by the bedroom window. I thought, he's missing. Disappeared. All these terrible thoughts in my head: if Gerardo's been kidnapped, who would pay the ransom? Gerardo has no family. I don't know where his money comes from. Then again, Gerardo always seemed to have money: money to move from country to country whenever he wanted. Maybe he was involved in some business I know nothing about?

I never knew him to do any drugs. No marijuana. No coke. Nothing. A criminal would have been better off kidnapping me, because my parents have money. The sweat turned cold on my skin. The terrible anxiety at not finding him just flooded into me.

I love him so dearly… like… what? I don't know. It was the work he did with me… he made me bring things out on stage I had no idea I was capable of doing. He's so much older than me but he always related to me in the theater space with so much respect. I love him… I mean… but he's about the same age as my father, you know. There's such a difference between them: my father's a businessman, he makes a lot of money, and Gerardo only just about makes a living as the director of the company… Gerardo lived in exile during the years of the dictatorship while my father never seemed to have been affected by it at all. I think my father knew people in the junta… but I'm not going to talk about that… Gerardo was gone. I wanted to call someone with my cell phone. Get some advice. Sara up at the colony. She's always so practical. Pragmatic.

I thought, well, she'll know what to do.

I took out the cell phone. No signal, of course.

I thought, should I lock up the house and find a place where I can call? Or wait for Gerardo to get back? He's not coming back. I knew that. I went into the bedroom again. Crossed to the window. The fox had gone from under the hammock. Maybe Gerardo had turned into a fox and disappeared… I wish…

[Extract from the casebook of Juan Manuel Pérez
January 10th 2006
Hours: 17:30 to 18:50

'How old is Gerardo?' I said.

'Close to sixty, I guess,' Ana said.

I couldn't see this young woman, at most in her late twenties, with dreadlocks and tattoos sleeping with a sixty-year-old guy... but you never know.

'Is there anyone who might have a grudge against him among the people here?'

Ana's blue eyes fixed on me. She shifted back on the kitchen chair.

'I don't think so.' She shook her head. Maybe there was someone but she didn't want to say.

'I have to ask you this. Have you noticed any strangers poking around?'

That brought back memories of Pablo Arenas for both of us: the robberies, the brutal beatings, the killing... back then she'd been one of the colony residents that I'd had to interview. They'd all been shaken up. Some of them had been relieved it wasn't their houses that had been robbed: that it wasn't they who'd had to face the robbers. But it had left most of the colony residents, Ana included, angry, shaky, but most of all, the robberies had brought them together. They wanted to look out for one another. Ana was fiercely protective of her friends. I admired that in her. She was pretty, too. But I was a cop with a job to do. No chance to explore anything more friendly with her.

'No. No one I can think of.'

'I'm going to take a look around the house.' I went down the corridor: two bedrooms, one on either side. I went into the one on the right, Gerardo's bedroom, the master bedroom. Just like Ana said, the pillows were still on the floor. The bed was rumpled with no sign of any kind of struggle, amorous or otherwise. I checked the bottom sheet for stains. Nothing.

Three books lay on the bedside cabinet: Ricardo Piglia's *Assumed Name*, a collection of short stories from 1975; Juan Rulfo's novel, *Pedro Páramo*; and *Illuminations*, a collection of essays by Walter Benjamin. I knew the first two books but not the third. I flipped through the pages of all three books in case there might be a note tucked in among them. There wasn't. I opened the door of the bedside cabinet. Empty. So I tried the wardrobe: a sports jacket, a raincoat; two pairs of trousers, one cotton, one linen; a small pile of dirty laundry; some socks on one of the three shelves. I checked the pockets of the jacket, coat and pants but there was nothing, not even a dirty tissue or an old train ticket. But Fischer might have packed a bag and left these things. Maybe he'd just been careless and left the doors and windows open knowing that Ana would arrive just after he'd left so she could lock up for him.

I couldn't see anything else of any interest in this room.

I looked under the bed just for good measure but there was nothing there either but a few dust balls clinging to dead hair.

In the spare bedroom, the metal-framed bed wasn't even made up. It was little better than a camping cot with a thin foam mattress. Nothing under the mattress, nor under the bed. I knelt down and opened that bedside cabinet: nothing. It was a house for guests, a rental place, and Fischer seemed to travel light.

I opened the closet just inside the bedroom door: old adventure books for children, dusty, untouched for years; a pile of magazines;

a pencil case with some colored crayons and crumbled shavings. I closed the door. I quit the small bedroom, went down the corridor and through the door onto the terrace.

The terrace faced north and was lit up by the bright sun. I ran my hand above the dry-stone wall that kept people from falling off the terrace and onto the overgrown lawn three meters below. Directly opposite the open window of the master bedroom, a single stone had been dislodged from the wall. I went to the end of the terrace and down the steps to where the stone and some crumbled mortar remnants were lying in the grass. The uncut grass from the bottom of the wall to the hammock might have been bent down by footfalls. Could Fischer have dislodged the stone as he jumped off the terrace into the orchard, and then ran toward the trees at the perimeter of the property? Why hadn't he gone down the steps? Or had the stone been dislodged by a struggle on the terrace.

I followed what might have been the faint evidence of footmarks in the grass as far as the hammock. There was no sign of the footmarks continuing any further than that, but the ground was less grassy in this part of the garden, just hard-packed dirt, so scuffs and traces might not show. At the edge of the orchard, a grove of trees led down to the stream below. I ducked under the rope that tied the hammock to one of the plum trees. Lots of fallen fruit lay around the roots. I guess this had been what Ana's fox had been eating. Where the orchard ended at a stand of eucalyptus and pine, the branches had been broken and the earth scuffed up. That was recent, too. But all this breakage could have happened more than a week ago. No rain in the last few days. Just dry thunder. I skirted the stand of trees and made my way down to the streambed by the small path that was closer to the house. The streambed was dry, mostly rocks. Spiny shrubs, silica-sparkle in the dry dirt. Impossible to tell whether anyone had been through there or not. If Gerardo Fischer had been frightened by an intruder, he might have grabbed his laptop, slipped out the bedroom window, jumped the terrace wall and dragged a rock off the top of the wall as he tumbled into the garden. He could have run toward the hammock and veered off into the woods, broken through the tree line, skittered down to the streambed and kept on running until he reached the road. He could have gone anywhere from there.

If Gerardo had got away from someone chasing him, any minute now, he would probably call Ana or Sara to let them know where he was; unless someone really had been chasing him, and they'd caught him. They could be holding him for ransom or they might have killed him. But why would they want to kill him? Up in the eucalyptus trees that overlooked the orchard, the black shapes of vultures squatted in the branches, heads bent between humped wings. No corpse around here or they would already be bothering it. If he'd been killed for his laptop – and around here people can get killed for less – his body might have been dumped anywhere out there in the wilderness: maybe by the side of some dirt road deep in the hills. If someone wanted a ransom, they'd be in touch pretty soon.

But right now, Gerardo Fischer might just be with some woman in a neighboring holiday home. He still might turn up. I wanted to believe that for Ana's sake. Somehow, I didn't.

I made my way back up the path from the streambed to the orchard. Ana was sitting on the side of the hammock, easing it a little, back and forth.

'Are you okay?' I asked.

She nodded. She was so tiny. She stood up. I'm not a really tall guy but her dreadlocks only reached up as far as about elbow-height on me. We climbed back up the steps to the terrace and into the house. This could still be just a missing person case no matter how worried Ana was. I told her that. I could see that she wanted to believe it but she didn't. I wanted to give Gerardo time to show up if he was going to show up. I was still enough of a cop for that. But Ana was so spooked I knew she was convinced that Gerardo Fischer had been kidnapped.

I went back into the house, along the corridor and into the

kitchen. Ana sat down next to the table. I opened the single kitchen cabinet. Nothing but a few boxes of pasta, cans of tomatoes, olive oil, a pack of *yerba mate*, onions, potatoes, flour, and an unopened bottle of wine: a decent Malbec, from Mendoza.

On Ana's side of the table was a drawer with a round wooden knob, probably a cutlery drawer.

'Do you mind?' I said.

Ana got up from the table. I opened the drawer: no cutlery, some string, a corkscrew, some old ballpoint pens on a cardboard folder, and a set of car keys.

'Is this a spare set?' I asked Ana.

'I don't know,' she said.

'We'll take them. I want to check on the car.' I pocketed the keys. I was about to close the drawer but I stopped. Maybe the cardboard folder contained invoices, records of what he'd bought, evidence of where he'd been during the past few days... or last few weeks. I slid the folder out of the drawer and opened it on the tabletop. It wasn't an invoice book. It was some kind of notebook. It was pretty thin, and not all the pages had been used up. The pages were covered in a tiny crabbed calligraphy. I'd have to use a magnifying glass to be able to read the words. From what I could make out, some of the entries were in diary form. The rest seemed to be just random thoughts and notes. A lot of the entries had something to do with the Middle East. Among the scratches I could at least recognize the words Israel, Lebanon, Syria, Palestine... I didn't have time to read it now.

Inside the back cover of the folder, in a kind of pocket, was a packet of postcards and a few old photographs of people – from the 1980s by the look of the clothes – and a Jewish New Years greeting card – that wasn't too recent either. Nothing in the book seemed at all recent. I held the pages open for Ana to look at.

'Is this Gerardo's handwriting?'

Ana nodded. 'I think so.'

'You know this book?'

She shook her head.

'I'm going to keep this, just for a short time. There might be something useful in here.'

'Okay,' Ana said.

If Gerardo Fischer suddenly showed up, as still he might, he might not be too pleased that I'd been poking through his personal writings. I could deal with that. I'm a curious son of a bitch.

'Why don't we lock up?' I said.

Ana picked up the house keys from the table, her small white hand closed around them: the tattoos on her forearm deep blue against her pale skin, her dreadlocks swaying forward. I could really go for a woman who looked like that; at least to get to know her a little better. Under the grape arbor, outside the kitchen, Ana turned a separate key in each lock of the steel-grilled gate.

If Fischer had been sleeping with her, he was one lucky old man.

Ana and I walked back up the hill under the fierce sun.

'There's no one that Gerardo might be seeing who could have come up here and taken him off on a trip for a couple of days?'

'He never misses rehearsals,' Ana said. 'And he hasn't called us.'

I nodded.

'What state of mind was he in the last time you saw him?'

'State of mind?'

'Yes, was he agitated, nervous, distracted?'

'It's difficult to imagine Gerardo distracted,' she said.

'He didn't seem scared at all?'

'No, but he doesn't really show what he's feeling… if he doesn't want to. Especially not fear.'

'Did he have anything to be afraid of?'

'Up here? After the robberies? Don't we all have something to be afraid of?'

'Okay. So nothing unusual about his state of mind?'

She shook her head.

We walked along in silence until we reached the parking lot.

'It's that one,' Ana said. 'His car.'

She pointed to a Fiat Fiorino. The small white van was covered in dust. I found the key opened the driver's side door. It wasn't too messy in there. I popped open the glove compartment: documents for the car, a small pack of tissues, some old cassette tapes, Arvo Pärt, a Bach Cantata, and Gerardo Gandini's *Flores Negras*. In the back of the van were a thin mattress, some literary magazines in English, a coil of rope neatly tied off, and a car jack. I locked up the van.

We walked back to Sara's house. It was cool inside and the dogs were locked away, maybe in her study. She had some *mate* ready. Ana and I sat down on the easy chairs in there. I put the folder down on the arm of the chair.

'Are you in the theater company, too?' I said to Sara.

'No, I'm not.'

'Are you a writer, a painter?'

'I'm a psychologist. Everybody up here just puts up with me. They don't really consider me an artist, you know, but psychology is an art, isn't it?'

'Psychology an art? I never would have thought that.'

'Well, I mean... psychiatry, psychosis, that's hard science, up to a point... maybe if you have to prescribe medication. But understanding the mind itself? Consciousness? Nobody has ever explained consciousness... or what it is, have they?'

'I guess I never tried.'

'A lot of people have tried, but the best you get is a model and then you find out that the model is limited... like everything else in the scientific world. There aren't any answers... there's always more to discover... until you find you can't know... we'll never know.'

'Is that what you're doing up here, a study on consciousness?'

Sara laughed.

'Not at all. I'm writing a thesis for a doctorate: "The Psychological Impact of Immigration to Argentina on European Jews and their descendants".'

'Was Gerardo helping you with that?'

'It's difficult to pin down Gerardo for a long interview.'

The dogs started snarling and barking from behind the door.

'Do the dogs disturb you?' she said. 'You shouldn't worry. They're under control.'

'I'm glad.'

'I like to feel secure... since the robberies. My dogs give me that.'

'It's okay.'

'And now Gerardo has disappeared.'

'How did you find out he'd disappeared?'

'Ana.' Sara waved a hand at her. 'It was about three o'clock. I was on the shady side of the terrace, watering the plants.'

'How long have you been at the colony?'

'Since the Saturday before Christmas. All the cottages are full. Everyone is up here to escape the heat of Buenos Aires. Everyone in the village knows we're here because regular deliveries have started again: drinking water, vegetables, bread.'

'You think someone in the village is responsible for Gerardo's disappearance?'

'I don't know. It crossed my mind. When I saw Ana hurrying up the path, breathless, close to tears, I knew something terrible had happened. "Gerardo's missing," she said. The way she said it, flat, it gave me the chills even in that heat. I thought: Oh my God, not again. I couldn't help thinking about those robberies a few years ago; how we were just getting over them, feeling safe again at the colony.'

'What did you do when you found out that Gerardo was missing?'

'I just told myself that I had to stay calm because there were a hundred or more possibilities that might have happened to Gerardo and many hundreds more of which I couldn't even conceive and all of them would be better than him being kidnapped; or almost any of them. Then for a moment I wondered if Gerardo might be capable of suicide.'

'You think that's possible?'

'I don't think so. But how can anyone tell what might drive him to an overdose, or to shoot himself... or whatever? At least a kidnapping would be better than that. We'd get him back in one piece after paying out a little money. Or a lot of money. "We're going to start with the cops," I said to Ana. Then I went into the house and I dialed from my landline. I explained to the desk sergeant what had happened and I asked if anyone had reported any accident or arrests, anything. Nothing. The desk sergeant just told me to call back the next morning and he'd file a missing persons report. "Wait until tomorrow," the desk sergeant said. "Then we can list him as a missing person." "Yes, of course," I said to him. I mean, what was the point of arguing? "He'll turn up," I said to Ana. "No, he won't," Ana said. And then she burst into tears. I put my arm around her but she was inconsolable. I suggested calling you. You helped us a lot after those robberies up here. I thought you were still a federal cop but Ana had seen your ad in the newspaper... she knew that you ran some kind of investigation agency, now. So that's how come we called you. You're a decent guy. I trust you.'

'Thanks,' I said.

'I trust you, too,' Ana said.

She's a very beautiful young woman.

'If Fischer shows up, no matter what time of the day or night, you let me know right away, okay?'

I got up and tucked the folder under my arm.

'We will,' Ana said.

I really wanted to get to know Ana better but right now I thought that I ought to keep my mind on finding Fischer. If Fischer had been kidnapped, it would make sense to talk to some people in the area who were in the kidnapping business.

Pablo Arenas knew the kidnapping business very well. He was a veteran of the Dirty War. He'd been in the Argentine Anticommunist Alliance. He'd robbed the colony twice. Maybe his kind of trouble came in threes. If Arenas had Fischer, it would be better to talk to Arenas soon. Very soon. Like immediately. But I wouldn't visit Arenas alone.

'Right now,' I said to Ana, 'I need to call my partner at the office. I have some ideas I need to follow up on with him: routine checks, but they might just turn up something useful, okay?'

Ana nodded.

'Try not to worry now. We'll find Gerardo, I'm sure.'

They accompanied me out to the terrace and across the parking lot to my car.

I leaned down to kiss Sara and then Ana on the cheek.

Through the dusty windshield, I watched them walk back across the parking lot toward Sara's house. I opened the glove compartment and took out the hip holster with my .45 caliber Colt automatic. I hooked it onto my belt. The M1911 is a heavy weapon but I like the heft. The design has hardly changed since before the First World War in Europe. It has a lot of stopping power.

I got out the cell phone and called my partner, Rangel.

'Can you meet me in thirty minutes at the grocery market on Route 60 next to the Alfajores factory?'

'Sure, why?' Rangel said.

'We're going to see Pablo Arenas.'

'Don't you have some kind of history with that guy?'

'I'll fill you in on the way,' I said.

I hung up.

Extract from the casebook of Juan Manuel Pérez
January 10th 2006
Hours: 18:50 to 19:20

I started the car and backed it around to get down the drive of the Artists Colony. I headed down the dirt road toward Route 60. Knowing the criminal talent in this area, Arenas was a good bet for a kidnapping and ransom case. That said, it was doubtful that even if Arenas had kidnapped Fischer he would have brought Fischer to his house. Still, a visit to Arenas would be a simple way for the word to get around the criminal world that I was looking for Fischer and I could help negotiate a deal for him. After all, I wasn't a cop any more.

Rangel was already at the grocery market when I arrived. He was leaning against the hood of his gray Volkswagen. When I pulled up, he ambled over. Rangel's belly, framed by his open suit jacket, overhung the belt of his pants and his chins had begun to hide the knot of his tie. He clutched a can of Coca Cola in one hand and a cigarette in the other. His face was red and sweaty and his thinning hair was plastered across his tanned skull. His moustache was neatly trimmed. How could a guy in this condition have a wife and two kids?

'You just come from a funeral?' I said.

'I thought maybe we were going to one.'

'Yours if you don't get in shape.'

'Fuck you.' He flicked his butt toward a garbage bin in the grocery car park and got into the passenger seat of my car. We drove down toward San Sebastian, which was about twelve kilometers away.

'So what's the deal with Pablo Arenas?' Rangel said.

'He's just out of jail. Probably hungry.'

'He's a political type, right?'

'Argentine Anticommunist Alliance. Recent conviction for armed robbery. Previous in Bariloche and Buenos Aires Province.'

'You put him away for robbery?'

'Correct. Flamboyant son of a bitch, three years ago, he arrived in a Ford Falcon outside the house of this Melissa Auerbach, a German woman staying up there. Three guys got out of the Falcon. Two of them had ski masks, the third had one of these rubber masks, you know... full head... like a werewolf.'

'A werewolf?' Rangel said. 'The Rocky Horror Show. This was Arenas?'

'No. His nephew. This guy was young... built. And he had a tattoo.'

'Distinguishing marks, right?'

'A snake around a dagger.'

'Old school,' Rangel said.

'Right, and the other two guys, one of them was a skinny kid in jogging pants and a Los Angeles Raiders tee shirt; the third guy in a track suit was short and fat and a good deal older and he was the main guy, the boss. He was the main son of a bitch.'

'Arenas?'

'Right.' I'd told this story a lot back then: to the judge and jury mostly. 'Nobody was around. It was sunset. These three sons of bitches were on this old woman's porch and they had guns... handguns. They went up onto the porch and just knocked on the door. This Melissa thought it was one of their people, you know, artist or writer or something... she opened the door and she's faced with these three guys in masks and the fat guy put a gun muzzle to her forehead and pushed her back in the house.'

'And how old is this woman?'

'About sixty. Hippy type, all wrinkled and brown... and she hennas her hair and she wears these flowing colored smocks that hide her weight. Get the picture?'

'Sure.'

'So they were all in her house and it's just like one big room for living and eating and the kitchen and an open stairway that goes up to the loft where she sleeps. Melissa saw that the fat guy was really calm but the two young guys were real jittery. She thought they were local. They seemed to be looking for something in particular but they said nothing. She got her purse and opened it and emptied all the money in it onto the dining table. The kid in the werewolf mask grabbed it and pocketed it. The other young guy in the jogging suit was shaking. He held the gun pointed at Melissa and his hand was shaking. She was terrified that he was going to shoot her out of fear. Melissa was still holding her purse open. The old guy, Arenas, plucked out the credit card and pocketed it.

'He said to her, "You got more money?"

'Melissa said, "No." So the bastard smacked Melissa across the cheek with his pistol. You should have seen the mark it left: livid, red mark on her white cheek. I saw it.'

'A sixty-year-old woman.' Rangel interlocked his fingers behind his head, leaned back. 'Cute son of a bitch.'

'Yeah. After that she was terrified of getting badly hurt. "Wait," she said to him. Melissa went over to the stairs that led to the loft. She shifted a tile at the side of the stair stringer. She pulled out a small wad of new bills, about two thousand pesos.

'The old guy said, "This all you got?"

'Melissa said, "Yes, I swear."

'So then the old guy asked her where she's from.

'"Germany," she said.

'You know what he told her? "I like Germans," the old guy said. Can you believe that?'

Rangel just shrugged at me.

'The one in the werewolf mask was holding his gun sideways like some hip-hop gangster from a Hollywood movie, and the skinny kid in the ski mask was still shaking.

'"Don't call the police for at least an hour," the old guy said, "or someone will come back here to see you, you understand?"

'Melissa understood. "Okay, let's go," the old guy said and the two young guys backed out of the door and the old guy followed them. She heard the car start up and she went to the window. She saw that it was a rust-colored Ford Falcon with a busted taillight. She was still too terrified to call the police. Then she saw the Falcon go back over the hill and drive away.

'Melissa ran down to her friend's house after an hour. They called the cops, the local cops, but the cops just said it must have been some criminals from Buenos Aires up for the summer. They did come to take a look around but then they just shrugged and drove off.'

'And the guys in the masks came back?' Rangel said.

'Two weeks later, the same three guys and the same car, in the late evening, just like before. But this time they went to a neighboring property: the house of one Ramón Gorriti. He has two people living with him, Carlos Brescia and his mother, Miriam. They were on the porch. Ramón, who is Carlos's lover, was in the garden. He was just watering the plants.'

'Carlos's lover?' Rangel sounded surprised.

'Yeah.'

'He's gay?'

'Yeah.'

'And Miriam is Carlos's mother?'

'Yeah, she's real old, and she hasn't been well and Carlos had brought her to the property to look after her for a while.'

'Wait a minute. Carlos brings his mother to live with him and his gay lover?'

'Yeah.'

'How does she like it?'

'She's fine with it.'

'How old is she?'

'She's seventy-something.'

Rangel shook his head. 'This fucking country…'

'So Carlos and his mother were on the porch. She was on the swing-seat and Carlos had his bench and his weights out there. He was doing his reps: barbell flies, bench presses, squats… you should see this guy work out.'

'In front of his own mother?'

'Yeah… in front of his mother, in the shade, the fresh air, the evening breeze, the red sunset, what the fuck? Do you have to keep interrupting?'

'Sorry,' Rangel said. He looked horrified, his puffy eyes glazed and mouth open like some kind of bottom-dwelling fish.

'Then the Ford Falcon pulled up and the guys with the masks and the guns got out. In the garden, the masked guys all pointed their guns at Ramón and forced him onto his knees. So Carlos dropped the weights, grabbed his mother, pulled her inside the house and locked the door. The fat guy, Arenas, held a gun to the back of Ramón's neck. He called out: "Open the door or I blow his head off." Carlos, inside with his mother, wouldn't open the door. The fat guy yelled out that he wasn't fooling but Carlos still wouldn't open up and the next thing you know the fat guy pulled the trigger.'

'He killed Ramón,' Rangel said.

'The gun jammed. It didn't go off.'

'Christ.'

'So the fat guy, he called out: "Open the door. I'm not fooling. Next time it won't jam. This guy is dead." But Carlos was afraid that something would happen to his mother. He refused. So the fat guy pulled the trigger again.'

'And?'

'The gun jammed again.'

'So how did Ramón feel about this?'

'I've never asked him. But at this point, Ramón realized that he might not get a third chance, so while the old guy struggled to un-jam his gun, Ramón got up off his knees, made a run for it and jumped over the garden fence and kept running.'

'Over the red earth, and through the pale green shrubs and disappeared into the red Sierra sunset.'

'Right, and then the three guys forced their way into Carlos's house by shooting the lock off the front door.'

'Fuck,' Rangel said.

'What they didn't know is that Ramón had a twelve-gauge double-barreled shotgun in the house. And Carlos had loaded it.'

'How come Ramón had a gun? I thought we're in a nice New Age hippy place here.'

'This is the Sierras. Two gay guys... out in the mountains, afraid of kidnappers and thieves: who knows what can happen?'

'If three guys in masks show up to rob the place,' Rangel said.

'Right... which they already had done... two weeks before, at Melissa Auerbach's house.'

'Okay.'

'So Carlos had got the shotgun and when the fat guy shot the lock off the door, the guy in the werewolf mask ran into the room with his pistol raised and Carlos let him have it with both barrels. He blew him clean off the porch. As good as dead.'

'As good as?'

'He died about twenty minutes later.'

'Right.'

'So Carlos reloaded and then the fat guy tried to come in.'

'Ramón got him, too?'

'Shot off a finger and part of his ear, and various upper body wounds. The fat guy had had enough. The young kid helped him, it's his uncle... the kid helped him to get back to the car and the kid and the driver took the uncle to the hospital.'

'Where they got arrested.'

'Right, because Carlos called the police... he has a body on the porch.'

'Meaning you got called... at that time,' Rangel said.

'Exactly,' I said. 'Homicide is a Federal case. We came to find out why the guy with the werewolf face, on the porch, was dead. By this point we... the Feds... had checked on the old guy with gunshot wounds at the hospital... and we found out that his name is Pablo Arenas and he's a friend of the town police chief from back in the old days of the dictatorships, and he's connected to the Argentine Anticommunist Alliance. He's a Triple A man.'

'But why was this Arenas after Carlos and Miriam?'

'That we don't know. Maybe Arenas just don't like gays or old hippy women. Maybe he just needed some money.'

'But we don't know.'

'No, and the charge at the trial was armed robbery with violence, Arenas was convicted for the robbery of Melissa, and the attempted robbery of Carlos, Miriam and Ramón. With good behavior and taking into consideration he's still got some friends in powerful places, he came out on parole three weeks ago.'

'Shit.'

'Maybe Arenas felt like he had a score to settle. Maybe Arenas decided to kidnap this Gerardo.'

'Which is why we've come to talk to him,' Rangel said.

'Exactly,' I said.

I turned into a dirt driveway.

'And here, my dear Rangel, is the house of Pablo Arenas.'

[Extract from the casebook of Juan Manuel Pérez
January 10th 2006
Hours: 19:20 to 20:00

A battered Ford Falcon was parked in the narrow driveway of Pablo Arenas's one-story house. I pulled in behind it. By the time we slammed the car doors shut, Arenas was out on the porch. He came down the driveway towards us. He'd lost weight in prison. His pale blue tracksuit top hung loose over his short frame; the knees of it bulged. His hair was gray, close cropped. Pouches under his eyes, jowls that sagged a little, the dark lines over his cheeks and jaw made darker by stubble. Half of one ear was missing, the right one. I couldn't see his fingers.

'Well, the ex-Detective Sergeant Pérez, to what do I owe the honor?'

This scumbag had got me thrown off the force.

'I'm looking for a friend,' I said.

'You have friends around here?'

'His name is Fischer, you know him?'

From the wry smile I assumed he did.

'How come a *former* policeman got friends like that?' Arenas said.

'Like what?'

'Faggot... commie... *artiste*... you know...'

'So you know him...'

'I know all those people up there.'

'You been to visit them?'

'Not recently.'

'Thought about it?'

He shrugged.

'I think about a lot of things.'

'Why don't you invite us inside?' Rangel said. 'It's too hot to talk out here.'

'Why should I invite you in?' Arenas said.

'Maybe you could help us locate this friend of ours,' I said. 'We're a little anxious about him. Some information we might be able to get paid for.'

Arenas cocked his head. You could tell that the little cogs and gears of his brain were trying to process my discreet offer to negotiate a ransom if he had Gerardo Fischer or knew of his whereabouts. If he didn't know where Fischer was, I was sure he'd try to find out who did have him. He'd figure there was a percentage in it.

'Would you like to come in?' Arenas said. 'How's that?'

'That's very kind of you,' Rangel said.

Arenas turned his back on us and walked up to the house. Fischer wasn't here. That much I knew. Rangel and I followed Arenas into the living room. A young woman, late twenties, I'd say, with thick curly black hair, was sitting drinking *mate* at a dining table, the thermos flask right next to the gourd; she had a pack of cigarettes and a lighter next to an ashtray with two recently crushed butts.

'My niece,' Arenas said.

I nodded. She looked back at me out of very dark eyes. She had dark diagonals below them and her skin was a little waxy: late nights and too many cigarettes. She was attractive in a wasted kind of way. I thought it might be interesting to talk to her: to examine her family connections.

'You live in San Sebastian?' I asked.

'Next to the laundry,' she said. 'Why?'

'Just curious.'

'Take a seat,' Arenas said.

He waved at the other chairs around the table. I didn't sit down, neither did Rangel, nor Arenas.

'How are you getting by since you came out?' I said.

'What are you, now,' Arenas said, 'a social worker?'

'Just passing by.'

'I have a very loving family,' Arenas said. 'Thanks for your concern.'

The girl sucked on the *bombilla* until the gourd was noisily empty. She reached for the cigarettes and lit one. Then she opened the top of the thermos and poured more water on the *yerba*.

'Maria Dos Santos, right?' Rangel said.

Her head tilted and pulled back. 'Do I know you?'

'I seen you in the clubs around the lake,' he said.

'You a cop?'

'Private businessman,' Rangel said.

Arenas was interested in us. Maria Dos Santos didn't give a damn.

Arenas leaned on the back of a chair. A leather belt was slung over the chair back. From the belt hung a big gaucho knife in a silver studded sheath. The blade was about nine inches long and, knowing Arenas, it would probably be honed like a razor. That knife connected Arenas to a bloody strand of our beloved country's history and literature. And Arenas would be aware of it. He was a traditionalist. I like books, too. One day I thought maybe I'd write a novel instead of investigating people's dirt.

On the wall behind Arenas's head was a wooden crucifix with a garishly painted Christ in torment: on a high shelf to my left, a statue of the Virgin Mary. A double-barreled shotgun was propped up next to a dresser in the corner. On the right-hand wall, there was a photograph of Arenas shaking the hand of a tall man who was going bald. The bald man wore a sheepskin jacket. Behind Arenas and his companion in the photograph, there was a hotel on the side of a mountain. The mountain was covered in snow, the lines of a ski lift crossing the slopes.

'That a relative of yours?' I said.

'A friend,' Arenas said.

'Not from around here.'

'No.'

'Where from?'

'My home town.'

'Oh. What's your friend's name?'

'You want to talk about business?' Arenas said.

'Do we have any business to talk about?'

'We might. After I make some enquiries.'

'I'd appreciate that. Here's my card.'

'I'm a friend of your father. Did you know that?'

That caught me by surprise and he knew it.

'He's a good man,' Arenas said. 'He knows which side he's on. Things were a lot simpler once upon a time. You could count on people. We used to be on the same side once upon a time. Then we weren't when times changed. But then again, times keep changing, don't they?'

'What's my father got to do with this?'

'I'm not saying he has.'

I wanted to slap the evil smile off Arenas's face.

What did he have on my father? From now? Or from back when they would have had a common enemy...

'Better not to dig up the past, eh?' Arenas said.

My father had said that to me more than once.

'I'm interested in what's happening right now,' I said.

Maria stubbed out her cigarette, blew smoke at the ceiling.

'Look,' Arenas said. 'I don't know anything about this guy you're looking for but if I do find something out and we can do business, I'll let you know. But go talk to your old man, maybe he can help you.'

My old man? No way. Arenas had to be cranking me up. I'd sent Arenas away. Maybe he wanted to have a little fun with me.

Rangel walked around the room, looked at the Virgin, the

crucifix and the photograph on the wall. Okay, so Arenas wasn't hiding Fischer in his house. I only hoped that my father knew nothing about this disappearance. But I was going to ask him, wasn't I? Rangel caught my eye. I nodded and we went back out through the kitchen to the porch and down to my car. Arenas and Maria came out on the porch to watch us drive away.

'He don't know shit,' I said to Rangel.

'I'm not so sure.'

'How come?'

Rangel shrugged.

'Who was that in the picture with Arenas? Do you know him?'

'Not personally, no.'

'But you know who it is?'

'Sure. Erich Priebke.'

'Who's Erich Priebke?'

'Erich Priebke,' Rangel said, 'one time Nazi, born 1913, extradited to Italy in 1995 – after years of living in hiding in Patagonia – to stand trial for the murders of 335 Italians, executed in reprisals for an ambush on the German SS in Rome in 1944. They found the bodies in a cave at the Fosse Ardeatine outside Rome, and the Italians had been looking for Priebke ever since.'

'But they found him.'

'They tracked him down to the Olympic Hotel in Bariloche. He was running a ski resort in Patagonia. It took years to extradite him. He had a lot of friends in the police force and the judiciary down there. And even in Italy it was difficult to prosecute Priebke. He still had a lot of friends in high places. They got him in some sort of house arrest. You couldn't have been more than thirteen or fourteen when they finally nailed him.'

'So that picture was Arenas and Priebke?'

'Standing outside the Olympic Hotel in Bariloche. I'd say it was taken not long before we shipped him off to Italy.'

'Son of a bitch.'

If Pablo Arenas, or any of his friends or associates, guys like

Priebke, had gotten their hands on Fischer, it would be good news if we heard a ransom demand very soon. Still, who knew? I just hoped that Fischer was out visiting a woman somewhere around the hills and he would eventually turn up. Why couldn't I believe that? Because no one around here would leave the house unlocked. It was as simple as that.

My father involved with a man who had photo ops with Nazis: I didn't want to think about that. I just wanted Fischer to turn up so I could forget all about Arenas and his dirty associates.

'You know what,' I said. 'I'd like to talk some more to that Maria Dos Santos.'

'Yeah, I'd like to talk to her, too,' Rangel said,

'I'd like to talk to her alone.'

'I can imagine.'

'I'm sure you can.'

'You want a cigarette?'

'Yeah.'

'Maybe Fischer will just turn up.' Rangel had that resigned looked on his face that made the bags under his eyes droop, his moustache droop, his red and spider-veined jowls droop.

'I don't think so,' I said.

'Me neither,' Rangel said.

'Do me a favor. Can you check on all the bus companies in town and find out if Gerardo Fischer has bought a ticket to any place?'

'Sure,' Rangel said.

'And the car hire companies, too. Fischer's car is still in the colony's parking lot.'

'Will do.'

'You really think Arenas got something to do with it?'

Rangel shrugged. 'I wouldn't discount it.'

I backed the car down the driveway.

Maybe Arenas had been playing a little cat and mouse with us. But I still didn't much relish talking to my father.

Extract from the casebook of Juan Manuel Pérez
January 10th 2006
Hours: 21:00 to 24:00

I have a nice apartment in Ciudad Azul that overlooks the lake. It's got four bedrooms, a living room, a big kitchen and a dining room. One of the bedrooms I've converted into a study. It's full of books. As a kid I spent all my allowance on books: crime books mostly, but not just. My old man and the old lady always complained about the piles of books beside my bed. Now I've got a library. But my apartment is too big. My wife chose it. My ex-wife, that is. When I had all that trouble in the police department that led to me losing my job, I guess I wasn't such a pleasant guy to live with. Add to that a second miscarriage, and our marital plans all seemed to go awry. Teresa was a Porteña, and still is. She missed the city, she said. So she moved back to Buenos Aires. I miss her from time to time but the apartment is quiet now and doesn't echo with screaming rows, or plates breaking, or low-level bickering. It's a relief in a way. I bring a woman here once in while but no one I've ever wanted to ask to stay for more than the odd night. I guess I'm still in mourning. But I must be a glutton for grief. Why else would I set up a private investigation agency in Ciudad Azul of all places? I guess it seemed so easy when I left the force: I still knew a lot of cops who liked me. I still knew a lot of criminals, too. That's useful in this job. This job is about information: true and false information. True information that incriminates cheating lovers. And false information for the sideline I have in arranging bogus business trips for executives who want to escape from their wives for a week, or a weekend, or a month. I provide tickets, hotel reservations and documents for imaginary conferences in any city in the Americas. The wife – or husband if the client is a woman executive – would never suspect their beloved spouse is hidden away with a lover in Rio or Miami or Santiago or New York. Those jobs pay really well. But they don't come by so often. Maybe Gerardo Fischer had employed a business rival of mine who wasn't so good at his job. Not really. I didn't think so.

This Fischer investigation could pay my bills for a few months maybe, if he didn't show up. Maybe it was in my interest that he didn't show up. But somehow, I liked the people at Temenos. Decent people. Artists. I liked putting away the son of a bitch who had terrorized this Melissa Auerbach, and Ramón and Carlos and Miriam. Maybe I had a soft spot for gays. Maybe I was a closet case. Probably not. That made me think about Ana. She's very cute. And the Temenos world didn't seem as horribly corrupt as mine. I might be wrong.

I sat at the desk in my study, pushed back the books and my laptop computer to clear a nice white space and I opened the folder I'd found in Fischer's kitchen table. I took out the notebook. It fell open at a yellowed newspaper cutting that dated from July 1994. It was about the bombing of the AMIA Jewish Community Center in Buenos Aires in 1994. Over eighty people had been killed, and hundreds injured. It had been the worst bombing ever in Argentina. I read the report. This case was back in the news right now. Since Kirchner had come to power, he called the investigation a national disgrace. The new prosecutors were still trying to find out who was responsible for it. It was a murky business, implications of a cover up: people in the government of the time, the police... even the main judge in the new proceedings had been impeached and removed, and yet another appointed.

Fischer had made some notes on the page below the old cutting about the AMIA bombing. I got out a magnifying glass and held it over the scratchy lines.

Some connection with Iran? Hizbullah? Revenge for Mussawi's killing in Lebanon. Local assistance from some members of the Buenos Aires police force? Or the Argentine Secret Service? How much of this is true? How much money has been changing hands between Lebanon or Iran or Syria and Argentina? And how much obfuscation has been bought down at street level?

A few pages toward the front of Fischer's book, there was another newspaper cutting. This one was on the Israeli embassy bombing in Buenos Aires in 1992: a truck bomb, 29 dead, over two hundred wounded, many of them children from a school close by the embassy. No notes there. Just a few jottings on characters for some plays: a short piece on *Antigone*; another on *Elektra*. Was Fischer using the cuttings as research for these plays? There didn't seem to be any connection. And these theatrical notes weren't getting me any closer to finding him.

From the back of the folder, I opened the paper packet with the set of postcards and pictures that Fischer had presumably collected over a number of years. Not all of the pictures were dated. Some of the postcards were. I spread them over the surface of my desk. I picked up a Jewish New Year's card with the words

L'SHANAH TOVAH

printed across it and beneath it what I thought of as a kind of altar that you'd see in a synagogue, the place where they keep the scrolls of the Torah. Inside the card a message was printed in English:

Wishing you happiness
And good health
Throughout the coming year

The rest was written in good Spanish and signed from Melanie and Joe. It wasn't meant to be just for Fischer but for Melanie and Joe's '*Dear Friends.*' Maybe it was to the whole theater company. There was no envelope to indicate where it had been sent. Gerardo or the company might have got it in Buenos Aires, Montevideo or Rome. The card had been printed in Cleveland, Ohio, but it could just as easily have been bought in a store in any city in the United States from New York to San Francisco. *Thanks be to God,* they'd written, *we can celebrate being alive and in good health for the coming year.*

At Rosh Hashanah, Jewish believers maintain that God decides who gets to live and who gets to die for the next year and I guess that Fischer and most of the company made it through when that card was written. I wondered if 2006 in the Christian Era was the year when Fischer's name had been crossed off the list in the Book of Life. I had no inkling one way or the other. Wishing people health and long life: given that a lot of the other postcards were from the late seventies and early eighties, the greeting card seemed particularly poignant.

I put three postcards from Israel down on my desk. Each one had that crude coloring where the sky is too blue, the blonds too blond, and the foliage a messy green. There were no addresses on them and the messages were scrawled right across the backs of the cards, which meant that they must have been mailed inside envelopes. They could have been sent to any country in the world – there were no envelopes to indicate which – wherever it was that Fischer was living at that time. The first of the postcards I looked at was dated 12th June 1982. It was a picture of a lot of guys with bushy hair and sideburns, some of them dressed in fatigues, all leaning on the hoods of cars beside an olive grove and a barbed wire fence; with the words *The Good Fence Metulla* in red on a white background and below those words in English and Hebrew was a bible quote in red: *And they shall beat their swords into plowshares and their spears into pruning hooks. Nation shall not lift up sword against nation neither shall they learn war any more.*

On the back was a message.

12th June 1982

Dear Francesca,

I'm working with a medical team here in Metulla. Just north of us, the situation in Lebanon is atrocious. Every day hundreds of refugees come through the gate to receive treatment for bullet wounds, shrapnel wounds, terrible burns. It's impossible to work out who is fighting whom and for what. The PLO is attacking the Lebanese Army and Christian villages. Christian Phalangists are shelling PLO refugee camps. Druze and Shia all have their militia groups and are driving 'disloyal elements' out of their villages and areas of influence, or simply shooting them dead. This is what I've heard. The refugees tell us that whole neighborhoods of Beirut are in flames. At least for now, Israel has a peace accord with Egypt but Lebanon seems like hell on earth. I receive little news from Buenos Aires. I believe my family is still well, but every time I receive a letter from them, I'm terrified to open it. My whole world seems to be at war. I'm doing what I can here because back home… what's there to do? I miss you, Francesca. Maybe some time I can come to see you in Italy.

Love,

Isabel

It was bizarre reading these words with hindsight, here in my office in 2006, when I knew that in June 1982, the Argentine armed forces were fighting against the British in the Malvinas. Every kid watched that on TV. I was only six years old and I remember marching around with my toy rifle and firing at imaginary British sailors on the lake. Here in these postcards were chronicles of another war. How was Fischer involved in that? Should it have any bearing on his disappearance now?

The second postcard from Israel that I'd plucked from the folder had a picture on the front of two blond women on Atarim Square in Tel Aviv. The architecture was ugly. Maybe at the time it was supposed to be chic and modern. Back then it was worth someone printing a postcard to sell to admirers of the new development on the Tel Aviv seafront. The card was dated September 30th 1982.

Dear Francesca

Last Saturday saw the biggest demonstration ever against the policies of the government in its war in Lebanon. Four hundred thousand of us were in the streets of Tel Aviv. We are all of us in shock that Sharon allowed the massacre of so many civilians in the Sabra and Shatila refugee camps in West Beirut by the Christian Phalangists. How can anyone be called Christian who systematically murders so many people? And the Israeli army stood by and watched it happen. Encouraged it? If I feel safe here on Israeli soil, it's because I feel like I am living in a fortress state whose armies periodically venture outside to wreak destruction on the neighboring states. This will never lead to peace in the region. And in Lebanon, each faction is still intent on murdering the sympathizers of every other faction. It's like gang warfare with heavy weapons supplied by rival regional powers: Syria, Israel, Iran. The peace movement is growing. So many people on the streets. Even if at times I feel like I should get out of this state that is headed by warmongers, I still feel that I should be here in Israel. This is my adopted country and we all have a right to be here whatever happened in the past, and I must help in the struggle for justice for Israelis and Palestinians both. At least I can demonstrate on the streets here without fear of being picked up and tortured. But I feel so powerless against the atrocities being committed in my name in Lebanon. I hope all is well with you in Italy. Write me soon.

Love

Isabel

The last of the postcards that had originated in Israel was a picture of the ruins at Masada. The message on the back of that card was bleak. It was written to Gerardo and it was much more recent. There was no date and the card was a little beaten up but the content suggested it had been written within the last few years.

Dear Gerardo,

Thank you for your card wishing me peace. The truth is that it's in no one's interest to have peace in the Middle East: not the Israeli government, not Hizbullah, not Hamas, not the Syrians, and not all the various gangster factions in Lebanon that grew out of the civil war. The PLO wants to get rid of the Israelis, and so do all the other Islamic groups, even if they hate every other Arab faction with as much passion or more. The Iranians have no interest in peace because they want to lead the Islamic world against the Israelis and the Americans. The Americans have no interest in peace because they want to keep control of Middle Eastern oil. Having failed to convert post-Saddam Iraq into something resembling Texas, the next best thing is a state of perpetual war among all the factions: Shiite, Sunni, Kurd, or any gang of sycophants that can hang on to power and guarantee the oil supply. The Middle East will continue to be in a state of warfare because it is willed by all parties: Islamic Jihadists, the world's oil and military interests, Shiite Islamic revolutionaries, Hamas, the Muslim Brotherhood, Al-Qaeda, NATO to maintain control of Afghanistan and Pakistan, Russia to keep control of Chechnya, Uzbekistan, and Kazakhstan, China to maintain control of Xinjiang. And oil, and oil, and oil. Who wants peace? Nobody. While we are all at war then all of these interests are being served economically and ideologically.

Perpetual warfare is the natural state.

Love,

Isabel

Perpetual Warfare? That was one pissed off woman.

I sifted among the pile again.

I pulled out a card from Bariloche.

Arenas? Priebke?

The postcard was in Isabel's handwriting: it was an old postcard from the early nineties.

Dear Gerardo

We brought the American here today. I think we've found the long lost relative we've been looking for. We couldn't get reservations at the Olympic Hotel which was disappointing. We're in a place close by and it's a little frustrating that we can see the place where we wanted to stay but we were told that it was totally booked up with delegates for a private conference. The delegates and their wives seem to be very well off. We've seen number of officers in uniform, too. We're sending a photograph of a well-connected gentleman we met up here. He's been very kind to us. The American wants to talk to the manager of the Olympic. Maybe when the conference is over. We're so excited to be here in the Andes. Do let Melanie and Joe know that we'll be staying on for a few weeks more.

Love

Isa

This had to be connected. So Isabel had come back to Argentina after the fall of the dictatorship and had gone to Bariloche to take a look at the Olympic Hotel. It had to be connected to this Priebke guy.

Who was the American?

Behind the postcard was a photograph of a gray-haired man wearing shades and in fatigues. He stood beside a lake that was surrounded by mountains, which were probably the Andes. There was nothing written on the back of the photograph. Whoever was in the photograph, the man in fatigues, I had no idea. It wasn't Priebke. He looked nothing like the man in the photograph at Pablo

Arenas's house. Was he the one who had helped Isabel identify Priebke?

Fischer must have known who this man was to have a photograph of him, and Fischer was involved with Isabel and her companion, and whoever or whatever they were searching for. But did it necessarily involve Arenas? Or did Arenas become involved later after Priebke had been flushed out of hiding and extradited?

What was the link with the Jewish New Year's card from the United States? Maybe nothing. Isabel would have mailed the first two postcards from Israel to this Francesca who was in Italy, and Fischer had kept them for all these years. That would make Fischer something of an obsessive: not necessarily surprising considering that he was a playwright who had kept writing and producing plays for around forty years so far. There had to be a streak of obsession there somewhere.

And if Fischer had been in Italy, a possible link that would tie him to Priebke in Bariloche would be the massacre at those caves in Rome: for which, Rangel said, Priebke had been extradited. But why would Fischer become involved in the hunt for Erich Priebke? Why should it have any relevance to his disappearance now over ten years later?

What was obvious here was that Fischer's politics, or the politics of those with whom he kept company, were a little complicated. On the one hand, if he had been connected with trying to expose Priebke, he was obviously looking for justice, or punishment, for an ex-Nazi; while on the other hand, even if Isabel had found refuge in Israel, she was still critical enough of the Israeli government to get herself arrested in Tel Aviv after the Sabra and Shatila massacres in Lebanon.

Why was it that Fischer had this folder with him, up here in a house that was a short-term rental, while he worked on a play? Was this material for something new but based on the past? Did this folder have any significance for his disappearance? There was plenty in it. Two postcards had been sent from Iguazu: spectacular views of the waterfalls where the borders of Argentina, Paraguay and Brazil all meet up. Away from the tourist villages, the area is notorious for arms deals, drug deals, and all kinds of shady business from contraband to prostitution.

I couldn't tell which of the Iguazu postcards had been sent first. They both had one-line cryptic messages.

We've lost Araujo and Sadiq.

The two boys plan on going to Buenos Aires.

Neither was signed. Why did Isabel communicate by postcard?[2] Was it because she was afraid of her messages being intercepted? No cell phones in those days. If this was around the time of the Jewish center bombings was there any connection?

If Fischer had involved himself in digging in the dirt of an investigation into the bombings – which was still going on at this very moment within the prosecutors' jurisdiction in Buenos Aires – which has a ten year history of being covered up, with a lot of money changing hands – maybe that had provided a motive for someone to make him disappear.

I checked my watch. It was only just ten pm. I took out my cell phone and found Ana's number.

'Hello?' she said.

'Listen,' I said. 'I've been looking at these postcards and diaries. Do you know who Isabel might be?'

'Isabel? A friend of Gerardo's? That could be Sara's sister.'

'Is she at Temenos?'

Fischer's postcards

2 http://bit.ly/farsouth3

'Who? Isabel?'

'Yeah.'

'No, she lives in Buenos Aires.'

'I'll ask Sara about her.'

'Okay.'

'Hey, listen,' I said. 'You want to have a drink?'

'Now?'

'Yeah.'

'Maybe another time, okay? I'm just so worried right now. I want to stay with Sara.'

I let the air out of my lungs quietly.

'Yeah, sure. Is Sara there now?'

'Yeah,' Ana said.

'Can I speak to her?'

'Sure.'

Sara came on the line.

'Can you give me your sister's number in Buenos Aires?' I said.

'Isabel?' Sara said.

'Yeah. I picked up a folder at Fischer's house with a lot of correspondence from her to him over the years and it might be useful to talk to her.'

'Okay. But she's away until late on Friday night.'

'Where is she?'

'Israel.'

'Oh... does she know about Gerardo?'

'Yes. I sent her an email right away.'

'And she's back on Friday?'

'That's right.'

I could wait until Saturday before trying to talk to Isabel. What time would it be over there anyway, four in the morning?

'Look,' I said. 'Can we meet and talk about her a little? It might lead somewhere.'

'How do you mean?'

'I think there's a possibility that your Gerardo might have

skipped out of his own accord. And it might be somehow connected with the past.'

'You really think so?'

I didn't want to say that Fischer might have got himself involved in some murky political investigation that might have led to him being taken out of the picture. It's better business to be optimistic with a client.

'I think it's a possibility worth investigating.'

'But why wouldn't he call us?' Sara said.

'Maybe to protect you. Sometimes it's better if people don't know what you're doing. Cell phones are traceable, emails are traceable, laptops are traceable. Do you understand?'

A long silence at the end of the line, then Sara spoke. 'Oh... okay.'

'I'll come around after lunch tomorrow.'

'That's fine,' Sara said.

'Thanks.'

I hung up.

Priebke on the wall of Arenas's house: Isabel was at the Olympic Hotel in Bariloche.

I called up Rangel.

'What happened with the car hire places and the bus companies?'

'No Fischer, and no one who looked like Fischer to the people who would give me answers to the questions I had. Then again, maybe he used a false name.'

'Thanks. See you in the morning.'

I looked around the empty apartment: the art books on the coffee table, the deep pile white carpet, the panoramic window with its view over the lake. No Ana or Maria Dos Santos. A pity that. I guessed that I'd be drinking alone for the night. I didn't really feel like reading. I had an afternoon date to talk business with Sara.

Arenas had got under my skin.

First thing in the morning I'd have to go to see my old man.

[**Extract from the casebook of Juan Manuel Pérez**
January 11th 2006
Hours: 09:00 to 11:30

Last night I dreamed I was in Lebanon. My girlfriend – a dream girlfriend... I'd never met her in my everyday life... maybe she looked a little like Maria Dos Santos – had been shot in the shoulder by some gangster and then the gangster had been arrested by some cops that I knew. An ambulance came and took my girlfriend to the hospital. For some reason, I had to cross the city with a male friend in order to go see her. This was in the middle of the civil war in Beirut. Two things I had to transport across the city: a bottle of excellent white wine, and the hand and forearm of a female mannequin that was decorated with rings and bracelets that had all been made with precious stones. The plaster hand served two purposes: one was to safeguard my girlfriend's jewelry; the other was that the mannequin arm would help in the healing of her shoulder. I don't know how. This was a dream, dream logic. I wrapped up the plaster arm in linen and hid it in the belly of my girlfriend's teddy bear. I re-stuffed the bear and sewed it up. I took off with this male friend of mine. The streets were a running battle: some Islamic militiamen fired rocket propelled grenades into a house and dragged out the women of a rival faction. One of the fighters was about to rape a woman in a headscarf. I was horrified. The woman had some scarring on her face from previous battles. I was powerless to stop the assault on her. I thought, he's doing that because for him the woman isn't a Muslim... she's part of a different sect to him: a Druze or a Shiite. So she's an infidel. An apostate, she deserves death. I wanted to help out, but my friend grabbed me by the arm and said, 'This isn't our fight.' A bus came by, a kind of Ford people carrier, and my friend forced me to get on the bus. I was still traumatized by the attempted rape and I was worried that we'd get kidnapped if we got on the bus but he insisted we'd be safe. There were some Muslim women in head-scarves on the bus so I thought that he was probably right. It was shocking that a semblance of normal life was going on – a city bus picking up passengers at a regular bus stop – while this civil war was in full spate in the city streets. I woke up as we arrived at our destination. Those postcards must have affected me.

I showered and cleaned my teeth; put on a clean white shirt and a light brown linen suit.

When I picked up the holster with the M1911, the story of Arenas and his jammed gun played on my mind. I went into my study, cleared a space on the Formica-topped table, laid out a cloth and disassembled the gun. I can do that in a flat thirty-nine seconds. I opened up my cleaning kit: nylon brush, copper brush, a patch rod, patches solvent, rag and oil. I wiped the barrel down with the rag and ran a patch through with some solvent. I wiped off the frame and ran a rag through the mag chamber. I oiled the slots in the slide and set it aside. I rubbed a thin film of oil onto the barrel and the locking lugs; a little onto the recoil guide rod; and with the oil having run down the length of the slide slots, I reassembled the weapon in a flat forty-five seconds. I emptied the magazine, lining up the rounds at the top of the cloth. I released the mag spring and wiped it down, ran a rag over the magazine, inside and out – it was pretty clean – and reassembled it. I haven't use the gun much in a long time. I reloaded the magazine and snapped it back into the stock. I repacked the cleaning kit. I checked the weapon and clipped the hip holster onto my belt. It shouldn't jam.

Over coffee and *medialunas* at the local bar, I called Rangel at the office.

'I'm going to talk to this Sara Suarez at the Artists Colony. But first of all, I want to pay a visit to my father.'

'That bastard Arenas poured poison in your ear, my friend.'

'Maybe. But I need to broach the subject with Pa.'

'Your call.' Rangel hung up.

I got in the Ford Executive and I drove out to Route 60, and then the thirty kilometers or so to my father's property near San Pedro. Pa has a small farm in a valley reachable by an all but washed-out dirt road. The farm is bordered by stands of pine that surround the open paddocks for his five horses. Pa divorced my mother fifteen years ago. He left her the family house in Ciudad Azul and bought this little spread up in the hills where he set up with his horses; and with his new woman, Costanza, for whom I'd had no kind word to say for about seven years after they got together. I've kind of got used to her now. Costanza is ten years younger than my mother – which put her in her late forties – and just because she had bottle blond hair, a nose job, and silicone breasts, the cosmetic surgery didn't automatically make her a monster. Fuck it, so many women do that, now. There's a cosmetic surgeon on every street corner in Buenos Aires and every other in Ciudad Azul. And, despite it all, Costanza still looked like a countrywoman. And she could ride, which my father likes a lot.

I turned off the dirt road, rattled over a wooden bridge over the stream that is the southern boundary of the property, passed a shrine to the Madonna on my right, and turned left again down to the main gate where I parked the big black Ford. The wall around the house is about ten feet high. The green paint on the main gates is blistered and flaked, and some of the slats are rotten and need replacing. I lifted the right door handle and pushed. The gate scraped across the dry earth. I lifted it shut behind me.

The fruit on Pa's cherry trees and plum trees were ripe. He keeps the lawn cut short on the slope down to the stream that runs along the bottom of the garden. Across the stream, in the next paddock, a mature pair of bay thoroughbreds, and their three close-to-full-grown offspring, lifted their heads to inspect me from a distance; and then dipped them again to continue their grazing.

Pa came around the side of the house to see who'd driven up and opened the gate. He's proud of this flat-roofed ranch house from the nineteenth century. Wisteria climbs the walls. The windows have the original wooden shutters that have been kept in far better condition than the gate and they've been strengthened by the addition of iron bars for the windows.

Pa raised a hand to me. The cuff of his plaid shirt, worn over a white t-shirt, flopped back on his forearm. His wheat-colored cotton pants bunched at the ankles over his leather sandals. He's a wiry man, a deep brown color from the sun, deep wrinkles, bald with a chiseled off chin that's shadowed with pale gray stubble. In that tanned face his eyes are a deadly blue. I'm taller and thicker set than him. Better fed in my childhood, I guess. And I wish I had those woman-killer eyes of his. My own eyes are dark. I must take after my mother in that.

'Juanma! To what do we owe the honor?' he called.

Costanza appeared behind him, her blond hair tied up with a wide blue hair band, her denim shorts cut high on her tanned thighs, and her yellow cotton blouse stretched over those sculptured breasts.

'Hi,' she called.

I reminded myself to be nice to her. She's nice to my father, isn't she?

'A *matecito*, Juanma?' my father said.

'Sure,' I said.

We went round into the shade close to the stone barbecue that he'd built into the farmhouse wall. We sat down at the black cast iron garden table. A black and silver thermos stood next to Pa's leather covered *mate* gourd. Costanza reached for her cigarettes and lit one while my father adjusted the long silver tube in the *yerba* with his fist and poured the hot water into the gourd. It's always his job, preparing the brew. He has to be in control.

'You're working?' Pa lifted his chin toward my open jacket, his glance on the butt of the automatic in the leather hip holster beneath it.

'Up at that artists colony, you know the one... Temenos... one of those people has gone missing.'

He passed the full gourd over to me, bubbles foaming on top of it.

Bitter, not too bitter.

'How missing?'

'House open... and man and computer gone.'

He shrugged.

'I talked to Pablo Arenas,' I said.

'Arenas?'

'Yeah.'

'The guy you put away.'

'He's robbed them twice up there. Maybe things always go in threes.'

Pa pushed out his lower lip. I sucked at the silver tube.

'He's done his time. Why you got a hard-on for Arenas?'

'He got me thrown off the force.'

'You getting paid to do this work?'

'Yeah.'

Pa nodded.

'Anyone ask for money yet? For this guy.'

'Not that I know of... I don't even know who might pay a ransom for him. No family to speak of... doesn't seem to have much money.'

'Or if he just took off with a woman... or if he got involved in an accident somewhere...'

'The house was open,' I said.

'Right,' Pa said.

I sipped at the brew. Costanza smoked her cigarette.

'Arenas says he knows you.'

'I know Arenas.'

Now it was my turn to say nothing. I finished the brew and passed the gourd back to my father. He took the thermos and filled up the gourd again. He passed it over to Costanza. She took it from him, crossed her legs, drew on her cigarette, blew out smoke, posed with the cigarette, and sucked at the silver tube. I waited for my father to say something. But he didn't say anything.

'You think Arenas might have anything to do with it?'

My father shook his head, not in denial, simply an expression that he wasn't interested. I wanted to ask him what he knew about Arenas and why he knew him but I also knew that my father wasn't going to tell me or he already would have said something.

'You know Arenas has a picture of himself with this Nazi war criminal, Erich Priebke, on his wall. The SS guy we extradited to stand trial in Italy back in the nineties.'

Pa shrugged.

'Who else wants to see this guy gone?'

I shook my head: my turn to be inscrutable. A possibility of murder, that's what my father was implying. But he wouldn't be drawn on Arenas.

'Maybe he just skipped out,' Pa said.

'I'd like to see Fischer's police records. He must have a record somewhere if he went into exile in the seventies. We kept records on every potential subversive. It would be good to see Arenas's file again, too. I don't remember a lot about it but the strange thing is, I know I saw that Arenas had a record of being in the Triple A; but there was no mention of anything to do with Priebke. Maybe there was some other stuff missing, too. Or maybe there are some things in his file that I didn't pay any mind because the robbery case was so cut and dried. I'd like to see it again.'

My father shook his head. 'Difficult. You're not a well loved man in the precinct.'

'No, I'm not.'

'I'll do what I can for you.'

I sat upright in the garden seat. I couldn't believe what I'd just heard.

'Just leave it to me,' he said. 'I'll find out if anything is going on.'

I knew better than to push it any further.

'The colts are looking good,' I said. 'They're coming along fine.'

'Costanza is already excited about breaking them in.'

'They'll be a good ride.'

My father smiled, a look of love on his face. Costanza poured water from the thermos into the gourd, and offered it to him to drink.

I got up from the table.

'I gotta go.'

'Come back soon, Juanma,' my father said.

'Bye, Juanma,' Costanza said.

'Bye.'

Across in the paddock, the bay mare whinnied.

I let myself out of the gate, got in the car and drove back towards Ciudad Azul.

[
Extract from the casebook of Juan Manuel Pérez
January 11th 2006
Hours: 11:30 to 12:00

On the road from San Pedro to Ciudad Azul, I pulled off Route 60 and drove through the village of San Sebastian. I passed the local police station and followed the main road up towards Plaza Lavalle. I glanced at the hardware store and the pharmacy on my left and then I passed by the laundry. I felt a rush of adrenalin when I saw Maria Dos Santos, all hair and hips in a light summer dress. She tottered on her high heels toward a bus stop. She had a sky blue and white-striped shopping basket slung on her left shoulder. I slowed the car. When Maria reached the bus stand and stopped walking, I touched my foot on the gas, then braked and pulled up just in front of her. I pressed the button to lower the passenger side window.

'Hi, Maria,' I called out.

Maria dipped her head and squinted through the frame of the window. Her dark hair fell forward. I couldn't help notice the swing of her breasts under the light cotton. She didn't seem terribly surprised when she recognized me.

'Where you going?' I asked.

She stayed leaning over, put one hand on the window opening to steady herself as she tottered on her heels. She has such full lips, I thought. Dark eyes.

'Ciudad Azul,' she said.

'Get in. I can give you a ride. I'm going back to my office.'

She looked uncertain for a moment, glanced back the way she'd come, another glance ahead, raised her head to look over the roof of the car, and then reached for the door handle and opened it. She slid onto the passenger seat and slammed the door a little too hard.

'Thanks.' She looked straight ahead through the windshield, her hands resting on her knees. Her legs were brown. The straps of her high-heeled shoes cut into her instep a little. I didn't think that they'd be comfortable shoes to walk in. I checked the mirrors, let out the clutch and eased the car forward into the street. There was hardly another vehicle on the road. A lot of the stores would be closed soon for lunch.

I kept my mouth shut. I eased through the gears, left behind the last of the stores on Main Street, and then began the climb from the other side of the village up toward Route 60. When we passed the soccer field I saw that the Ford Falcon was parked outside Arenas's house.

'How's your uncle?'

'You don't like him, do you?' Maria said.

'He beat up some old lady, I put him away for it.'

'And for robbing those queers.'

'Yeah, and for robbing the queers.'

'The boy that the queers killed was a cousin of mine.'

'I'm sorry.'

I didn't think I was really sorry but the words just slipped out of my mouth.

'I don't think you're very sorry,' she said.

'I was doing my job. I found out who it was robbed the old lady and the queers and then I had to testify and then they went to jail.'

'With a couple of cops.'

'Yeah. With a couple of cops.'

'You aren't a cop any more,' she said.

'Well, yeah. That's right.'

'So why you come round and ask my uncle all those questions?'

'Some guy's gone missing. I'd like to know where he is.'

'Why?' Maria pulled her hair back from her face.

I pulled onto Route 60 and stepped on the gas a little. That was a good question she'd asked. Why? Because I was getting paid to do it was the correct answer. Except it wasn't just the only correct answer: because I was involved in something, now, with a little more dignity to it than a simple divorce case. And then there was the angle that Arenas had brought my father into this. And now my father had agreed to look for Fischer and Arenas's records. My father's involvement meant something to me.

'I'm getting paid to do it,' I said.

'You're fucking with my family,' she said. 'For money.'

It was pretty obvious I wasn't going to be doing any of that with her.

'Do you know anything about this guy who's gone missing?'

'Is that why you picked me up?'

'I picked you up because I thought I might give you a ride into town. And I might like your company.'

'Well. Do you like my company?'

'It's very enlightening. But not what I expected.'

'What did you expect?'

'I wasn't sure. I was willing to take a risk.'

'Was it worth the risk?'

'Sure.'

'You just might regret it.'

'I don't think so.'

'Do yourself a favor. Stay away from my uncle. He doesn't like you.'

'Is that why you got in the car? To tell me that.'

'No. I thought I'd get to Ciudad Azul quicker in your car than if I waited for the bus.'

'You're in a hurry?'

'Yeah. I'm meeting my boyfriend.'

'Does he know anything about this guy disappearing?'

'Do you think I'd tell you if he did?'

'No, I guess not.'

The road curved down along an inlet of the lake and passed the first of the high-rise hotels. We reached the town clock. It's a big ugly mock-baroque affair.

'This is my stop,' she said.

I pulled over. She opened the door and got out without a backward glance. The door slammed shut. As I watched the sway of her hips and the tilt of her hair I realized what a pathetic fantasy it had been to think that I could have seduced her, won her to my side, and got her to talk about her uncle's involvement in the robberies and possible disappearance of Fischer. The clock clanged for midday. I figured it was time for lunch. I'd get a steak sandwich and a cup of coffee.

Then I had to go back out to the Temenos Artists Colony for my meeting with Sara Suarez. Priebke on Arenas's wall, the postcards from Bariloche in Gerardo Fischer's folder. It was a tentative link to explain Fischer's disappearance. I didn't know if I could trust a sense of intuition that the key to unlocking the motive for Gerardo Fischer's disappearance lay in the discovery of something dangerous from his past. So far, it was all I had to go on.

Witness Deposition: Sara Suarez

Isabel was picked up early on in the dictatorship. She disappeared for a month. And then she came back. God knows what they did to her in that jail. I was sixteen at the time. My mother put Isabel on a plane to Israel and told her to stay there until it was over. Until what was over? And how long would the Dirty War take to be over? We didn't know back then. And all of us couldn't leave. The family didn't have the money to just sell up and go. Go where? Israel, too? Barcelona? Mexico City? Always the question: is poverty better than… what?

Isabel was a friend of Francesca Damiani, one of Gerardo's lovers. The police picked up Francesca, and she was let go, too, and then she and Gerardo got out to Italy. This was in the early days. When people were picked up and interrogated and some of them were released. It got worse later. Much worse.

My sister Isabel had some kind of connection with Gerardo through Francesca. They wrote to each other, Francesca and Isabel: when Isabel was in Israel and Francesca in Italy. Isabel was involved in the peace movement in Israel. A lot of good that did. She lived on the border with Lebanon for a time.

Francesca turned up in Buenos Aires not so long ago. I don't have a telephone number for her but Isabel would. They're still good friends, I think, but Francesca has always been very secretive. It's an addiction of hers. I suppose you can't blame her really after all she went through back then.

For me the time of the dictatorships was like the thirties and forties… the time when our grandparents dropped everything and left Germany for Argentina. That was like a legend in the family. And in the seventies those shadows slipped back into our house in Buenos Aires. It was like a haunting: these black uniformed ghosts of my childhood imaginings: silver death's heads, lightning flashes, about to materialize at any moment. I was afraid of what might be behind the shuttered windows, the velvet curtains, the solid panels of the varnished front door. I was scared of the sound of every car that passed by in the street, terrified if a car stopped, the doors opening and slamming, and then the wait for the knock on the door, the ring on the doorbell. The wait. How many nights like that?

And worse and worse… for years it went on… and then we'd hear that someone close by had been taken away and disappeared… who was taking them away? The military because they were militants? At first, yes. And then there were the Montoneros to fear, and the ERP, because the family was bourgeois and we had some money so they might take someone away for ransom, or just for execution. Or it could be just some gangsters out for a ransom payment. And then we began to hear the stories, the rumors of what happened to the ones who had disappeared, heard about the discoveries of the bodies thrown from helicopters, floating in the Riachuelo, washed up on one of the delta beaches at Tigre. We were so glad that Isabel had gone. But we were terrified that some day they might come for one of us.

Thank God that seems to be over. But there are so many ex-cops and criminals… you can't just relax at all… you know what I mean… those robberies we had, and now this, with Gerardo… and Arenas out of jail.

The dogs are a comfort to me, especially now, with all this. We thought it would end after Melissa was robbed. But then they came back for Miriam and Carlos and Ramón, didn't they? They wanted to terrorize us, I'm sure. And Carlos and Ramón found out that Arenas had been in the Triple A.

I've known Carlos and Ramón for years. I was supposed to interview them for my book on the day that Arenas tried to rob them. Miriam is another subject I'd like to explore. Carlos had been looking forward to the interviews… Carlos is Miriam's son… so he's Jewish through Miriam's line… and he identifies with being Jewish… even if Dieter, you know, his father… you know that Carlos's grandfather is one of those Germans who left Germany in 1945… with a handy passport provided by the Argentine embassy in Berne, that got him to Bariloche with a different identity – Renato Brescia, a good Italian name – and an invented past that hardly anyone would ever talk about in public…

Carlos knew that I must have been practically foaming to get the story of his family. It's so rich, when you think about it… and complicated… like a soap opera in a way. And now we were all up here in this other soap opera with Melissa getting robbed by someone in a rubber werewolf mask, kinky enough, and the others in ski masks… Carlos admitted that he felt very nervous after Melissa was robbed. And he was glad he wasn't just living on his own with his mother.

Carlos used to live right here in the colony … that's where Ramón met him at a party one summer. They'd had drinks and one thing led to another… and now Ramón has been living with Carlos… and his mother… for a few years. That's enough of a soap in itself… Dieter, Carlos's father, had left Bariloche before Priebke's arrest… Dieter didn't want to be part of that scenario any more… the secret nods… the collusive whispers… all those awful parties that just happened to be celebrated on Hitler's birthday… Carlos is very proud of Miriam and Dieter for taking a stand…

Miriam is just amazing… Carlos couldn't imagine many mothers standing up for their gay son in Argentina. Dieter ran a travel business in Ciudad Azul… it ran itself, basically, after about ten years of Dieter's hard graft… and he sold it all before the crash in 2001. Smart enough to have a dollar account in Florida, too, not in a bank in Argentina. They felt so lucky to have survived when so many people lost everything. And then Dieter was diagnosed with cancer. This whole country is a series of disasters, isn't it? You think you escape one and the next one…

Carlos would probably get all philosophical about it. He's quite New Age, really. Just before Dieter died... maybe only two years ago, now... Dieter asked Carlos to look after Miriam when he passed. They had a kind of special understanding. Carlos thought that Ramón would object when he said he wanted Miriam to move in with them when she got ill. Miriam has always been reluctant to talk to me. I can understand in a way. Who wants to go into all those maybe unconscious reasons for her and Dieter's relationship – you know, a Jewish woman marries the son of an ex-Nazi, who turns out to be gay? Well, I do for one. And Carlos was happy to be part of it. He knew he was being narcissistic. But we're all a bit narcissistic, aren't we? Carlos just doesn't mind being honest with himself. He's such a good boy. And Ramón, too. They're very passionate about justice. I think doubly so since they were robbed. They've been part of a human rights group since before the robbery.

I don't know if Gerardo has some particular interest that he might share with them. Except that he's always interested in people. I don't think he's gay though. Maybe he wants to write a play about them. I mean, with those ingredients: the Nazism, the Jewish connection, the robbery, Miriam, and how Gerardo reconnected with her through Carlos seeing his play in Buenos Aires and Ana inviting him here to do those workshops. I want to write about them anyway.

Did you know that Gerardo is Jewish? I think so. But it's so hard to get a straight answer out of him. He's such a bastard. I know that he's interested in the Kabbalah. He studied it for years. He did a play, you know, based on the life of the alchemist, Francesco Bono. Bono disappeared in Rome... I can't remember when, back in the Renaissance time... If you read Gerardo's work, it's always connected with doors... entrances into other spaces... it would make a whole other psychological study... but I don't want to get distracted from my own subject... the psychology of immigration, yes.

And now he's disappeared. As if he's gone through some door in time and space. And everyone looking for him. He'd love the irony of that.

[Extract from the casebook of Juan Manuel Pérez
January 11th 2006
Hours: 17:15 to 18:20

The drive from Temenos to Miriam's house was a familiar one to me. Three years previously, I'd had to interview Miriam, Carlos and Ramón at some length about the robberies. And then there was the corpse of Arenas's buddy to pick up off the porch. The two gay guys and their mother had been pretty shaken up, but truth to tell who wouldn't have shot those two bastards, armed as they were, threatening murder, and firing through the door of the house? I pulled into the driveway and parked: only one car there, the old lady's. Maybe she'd say that Gerardo had gone to Buenos Aires with the boys.

But I didn't think she would.

Carlos and Ramón took good care of the plants and flowers in the garden: a beautiful border of azaleas and marigolds and tall gladioli. I called out a hello. No one answered. The curtain pulled back for a second and the old lady winced when she saw me but she raised a hand to me in recognition. The bolts on the other side of the front door clacked back and she opened up.

'Lieutenant Pérez,' she said.

'Señora Brescia. I'm not a cop any more. This is a private thing.'

There, I'm an honest guy.

'Come in,' she said.

Miriam's black dress and gold earrings gave her an austere and faded elegance. She was wrinkled under the chin and the delicately shadowed eyes. A pale liver spot stained her skin back toward her ear, close to her jaw. Her bobbed hair was dyed black. This was the woman who had seen her son shoot one man to death and wound another with a twelve-gauge shotgun. She leaned toward me, familiar enough to her that she inclined her head for a friendly greeting. Miriam's perfume was lemony. My cheek brushed against her face powder. She smiled a thin smile as I drew back.

'Sara told me about Gerardo,' she said.

'I'm just looking around to see if I can help. We've seen no sign of violence. Nothing of the sort... '

I followed her into her spacious living room. The farmhouse had been converted into a high-tech designer showpiece since the shootings. Red and shiny, a boxer's heavy bag hung from the ceiling about ten feet from the bookshelves on the back wall. Her boy's no doubt. The walls were painted white and hung with posters from art-house movies: *Hombre Mirando al Sudeste*; *Nueve Reinas*; an American movie, *Stranger than Paradise*. The white leather sofas and armchairs all looked as if they've been imported from New York, or at least from Buenos Aires.

Miriam sat down on the L-shaped sofa in the far corner of the room. The low glass table in front of her was scattered with foreign movie magazines in English and French: *Sight and Sound*, *Cahiers du Cinema*... She had a thermos and a gourd there, too.

'Would you like some *mate*?' she said.

'Yes, thank you,' I said.

She filled the gourd with hot water from the thermos and passed it over to me.

'So you're all alone up here?' I said.

'The boys have gone down to Buenos Aires. I can take care of myself.'

I wasn't so sure. But she did have that shotgun in the house.

'When did they go?'

'The day before yesterday... around lunchtime.'

'Just the two of them?'

'Yes.'

'Gerardo didn't go with them?'

'No. They would have said.'

'They know he's disappeared?'

'They're worried as we all are.'

'You knew Gerardo, of course.'

She smiled a wry smile.

'Know Gerardo? It's difficult to know much even *about* Gerardo. Always has been.'

'You've seen him recently?'

'A few days ago, he came over to talk with the boys.'

'Do you know what about?'

I sucked at the silver tube and the hot liquid scalded my tongue.

'I've no idea... they were talking on the terrace. I was inside. At one point I took a bath and when I came out Gerardo had gone.'

'You have no idea what might have happened to him?'

'None at all.'

'You've heard from the boys?'

I handed the gourd back to Miriam.

'They called from Buenos Aires the night before last. They arrived after midnight but they know I'm always awake until two or three in the morning.'

She filled the gourd again and cradled it close to her chest.

'So they're safe?'

'Yes, of course,' she said.

'How friendly are they with Gerardo?'

'Gerardo has known Carlos since he was a baby.'

'How did you meet him?'

'Gerardo?'

'Yes.'

'Through my husband, my *ex*-husband. Dieter was a little

younger than Gerardo. He'd arrived in Buenos Aires in 1968, early winter... it was June... Dieter wanted to get into cinema work but when he met Gerardo he fell in love... He fell in love with the idea of theater: live audiences, raw emotion, pure communication. Gerardo had just published his first book, *Los Delincuentes*, and he was making a name for himself in the federal capital. I was an actress with the company. Gerardo would take just about anybody with talent and ideas into the company. Always writing, composing, performing, theorizing, criticizing... Dieter got caught up in it. Everybody was caught up in something... 1968...'

'So Gerardo was involved in the politics back then?'

'Gerardo was an artist,' Miriam said. 'But everything anybody did back then was seen as political even if it wasn't. Just think... we'd had a military government since 1966 and young people were starting to organize into all these groups and factions: Marxists, Anarchists, left-wing Peronists, right-wing Peronists. Gerardo's theater group was seen as group of revolutionaries because we were doing experimental theater; but we weren't political in that way... so nobody liked us: the left or the right. Dieter was just a country boy who'd arrived in Buenos Aires.'

'Where from?'

'Bariloche.'

'Bariloche?'

'Dieter's father worked in the Olympic Hotel,' Miriam said.

'You're kidding me...'

'What?'

'He worked for Erich Priebke?'

'Of course... You know about Priebke...'

'Some,' I said.

'Priebke was the head of a whole nest of Nazis who were hiding out in Patagonia. The Olympic Hotel was a kind of haven for them. Priebke was the manager there. I don't know who owned it. But the hotel gave them all employment and a plausible cover and everyone in town from the police chief to the city council clerks were happy to have these heroes of the Third Reich become part of the town society.'

'So your husband's father was a Nazi on the run from Europe?'

'Dieter's father escaped from Germany after the war,' Miriam said. 'He got out via Switzerland with a new name and a new passport provided by the Argentine embassy in 1945. Dieter knew that the hotel was full of ex-Nazis but they all had new names by then, new identities. Even if you lived in Bariloche, no one knew the real identities of the Germans.'

'Was Dieter born in Argentina?'

'Yes, of course. In 1949... His mother had fallen for one of these handsome Germans who'd come to Bariloche. It was her way of living out the fantasy... the glamorous woman in love with the strong military man: like Evita and Perón... Dieter was born a year after his parents were married. Even if his father had an Italian name, Renato Brescia, he gave Dieter a German one. Dieter grew up surrounded by the Olympic Hotel clique... every year they all celebrated Hitler's birthday. They called it the Reich of the Andes. You almost want to believe it was some kind of a joke but then... Dieter was so ashamed, you see. The photographs... he showed me... when he was a child... Dieter loved his mother... she was a very... alluring woman. And to please his father... Dieter was six years old... his mother had him dressed up in a little uniform for an aunt's wedding... I saw the pictures... Dieter liked to dress up... but... well... by the time he was fourteen, he started to find out what the Nazis had done in Europe. And that his own father had been in the SS.'

'What was Dieter's father's connection with Priebke?'

'Dieter's father was in the same unit as Priebke. He was with him at the Fosse Ardeatine.'

'The mass execution,' I said, 'at the caves in Rome?'

'Over three hundred Italians,' she said. 'They were shot by the SS as a reprisal for a partisan ambush on a German police battalion in March 1944. The partisans exploded a bomb, which resulted in twenty-eight policemen's deaths. The SS took a couple of hundred Italian prisoners, suspected partisans and fifty-seven Jews, drove them out the caves at Ardeatine, and executed them with a bullet to the back of the neck. It took all day to kill them. The Germans blew up the entrance to caves to seal the bodies inside. They were found a year later after the liberation of Italy.'

'Your husband's father was one of the executioners.'

'Priebke used officers who had never killed anyone before. Some of them were horrified and testified later about the killings. But Priebke escaped along with others of his unit. The massacre was something Priebke, and the other SS men in Bariloche, were proud of. Dieter was devastated when he found out.'

'How did he find out?'

'They used to have a party on the anniversary of Hitler's birthday. A lot of them got drunk. They liked to boast about it among themselves. Dieter heard them just after he turned eighteen. He went straight to his father and asked him what he knew about it.'

'And?'

'His father told him that he had no idea what could happen in a war. He made no excuse for what he'd done, or Priebke or the others.'

'Dieter rejected his father?'

Miriam laughed.

'Dieter was beside himself. He didn't know what to do. He left for Buenos Aires.'

'Where he met you?'

'Exactly,' she said. 'I was an actor in Gerardo's first theater company.'

'And then Dieter met Gerardo Fischer through you?'

'Yes. Dieter had always been interested in theater at school, which his father thought was effeminate, but... it's funny... his mother encouraged him. After Bariloche, Dieter thought Buenos Aires was like heaven. At that time, in the late sixties, the company was a collective of around twenty people: you know, actors, designers, make-up artists, lighting technicians; but young as Gerardo was back then, in his early twenties, Gerardo was indisputable sole director. He was like a perpetual motion machine. He'd be developing a play in the morning with four people; another in the afternoon with six others; and rehearsing or performing a third piece in the night. But it all fell apart a few years later.'

'During the Videla dictatorship?'

'Before that... Just before you were born, I expect.' Miriam gave me a maternal smile. 'When I think back... just imagine what it was like to be in Buenos Aires back then... the Montoneros planning an armed insurrection to bring back Perón; the military in power and determined to save Argentina from the godless reds; and the USA didn't want communists in Latin America either so they supported the military. It was all madness. And then one of the actresses in the group had connections to the Montoneros. Her name is Francesca Damiani. She was having an affair with Gerardo. The awful thing was, back then, everybody thought they had the right to kill whoever they saw as their enemies: class enemies, enemies of the Fatherland, police, soldiers, or sympathizers with the revolutionaries. We all fell into one category or the other. But you know... left or right, both sides hated us, Gerardo's theater company. For the left, we were too bourgeois; for the right, we were dangerous subversives. And then there was Francesca, a Montonera... After Perón came back to Argentina in 1973, straight away they began killing the Montoneros who'd been bombing and killing to restore him to power. Francesca swore to us she had nothing to do with the Montoneros but she was lying. That could have been to protect us. When Perón died, and Isabelita and Lopez Rega got the power, Francesca was picked up. They gave her a terrible time in custody. But they released her. Maybe they made her talk. To be fair to her, she came back and told us it was dangerous for all of us to stay in Buenos Aires. Maybe she named names. Gerardo disbanded the company and advised us all to get out until it was all over. If ever it would be all over. The Argentine Anti-Communist Alliance, the military and the police had started making all kinds of people disappear.'

'Did you leave, too?'

'No, Dieter and I stayed,' Miriam said. 'We weren't picked up, but… for ten years… It was a nightmare. We went to live in Patagonia. We thought we'd be safer away from Buenos Aires. And we were, I suppose. Carlos was born a few years later.'

'You went to Bariloche?'

'No way.' Miriam laughed. 'I'm a Jew. Do you think I could stay with Dieter's relatives?'

I wanted to ask Miriam, how come the son of a Nazi marries a Jewish woman in Buenos Aires, but I didn't. But it was there in my head. I mean, what's the psychology of that?

'And Gerardo?' I asked.

'He went to Italy.'

'What did he do there?'

'What he did exactly… I don't know. He worked with an Italian theater company. And he taught drama in Rome.'

'Did he already know about Dieter's father and the massacre?'

'Yes.'

'Why didn't he do anything about it, then?'

'We had enough trouble surviving. The Nazis in Bariloche were under the protection of the police, the military, the government. What were we supposed to do?'

'But then Gerardo came back to Argentina after the fall of the dictatorship,' I said.

'Not right away… he was in Rome for a while… and New York… Australia… maybe other places. He came back to Argentina in the mid-nineties. When Gerardo came back, Dieter went to pick him up at the airport. Gerardo stayed with us in our apartment near Plaza Once. Carlos was about twelve years old by then. I'd been thinking about getting back into theater. Gerardo had an idea to do an Argentine version of *A Doll's House.*'

'The Ibsen play?'

She looked surprised that I knew of it.

'Yes, but he changed the Torvald character. Instead of being a doctor who tries to dominate his wife, Torvald becomes an army officer...'

'So a strong woman divorces an army officer,' I said.

'You can see how it would go down well at the time,' Miriam said.

'And you played one of the characters?'

'Nora, the wife. I was about the right age.'

'How long were you with the new company?'

'Five years.'

'What made you leave the company?'

'It was a bad time for Dieter.'

'How so?'

'Dieter decided that he needed to come out.'

'Come out?'

'Dieter was gay. That's how come we finally decided to get divorced. He was in love with Gerardo.'

'Is Gerardo Fischer gay?' I asked her.

She laughed. It was wry, sardonic, but it didn't answer my question.

'I decided to get away from both Dieter and Gerardo,' Miriam said. 'Carlos and I moved to Córdoba. It's a university town, it's cultured, it has theater, even if it's six hundred kilometers away from Buenos Aires. Then Carlos met Ramón and we moved up here, to get out of the city.'

'But you kept your married name... Brescia?'

'It was Carlos's name, and the name on my driver's license and the name on my credit cards and bank account. Why change? I didn't hate Dieter.'

'So how did Gerardo end up coming here, too?'

'Because of Carlos and Ramón... and me, too, I suppose. The boys and I became friendly with Ana and her theater group at Temenos. Carlos went down to Buenos Aires to see his father; and

Dieter took him to see Gerardo's production of *The Mercy Burlesques*. The production location moved around the city: warehouses on the docks, basement car parks, storage facilities. Carlos raved about it to Ana. Ana went down to Buenos Aires to see it. And not long after, Gerardo showed up here.'

'Small world,' I said.

'We're all linked up in some way,' Miriam said. 'Some links are stronger than others.'

'Do you have any idea why Gerardo might have disappeared?' I said.

Miriam shook her head.

'Gerardo's been around a long time. He's upset a lot of people. But I don't know.'

'Did you know that Pablo Arenas knew Priebke?'

She shook her head, held the *mate* gourd close to her heart, eyes wide, lips parted.

'Arenas has a photograph on his wall: himself with Erich Priebke.'

'I had no idea,' Miriam said. 'The first time I saw Arenas was on the day of the robbery up here.'

'Do you think that Arenas coming here to rob you might have had anything to do with Bariloche, Dieter's father?'

She shook her head again.

I'd frightened her. I wished I hadn't.

'Do you think that Gerardo Fischer's disappearance might have had anything to do with Bariloche?'

'I don't know,' she said.

'I'd like to talk to Carlos and Ramón,' I said.

'I'll give you Carlos's cell phone number.' Miriam went over to the desk behind the red boxing bag. She wrote the number down on a yellow post-it paper and brought it back for me.

I stood up. 'I'm sorry to have disturbed you. I'll do everything I can to find Gerardo.'

'You're going?'

'Can and I come and talk to you again?'

'Any time.' She leaned forward and kissed me on the cheek.

'I'll let you know if I hear anything.'

'Yes, do that,' she said.

I walked back down the garden path and she stood on the veranda until I got into my car. I waved to her from behind the windshield. I drove back toward Temenos.

Arenas targets a woman for a robbery whose husband is the son of one of Erich Priebke's SS unit. I nail Arenas for the robbery. Not the end of the story. Did Arenas follow her here? Did Arenas target Fischer because he was connected with Miriam and the boys, or because Fischer had something to do with Priebke being discovered in Bariloche? Or maybe Arenas had nothing to do with it? Could someone else from Bariloche want Fischer out of the way? Why now?

I wanted to talk to Miriam's boys.

What had they been talking to Gerardo about? I pulled over. I tried the number that Miriam had given me and my call was diverted to Carlos's voicemail. I left a message: 'My name is Juan Manuel Pérez. I was the investigating officer on the robbery a few years back. I got your number from your mother, Miriam. It's urgent that I speak with you about Gerardo Fischer. Please call me as soon as possible.'

As soon as I hung up, my cell phone rang.

It was Ana.

'Hi,' she said, 'I'd like to talk to you.'

My breath caught in my chest.

'I'll be right over,' I said. 'I'm about five minutes away.'

'I'll meet you in the parking lot,' she said.

She hung up.

Extract from the casebook of Juan Manuel Pérez
January 11th 2006
Hours: 18:45 to 21:00

I drove onto the colony's parking lot, got out of the air-conditioned cool of the car to affront the suffocating evening air. I locked the door. Even the wind was hot. No sign of Ana. The arms of the hillside pines lifted and dropped as each gust wafted by and the grass drifted. Shadows on the dark branches: vultures squatting in a flock, feathers ruffled by the wind. I walked to the edge of the parking lot, looked down into the dip of the valley. Ribbons of red earth wound among the rocks and pine trees of the property down towards the big meeting house.

Ana was alone on the far hillside, unmistakable, dreadlocks that crowned the tiny head, the small body. A tall male with long gray hair tied back in a ponytail limped his way up the slope below her. Dressed in denim, like a crocked and aged biker, he kept his balance with the aid of a black cane. A dark-haired woman, a lot younger than the longhair, followed behind him at a distance of about fifteen meters. I had the feeling that those two had had an argument. I guess I was disappointed that Ana wasn't alone.

I followed the path from the car park down through the pines toward Ana. I raised a hand in greeting and she waved back. The longhair was close to the top of the hill and the dark-haired woman had almost caught up with him. Ana, her arms folded across her belly, waited for me where she was. The longhair and the dark-haired woman disappeared over the ridge and I felt a sense of relief.

I'm no longhair. I'm an ex-cop trying to earn a living helping these people out. I'm from a family of cops. My father is a cop: his father before him was a cop, the whole family is either cop or military. Here I am trying to find a guy who went on the run thirty years ago not long after I was born. Knowing what I know of my father who was a cop back then, his job was to track down subversives. And Gerardo Fischer back then would have been a subversive. When I thought back to those bad times, I felt shame: shame at my father, and shame on us all for letting happen what happened. Maybe some people just feel some kind of righteous anger because it was people like them who were the victims of those years.

Ana stood on the hillside waiting for me. I stopped for a moment to light a cigarette, to look at her up there.

I wasn't just an ex-cop to her, was I? Or was that just my fantasy? Was she hiding some kind of hate for me and my kind? I was the guy who was helping her find this person she loved. Was I jealous? In what way did she love this Fischer? All of these artist people seemed to revere him in some way. I wanted to know the how and why.

Ana was like some kind of Medusa up there on the hillside. The thick cords of her hair drifted and lifted in the wind.

I lifted the cigarette to my mouth, took a drag.

Ana approached me down the path.

'Hey,' she said.

I bent down as Ana lifted her head to kiss me on the cheek.

'Come on,' she said. 'Let's go to my cabin.'

Ana took me by the arm. I intertwined my fingers with hers. She didn't object.

Dry thunder rumbled. It would pour with rain soon. Ana held on to me. The first of the rain began to fall. We hurried along the path to her cabin. It had a trellis over the veranda. Raindrops splattered on the vine leaves. She struggled to get the locks open and then we were safe inside. She pressed against me and lifted her head, eyes open, lips parted and I bent down to kiss her. This is what I hoped was going to happen. It wasn't going to find Fischer any quicker, but wherever he was, he would have to wait.

Witness Deposition: Ana Valenzuela (Extract 2)

... you want to know how I met Gerardo? The first time was five years ago... I didn't find him to be so endearing, to be honest. Gerardo likes to play games. Carlos and Ramón had gone down to Buenos Aires to see our friend Mariela in a play called *The Mercy Burlesques*. This great director, Gerardo Fischer, had written it, Mariela said, and he was directing it himself. Mariela played the part of Tamara, the lead, in as much as there was one. The play is set on Plaza Miserere in front of the Once railway station. It's the story of a Russian immigrant woman, who comes to Argentina and escapes from poverty by setting up a bordello that attracts the rich and powerful. She's on the run from a domestic nightmare back in Saint Petersburg that's only revealed in the last act... so I'm not going to tell you what it is in case you go to see the play some time. I guess it's a kind of equivalent to Gogol's *Nevsky Prospect*. Carlos and Ramón called me up from Buenos Aires and insisted that I go down to see the play at once. I could catch the second week's performances. It was being staged in a warehouse on the docks. To get there, the audience was brought in on coaches through some really scary parts of the city.

I saw the play three times: the first night I was convinced that I was seeing some kind of hilarious improvisation by a huge cast of seventeen actors. The dialogue was like fireworks going off; the actors were in constant movement. The second time I saw it I realized that it was not improvisation at all. It was all precision scripting and choreographic timing, and that made me feel even more exhilarated; even if I already knew all the twists in the plot; and on the third night there was a kind of pure rapture in the house. The cast just found some mysterious wavelength with the audience… and that made the drama terrifying… sublime. The euphoria of the performance left me high for three days. And I thought: if they'd produced that once, they could do it again. And I wanted to be part of it. I wanted to know how a company, the director, the writer, the actors, could bring an audience out of their everyday way of looking at the world and into a state that was quasi-religious, like some kind of medieval ecstasy. Or maybe like the ancient Greeks, like you read about, this catharsis. Do you understand, Juan Manuel?

I had to meet this Gerardo Fischer.

I told Mariela that I wanted to ask him about doing an acting workshop in Córdoba. What I really wanted was to join Gerardo's theater company. I risked putting pressure on him to meet me right away. I said, 'I have to leave the city within a few days,' which was true, in a way, because I was only in Buenos Aires to see Mariela and Gerardo's play which Carlos and Ramón had been raving about to me. So now I was raving about it, too.

And Gerardo agreed to meet me. I was so excited. He told me that I was to go to the English Clock opposite Retiro Station, in Buenos Aires, on a specific bench with a small memorial plaque at 12:30 on a Tuesday afternoon, three days after the last performance.

I said, 'Okay.'

So I took the subway to Retiro that day. I came out of the station and crossed the busy street. I found the bench. It was the middle of the day and there was no shade. The grass in front of the bench was dry and littered. The heat and humidity made me flushed and sweaty. I felt that I looked like a dog. My halter-top was stuck to my back. I kept shifting my bag from one shoulder to the other. This is not at all a very savory area of Buenos Aires.

To get out of full view – and the heat – I went across the grass to stand against the trunk of a eucalyptus tree. I watched the summer travelers struggling with their baggage from the subway station in front of the station façade; or guarding their suitcases by the seedy coffee kiosks and the fruit juice bars. I kept an eye on the shantytown boys from Fort Apache who were hanging around the CD shops that blasted out *cumbias villeras*.

You ever heard that stuff? This horrible scraping homemade sound that just files at your nerves. I hate it. And I dreaded the Apaches noticing me.

Why hadn't Gerardo picked a safer place for me to meet him? Some café in San Telmo or Belgrano, or down at the Puerto Madera waterfront where you've got security guards who keep the thieves and pickpockets and pimps away from the tourists? I thought: I'm standing around here looking like a prime victim. I was already beginning to resent Gerardo. He was ten minutes late. Not late if I was in a café, perhaps… but out there in the sun with these fucking animals staring at me...

The play had left me ecstatic but this was not the state of mind I was in under that tree, opposite Retiro Station. I just was irritated, hot… I was certain that Gerardo chose this place to make me feel edgy, even terrorized.

I thought: this guy is a psychopath. He's playing some kind of mind game. He wouldn't be the first theater director I'd met who enjoyed doing that.

From the shade beneath the tree, I stared at each reasonably dressed man who I saw approaching the bench, willing him to be Gerardo. Then these two ragged Apaches, about fifty meters away, began to stare at me. They were younger than me, maybe sixteen, no more than eighteen, but you never know… a skinny one like a speed-freak in a Chicago Bulls shirt, Michael Jordan's number 23; and a fat one who looked like he lived on burgers and fries. Maybe he was Peruvian. He was wearing a black t-shirt with some kind of heavy metal design on it. He scared me more. I reached into my bag for my dark glasses and slid them on so they couldn't see if I was watching them or not. They made some comments to each other, then laughed and stared at me again. They began to walk in my direction, shuffling hip-hop style, you know, in these untied basketball shoes. The skinny one grabbed the crotch of his baggy silk shorts, and he was making a gang sign with his hand. In the next ten seconds, I had to decide whether to leave the shade of the tree and start walking toward the crowded part of the station to avoid a mugging; or to stay where I was and risk that the two would walk by with nothing worse than an obscene comment. I had a few hundred pesos in my purse. I didn't want to lose that but it wasn't worth getting hurt to protect it. I'd left my credit cards at Mariela's house.

The Apaches sensed I was nervous, and they were coming for me, I knew, so I came out from under the tree into the full sunlight and I walked directly at them. They hesitated as I closed in on them. They were right next to the bench where I was supposed to meet Gerardo. The fat one put a hand in the pocket of his shorts and the toe of my leather sandal caught the tarmac path. I stumbled. The hairs on the back of my neck prickled. I regained my balance and stared past the two kids and marched straight by them. The fat one turned off the path as I got close to him. He scuffed among the litter on the lawn. The skinny one leered at me, head twisted on his shoulders, lips pulled back from these incredibly white teeth.

Then a tanned man in a dark linen suit and dark glasses darted across the busy street, dodging the cars. He was bald on top, his hair shaved quite short, gray. He had a trimmed gray beard. He was wearing an open-necked white shirt.

The skin-and-bones Apache in the Chicago Bulls shirt ran toward his fatboy friend and slapped him across the back of the head. He ran backward singing some *Cumbia* rap lyrics but I couldn't catch the words. Fatboy gave his friend the finger. They were ignoring me now. The man in the linen suit didn't seem to notice them. He stopped in front of the designated bench and I reached it a few seconds after him.

'Ana?' he said.

He wasn't what I'd expected at all. I hadn't seen him during or after the performances of *The Mercy Burlesques*. I had expected someone taller, younger, a little less formally dressed. I couldn't see his eyes behind the dark glasses.

'Gerardo?' I said.

'Yes,' he said. 'I'm sorry I'm late. The train was delayed from Tigre.'

He offered his hand and I took it and he leaned forward and the sides of our dark glasses clacked against each other as we kissed on the cheek.

'Let's get a taxi,' he said. 'We can have lunch together. Las Violetas. Do you know it?'

'Yes, yes, of course,' I said. 'I have breakfast there with my mother sometimes, if I'm down from the Sierras on a weekend.'

'I like the edginess of stations,' he said.

Fuck you, I thought. I might have been raped, or robbed or stabbed.

I tried to read him. Was he saying this by way of apology? I didn't think so. He had a naivety about him... he was ingenuous somehow. I was tempted to think him stupid but he was too alert, too present in his body. He navigated us through the levels of noise and confusion and bustle as we approached the taxi rank in front of the station. I'm from out of town. I'd been told that some of the cab drivers, if not all, are connected with the Mafia. I didn't want to be kidnapped. Did Gerardo know what he was doing? Was this just a calculated risk? A gamble? Was he doing this to keep me frightened? I was really pissed off with him. What kind of situation was this to have a first meeting with a woman you don't know? I was not long out of college for Christ's sake. What was he playing at? Was he so ignorant of what went down on the streets of Buenos Aires? Gerardo opened the door of a radio cab. Did he choose the precise cab and driver that he wanted by some instinct? Or was he leaving this all to chance? How could he know which was safe and which not? He must know the city better than I did. I felt like such a bumpkin.

Gerardo told the driver to take us to the junction of Medrano and Rivadavia and to take the Avenida Córdoba route and not to go across town. Gerardo was reciting a kind of ritual liturgy to tell the driver that he wasn't a tourist but a resident; or at least someone who knew the city well enough to find his way around. The driver hardly even glanced into his mirror at us. This made me a little more at ease with Gerardo and with the taxi driver.

'So you saw *The Mercy Burlesques*?' Gerardo said.

'I saw it three times,' I said.

'Three?' he said.

'It got better every night,' I said.

'Saturday was the best,' he said. 'I don't know what happened. They all just found it that night, everything dropped away. They were brilliant. All of them.'

'Nothing to do with you?' I said.

I couldn't see his eyes behind the mirrored lenses.

'All I can do is set them up,' he said. 'Rehearsals, suggestions... I mean you just have to work with what you've got... but it's the actors eventually, isn't it? It's their show.'

'What do you give them, then?' I said.

'Nothing much,' he said.

He was silent for a minute as the cab turned left off Avenida Córdoba and onto Medrano.

'You've got to help them to get the ego out of the way,' Gerardo said. 'There's the text, yes, I did write that, but they have to deliver on it. If you look, the words are quite ordinary, disjointed. Normal conversation, really. They know what to do. We've been working together for years.'

Oh, I thought: 'Working together for years.'

The words punctured the balloon of everything I'd fantasized. How could I possibly get into such a long established group where no one has to say a word to find out exactly what it is that makes the ensemble work?

'They know what you want,' I said.

'Yeah, I suppose they do,' he said. 'But they don't always get it right. There's no predicting it, is there? One night everything just zings. The next night it might be a great performance but there isn't that breakthrough that leaves you affected for days.'

'For days, yes,' I said. 'Saturday was amazing.'

His dark glasses were off now, waving in his right hand next to the window, the legs uncrossed. His eyes, I saw, are a bright green, his head and shoulders leaned in just a touch toward me.

'It's a mystery,' he said and he laughed; he sat back then, relaxed, and his hands lowered again onto the seat, his left hand close to my right.

'I love it,' Gerardo said, 'if it happens when the critics come to see a piece... they experience it and they can't deny it... least of all explain it... and if they're not complete bastards they give the show a great review. And we've had a lot of great reviews, so I know.'

He couldn't suppress the smile. He raised a hand. The green eyes disappeared behind the dark glasses again. He folded his arms as if he was trying to hold back his uncontrollable pride.

'We've had some bad ones, too,' he said.

'Reviews?' I said.

The cab pulled up on the corner of Medrano and Rivadavia. The facade of Las Violetas is all marble columns and plate glass windows and gilt moldings. The white-coated waiters let us choose a table for ourselves in the dining area, beneath the big staircase. The café was relatively empty. A waiter brought the menu and the wine list. My mother and I usually sat on the other side of the café near all the pastries in the glass cases.

'Did you see that documentary film about Macedonio Fernandez,' Gerardo said, 'the one that Ricardo Piglia presented?'

'Yes, yes I saw that,' I said.

I remembered some shots through the window of Piglia at one of the tables here. Macedonio was a big influence on Borges. He lived in an apartment near here, above a boxing gym on Rivadavia. I remembered some scenes from the documentary: the waterways of Tigre where Macedonio had his anarchist commune; but my memory of the whole film was vague. I hoped Gerardo didn't want to talk about it.

'So many layers of the city,' Gerardo said. 'We're here now, Piglia here a few years ago, something that we witnessed on a screen in a cinema, now in our memories. And the memories of the times you sat here with your mother eating pastries and drinking coffee. And Macedonio sitting here before the place fell into ruin. And then it gets refurbished like this… as if the ruin never happened.'

He's so ingenuous, I thought, not a trace of irony. Maybe I was wrong about that.

The waiter arrived to take our order. Gerardo had ravioli and a half-bottle of Cabernet. I ordered fish and a bottle of mineral water. 'You're *Porteña*?' Gerardo asked.

'*Cordobesa*,' I said. 'My mother lives here now with her second husband. I live in a kind of artists' colony in the Sierras, near Ciudad Azul.'

'An artists' colony, like a commune?' he said.

'We have a theater there,' I said. 'I do mime and modern dance. Sometimes drama.'

'How long have you been there?' he asked.

'Three years,' I said. 'We have painters, writers, a psychologist. I have a house there. Or studio. Just a little shack really.'

'And the theater?' he asked.

'Yes, big enough,' I said. 'A good space… about six people in the company.'

'A writer… director?' he asked.

'Three of us develop the pieces,' I said. 'Sometimes I do the choreography.'

'And you perform where?' he asked.

'There, at the colony,' I said, 'but also here. From time to time.'

'When next?' he said.

'Maybe in March,' I said, 'when the weather's a little cooler.'

'I'll come to see you,' he said, 'your next piece. You'll let me know, right?'

'Sure,' I said, 'but I want to ask you something.'

'Okay,' he said.

I couldn't bring myself to ask him what I really wanted to ask, I couldn't ask him if I might audition for his company, so I said, 'Will you come and do a workshop with us in the Sierras? Do you have the time?'

He leaned forward over the table, elbows down, fingers clenched under his chin. I saw him reflected in the mirror of the mahogany bar behind him.

'Yes.' He nodded once. 'Okay, I'll come.'

I felt a real thrill. He reached for the linen napkin. I reached out and squeezed his hand. He closed his fingers around mine. How old was he? A lot older than me? Fifty maybe… maybe more?

'What do those tattoos mean?' he said.

His fingertip slid above the shapes of the letters on my forearm.

You know sometimes it's such a drag when people ask you about your tattoos but not this time with him. I'd forgive him anything.

I pointed to the letters one by one.

'This one means essence,' I said, 'this one is nature, and this one is energy.'

'Essence... nature... and energy.'

He said it slow.

'I like that,' he said.

He didn't ask me any more because the waiter arrived. I was glad. I didn't want to get into a philosophical discussion with him about East and West… mysticism… nothing like that. People are always so clueless about it. Always asking me if it helps me in some way, as if I'm some kind of emotional cripple. It's how I see the world... it's that simple... but I didn't want to talk about any of that, right at that moment. I wanted... I don't know exactly what I wanted... something to do with Gerardo coming to the colony... something about him touching my forearm.

The waiter poured a glass of mineral water for me. Then he uncorked the half-bottle of Cabernet. Gerardo went through the ritual of tasting it. I was sure that he found me attractive... but he was a being a gentleman, a bit uptight to tell the truth.

I thought: maybe it's the age difference.

I thought: Maybe he's got some English blood. An Anglophile. Like Borges. He's probably old enough to be my father but that hasn't stopped other men making passes at me. I rather liked his hesitancy. But I didn't want anything stupid to happen that might make it seem as if I was trying to seduce him so that he'd give me what it was that I really wanted. That would be so clumsy. Even if he had no idea what I really wanted. Not yet, anyway.

A workshop. He'd agreed to do it. That way I thought we could get to know each other. I thought, maybe he'll want me in his company if he likes the way I work. Anyway, I'd got him to come to Córdoba. That's how it all started for me…

Extract from the casebook of Juan Manuel Pérez
January 11th 2006
Hours: 21:00 to 21:30

My cell phone rang at about nine pm. I picked up. It was Carlos. He knew who I was. We'd talked a lot back when I'd done the investigation into the Arenas robbery.

'I got your message,' Carlos said.

'Thanks for calling,' I said.

Ana propped her head up on her hand, pulled the duvet around her body. I slid my legs out of the bed, pulled some duvet into my lap and leaned over my knees.

'I'm trying to locate Gerardo Fischer,' I said. 'Nobody has seen Gerardo at Temenos for more than two days. Naturally, people are worried.'

Silence. I let it linger.

'We wanted him to come to Buenos Aires with us...'

I waited.

'We'd heard that Pablo Arenas had been released from jail and we were all a little outraged.'

'Who's we?'

'Well, me and Ramón,' Carlos said. 'We didn't tell Miriam because we didn't want her worrying. We've been trying to find out what we can about Arenas's background... We started to ask some questions around in Ciudad Azul. We knew about his connection to the Triple A. And Ramón and I have been working with a human rights group.

We tried to find out if Arenas could be prosecuted for, well... We'd like to see him behind bars for a long time, that's all I can say.'

'I can understand that,' I said.

I could also understand that Pablo Arenas would be very unhappy about a couple of nosy guys trying to get him put away.

'I guess you asked some pretty indiscreet questions around town,' I said.

'Yes, we did. It wasn't difficult to find out that he was involved in the drug trade in just about all of the clubs around the lake: weed, E, speed, coke, crack, smack... But something else that we found out... in Ciudad Azul, Arenas had some connections with the Artemisia Adoption Agency.

'Which is?'

'It was a genuine adoption agency that existed until the end of the nineties, when the business was sold and its name changed. All the previous records were put into storage. And fifteen years previous to the sale of the business, we think that these Artemisia people did a sideline in finding homes for the children of activists who had disappeared during the Dirty War; kids who had been born in custody and the real parents were never seen again. We thought that maybe something might stick to Arenas from that... if we could find out enough about it. And about Arenas who may have had a hand in the arrangements so to speak. We started to ask around to see if we could find people who used to work at the agency. A couple of days later, we were having a coffee in a café in Ciudad Azul when a woman called Maria Dos Santos came over to our table...'

'Maria Dos Santos? How do you know that was her name?'

'She dealt a little coke from time to time in the clubs. If you do the club scene in Ciudad Azul, well... do you know her, too?'

'I met her a couple of times, but go on...'

'Well, this Maria woman told us that the adoption agency had closed down long ago, and that it would be better for us if we gave up trying to find out about it because we might bring heartache to a lot of good people who would be upset at us for digging up the painful past. She said it all in a very sweet way. But I couldn't help thinking there was a threat behind it. A serious threat. It was quite scary.'

'What did she have to do with this Artemisia Adoption Agency?'

'Apparently, it was set up by her aunt.'

'And her aunt is the mother of the guy who was killed at your place?'

Carlos hesitated, obviously nervous. 'That's right.'

'Does Gerardo Fischer have anything to do with this?'

'Not directly... But he was with us when Maria Dos Santos warned us off. He'd been interested in Pablo Arenas, too. He wouldn't tell us exactly what about. It's always difficult to tell with Gerardo what he's up to.'

'Was there anything Gerardo said the last time he saw you that led you to believe he might leave the area... or go away for a while?'

'To tell the truth, Ramón and I were so frightened after speaking to this Dos Santos woman that we decided to leave Ciudad Azul for a while ourselves. We wanted Gerardo to come with us, but he said he had too much work to do. There were the rehearsals and then he needed to be there to do something with Damien Kennedy.'

'Damien Kennedy?'

'He's the set designer for the theater company,' Carlos said.

'And he lives at Temenos?'

'Yes, that's right.'

'But Gerardo didn't arrange to meet you in Buenos Aires?'

'He said that he'd see us next week when the company brought the theater piece down here.'

I'd got all I could from Carlos, I thought.

'Okay. Thanks for calling. That's been really helpful.'

Arenas *must* have something to do with this. And Maria Dos Santos? But there was no point in calling in on them again at this time of night, on their turf, in the dark...

'Please,' Carlos said. 'Wait a second, do you think he's all right?'

'I hope so. I'm looking for him.'

'Please. Let me know as soon as you find out where he is.'

'I'll do that. And if *you* hear from him, you call me right away, okay?'

'Okay,' Carlos said.

I hung up.

I turned to Ana. She'd listened to the whole phone conversation.

'Who's this Damien Kennedy?' I said.

'He lives just over the hill,' Ana said.

'What do you know about him?'

'He's been here about six months. He's known Gerardo since the eighties. Other than Miriam, he's the one who's known Gerardo the longest. Gerardo invited him from Europe to do some kind of special project.'

'From Europe?'

Ana nodded.

Gerardo probably just wanted him to paint some scenery for one of his plays. But I wanted to talk to him anyway. He might have been one of the last people to see Gerardo on the property.

'It's not late,' I said. 'You can take me over to see Kennedy after I've had a shower.'

'I'll call him now on his landline to see if he's home and if he's willing to speak to you. He's a strange guy. But if he does want to talk, he'll talk your ear off.'

'Where's the shower?'

'It's in the little cubicle under the lean-to.'

I climbed down the ladder from the loft.

I wasn't going to find Fischer tonight, but I could try to get as much as possible out of Damien Kennedy. Fischer had been digging up the past, too. This much was clear.

I stepped into the shower cubicle and turned on the jet.

I soaped myself up.

I really wanted to spend the night with Ana.

Extract from the casebook of Juan Manuel Pérez
January 11th 2006
Hours: 22:00 to 22:45

Ana took me up the hill in the darkness. She carried a flashlight. It was raining, not hard but enough. A set of steps had been made through the green bank behind her cabin. The path continued up, into and through a copse of pine and eucalyptus. The earth was dark and greasy underfoot. Drops of water fell from the branches, cold against the cotton of my shirt, my linen pants. From time to time, Ana grabbed my hand as my loafers slipped on the steeper parts of the path. She laughed at me. She was a very sweet young woman: bright, full of life, energy. Is this what made her an actress, a kind of dynamism in her small body? The oriental letters of her tattoos seemed to be alive, to crawl on the whiteness of her inner forearm. We came out of the trees and the path led up to a ridge and then continued through rounded mica-flecked boulders. The undersides of the clouds were dark as wine; blocks of rock were silhouetted on the horizon.

The house where Kennedy was staying looked like a construction site: bars on some of the ground floor windows, a pallet of bricks against the south wall, sacks of cement under a black plastic tarp roped down tight against the rainstorm. Kennedy opened the door before we got there. I don't know how he knew that we were coming. He was about five feet six, long grizzled hair, reddish stubble on big features. His woolen sweater was frayed at the cuffs and collar, and his blue jeans were a trifle paint-stained, his sneakers were worn across the instep.

'Come in,' Kennedy said.

We stepped across the threshold into the house. He ushered us through the small hallway into a kind of kitchen/dining area. The two-burner stove on a concrete shelf in one wall was a mess: a camping affair attached to a twenty-liter blue gas cylinder.

'Juanma wants to talk to you about Gerardo,' Ana said.

'You know he's missing,' I said.

'Sure,' Kennedy said.

'You may have been one of the last people to see him before he disappeared.'

'He might still show up,' Kennedy said.

'What makes you say that?'

Kennedy shrugged.

'I'll leave you to it,' Ana said.

I was disappointed that she wasn't staying. Kennedy took her back to the door. He waved to Ana as she went back down the path. He locked the door.

'You want some *mate*?' Kennedy asked.

I shook my head. I was a bit suspicious of a gringo making *mate*.

Kennedy lifted his chin to point out the living room. A large picture window on the west side of the house framed the darkness. In the day, he'd have a beautiful view of the Sierras. The room was spacious. So spacious that there was a large puddle of water in the center of the concrete floor right below a square hole in the ceiling.

'I haven't put the skylight in yet,' Kennedy said.

I nodded.

He poured hot water into the thermos flask, grabbed his *mate*.

'Let's go upstairs,' he said. 'The room up there is finished.'

I followed him up the concrete steps into his bedroom and

makeshift studio that was the entire loft section of the house. The room reeked of linseed oil and turpentine. Below the easel with a half finished painting, there was a blackened saucepan with the remains of a dried up brew of rabbit-skin glue. The paint-spattered floor was just plywood. A low double bed was at one end of the room. Along the north wall were Kennedy's canvases, nudes in a messy style that reminded me of the New York painter, De Kooning. A black drape covered what might have been another large canvas, or stage flat, that was about two and a half meters high and one and a half wide. There seemed to be some kind of box built onto the back of it, a box that was big enough to walk into.

'I'll move all this downstairs when I get the skylight in,' Kennedy said.

I wondered how he'd get the flat with the big box out of the room. Maybe it could be dismantled.

Kennedy waved at a wicker armchair. It had a thin embroidered cushion on the seat and a Bolivian woven cloth over the back of it. I sat down. Kennedy got himself a straight-backed chair, also paint-spattered.

'What did you talk about with Fischer before he left?' I said.

'He wants to do a revival of his play, *The Alchemist, Bono*. It was one of the first projects I ever worked on with him. For that piece he needs a replica of the Porta Magica in Rome. The actual marble doorway is still preserved on Piazza Vittorio in the center of the city.'

'Did Gerardo talk about going away anywhere?'

Kennedy pursed his lips, shook his head.

'Not at all.'

'Did he mention anything that might be bothering him, or worrying him?'

'No, we just talked about the scenery he wanted built. And then he left.'

'You met Gerardo Fischer a long time ago.'

'June 13th 1982,' he said.

'Precise,' I said.

'It was the same day I met up with a woman called Francesca Damiani. I still mark that day like an anniversary. For her… for him… who knows…'

'I've heard her name before,' I said.

He raised his head, the smile gone, eyes a little wider. 'Who from?'

'Miriam mentioned her, and Sara.'

Kennedy nodded. 'Miriam knew her in Buenos Aires.'

'You met Gerardo… and this Francesca… in Italy.'

'At a theater festival. Terme di San Tommaso. I was twenty-five and I'd just moved to Italy. I can remember the dates pretty well because Britain was in the middle of the Falklands War: Malvinas to you. I'm Irish, but I'd been living in London for years. And of course, because Francesca was an Argentine, it meant that the news had a personal interest for her. Gerardo, of course, is from Uruguay.'

'So Francesca was on the run from the Argentine military and Gerardo had joined her there in Italy.'

'That's what I found out, yes, but not right away.'

'Gerardo was Francesca's lover. Is that true?'

Kennedy's craggy face softened into a wry smile. He ran a hand through his long hair.

'I didn't find that out right away, either. You see, Francesca and I got involved with each other… that's the best way to put it… and she was involved with Gerardo, too… more than I realized… and not in any simple way of course… nothing is ever that simple with Gerardo… or with Francesca either… I was a bit naïve about the both of them, I suppose. Most of the people who talk to you about Gerardo will probably tell you what an amazing person he is: so creative, taking people right out to the edge… or beyond. Gerardo makes people drop their masks and be real for once in their lives. Would you like to do that?'

I shifted in the wicker armchair. 'What?'

Kennedy laughed. 'Drop your mask and be real for once in your life.'

'*What?*'

I wasn't sure that I liked this guy fucking with my head.

'It's true that Gerardo does that,' Kennedy said. 'A lot of the time maybe he takes people where they don't really want to go. He'd probably say it was only for their own good. Sometimes it was a little difficult to agree with him about that... especially over Francesca... But that may well be my jealousy... it's funny, isn't it? Even all these years later... anyway, whatever happened with Francesca, I ended up involved with Gerardo just the same, didn't I? He brought me here to Argentina... the grand reunion. What more can I say?'

'So you went to Italy to work in the theater and that's where you met Gerardo.'

'Oh no, not at all. I had nothing at all to do with the theater until I met Gerardo. I decided I'd move to Italy at the end of a trip to India and Nepal. May 1982, I'd been in New Delhi, euphoric, among all these bright colors of the Rajastani textile market... blue sky... dazzling sunshine...' He waved his hands about as if he might conjure the scene in the air for me. 'And the next day I dropped out of the gray clouds onto the gray tarmac of Heathrow airport, next to the wet gray rooftops of terraced London houses. And then there was a war on. And Margaret Thatcher was in power... I could have wept, really. I just thought: What the fuck am I doing here? What the fuck am I doing? So... what did I do? I enrolled in a five-day commercial course to learn how to teach English as a foreign language and I bought a ticket to Italy to work freelance. Teaching English would pay the rent while I lived in a garret and worked on my epic comic book diary.'

'Why Italy? What took you there?'

'When I'd been in Nepal, I'd met this woman, Liliana Franceschini. She was doing some kind of meditation course for a month near the Great Stupa in Bodhanath, and it turned out that she lived in Rome. We had this great long talk about Eastern philosophy over a few beers in a restaurant in Bodhanath.

I could easily imagine Kennedy having a great long talk.

'Then out of the blue,' Kennedy said, 'Liliana said to me, "If you ever come to Rome, you can stay for a few nights in my house." And she gave me her phone number. Well, some people say things like that and they don't really mean it, do they? But I was sure that she did. I was convinced. She'd given me her phone number, hadn't she? So now, I was in London, I was a fully qualified English teacher after a five-day course... what a joke... and I was going to Italy. Obviously. Why not? I was young. I had a place to start: sunshine and blue skies, good food and wine, the prospect of beautiful women. So I called up Liliana.'

'And she knew Gerardo Fischer?'

'She knew Fischer, yes. First of all I thought that was a problem for me because Liliana said she wasn't going to be home on the day I planned to arrive in Rome. She was going to a theater festival at the Terme di San Tommaso. Shit, I thought, now what? Maybe she didn't really mean I could stay at her place in Rome. "The festival," she said, "it's held every year. San Tommaso is one of those small medieval towns in Tuscany. Hot springs, you know? And the festival: it's all experimental theater. Do you want to go?" Well, of course, I wanted to go. It wasn't exactly looking for a job and a place to live to begin my new life but so what? "The house I'm staying in is full," she said, "but I can book you into a hotel." Well, I thought, an experimental theater festival in Tuscany couldn't be bad, could it? "Yes," I said.'

'And you met Gerardo Fischer at this theater festival,' I said.

'That I did,' Kennedy said. 'And Francesca, too.'

Witness Deposition:
Damien Kennedy

Liliana Franceschini picked me up at Fiumicino airport. She was waiting for me just past customs. If you saw Liliana from a distance, you'd get the impression of her being a big woman: she has these wide cheekbones… wide face… maybe that's good for an opera singer; the voice… and the laugh… it just erupts out of her. Up close, she was a bit less daunting. And it was great to see her again. We went across to the car park and I bundled my rucksack and drawing board into her Volkswagen and we set off for the Terme di San Tommaso.

The hotel she'd booked me into was in a converted building in the old walled town. It was beautiful. It was cheap. Liliana was renting a room in a farmhouse among the vineyards outside it. I got the impression Liliana would prefer to meet up with her friends first off without me hanging around with her. So I said, 'Look, I'm tired after all the traveling. I'll have dinner at the hotel tonight. Maybe we can have lunch tomorrow?'

'Sure,' she said, 'I'll pick you up at noon, on the town square, just outside the Bar Bagatto. You can come and have lunch with us.'

I was so relieved to be invited, I can't tell you.

So, on the Sunday, I took a walk around the town square: mist rising up off the hot sulfur pond, medieval walls with fancy food shops, pottery, gorgeously cut clothes. Opposite the Bar Bagatto, on one wall of the festival information kiosk, I saw a poster for a theater group called *O Berimbao*. That's not an Italian name obviously. Well, I thought, it must be Portuguese with that *'ao'* ending. This group was performing a new version of *Medea*, by a guy called Gerardo Fischer. It was on at the end of the week. I loved Greek tragedy but this seemed to be a new play by a guy I'd never heard of... Okay, why not? Here I was in Italy... experimental theater, a new life... Liliana pulled up next to me on the square. She leaned out of the car window.

'Ready?' she said. 'I have to pick up a friend of mine from church. We're late but we'll catch some of it. The monks do Gregorian chant for the midday mass.'

The church of San Tommaso stands out in the flat of the valley in a kind of natural amphitheater. The sun was slanting in under a few high clouds and the rays lit up the vineyards on the south facing slopes. It was like the bearded God up above was gazing down on his perfect creation. It was pure magic. Liliana parked the car in the gravel lane outside the church. We were in this basin below the walled town; open fields next to the church; the air was dry. And it was already unbearably hot. The church is a single round tower and below it are the straight walls of the presbytery. Bizarre gargoyles stare down from just below the roofline: lions with double serpents' tails; horned dogs; interlaced crosses. It's like something out of Umberto Eco. I wanted to come down here and draw this place for my comic book diary. The monks' cells are off in an adjacent building: stone, like a longhouse with cloisters. Some kind of Christian paradise.

'It's beyond real,' I said, 'so beautiful.'

'Would you like to be a monk?' Liliana said.

Something in my expression made her roar with laughter.

We went through the portal and into the shade of the ancient church. It was a relief to be out of the sun. On the altar, the mass was already going on. The priest was up there with a couple of monastic servers in black cassocks and white surplices. A few people in the back turned around to look at us as we come in and then turned to look at the altar again. The stone walls echoed with the chants of the monks in the choir stalls. A huge wooden cross hung over the priest, Christ suspended, chiseled out of raw wood and the painted features all faded by the sunlight: pre-Renaissance without a doubt. Stark.

About four rows in front of us was a woman in her mid to late twenties. My age. She had ash blonde hair that set off her tan. She was wearing a white cotton dress. She was a little on the plump side to tell the truth, but not fat… just the way that Latin women are happy to fill out their clothes, you know? This woman was serious, you could tell, about the mass, I mean. She was mouthing the words as the monks chanted them. She was following the lines. Liliana leaned over and whispered.

'That's Francesca, my friend from Rome.'

I nodded. I just knew it. I kept looking down the rows toward Francesca. At this point, I assumed she was Italian. She looked Italian. I wasn't really thinking that anything romantic might happen between us at that point. Not consciously anyway. The Gregorian mass is hardly erotic. And then we were at the offertory… and the consecration. Francesca kept her eyes on the host as the priest raised it and the server shook the bell; and she had the same beatific look on her face when the priest raised the chalice. I imagined how I was going to draw this in a set of panels in the comic book: no story yet, just the idea, the image of her rapture and the raised host and chalice. Like Bernini's *Saint Theresa in Ecstasy*.

Francesca was one of the first to go down to the altar rails to take communion. I sat back in my seat. Liliana did, too. I've got to admit, part of me wanted to join in with the ritual, to go down there and take the communion wafer in my mouth just like Francesca with her lips open and tongue out in front of the priest. Feel the host melting in my mouth. That state of grace I felt as a child, even if I don't believe in the Catholic faith any more. I wondered if that was what Francesca was feeling at this moment: one with God? Something like that.

I must be a bit like Martin Luther with the real presence, you know? Something like that. You know the history? I studied it in school… never forgot it… Luther couldn't bring himself to say that the host was Christ's body, which is what Catholics believe. But Luther said Christ is present in the host 'like fire in red hot metal.' And I was like that watching Francesca. I thought that to take communion I would have to be in an official state of grace, abiding by all the rules for taking the sacraments. And I really wasn't up for that at all any more. I'd have to go to confession. And how could I confess to some repressed celibate?

But here was Francesca, her eyes cast down, making her way back to her seat. And I wondered: how can a sexy woman like that be into the Catholic faith? Is she married? I assumed she wasn't. But I couldn't imagine that she didn't have a sex life. I mean the Church has rules. No sex before marriage. How could anyone abide by that? But this woman was taking communion. And Liliana would introduce me to her. So I wanted to observe her: Francesca that is, to see if I could get any clues to her, what she believed. I wanted to find out.

The mass ended, and the priest led the servers and the Gregorian choir off the altar and they went back into the sacristy. The congregation started to file out. Francesca still knelt there and prayed for a while. She really was devout. So in the aisle of the church, Liliana and I stepped aside to let the faithful and the tourists go by us. Then Francesca got up. She saw Liliana. She seemed genuinely surprised to see her so close. Francesca had been completely oblivious to us while the mass was going on. But that didn't put me off for some reason. Even if, when I think about it, perhaps it should have, now that I was definitely on the lapsed side of the religious equation.

'This is Damien Kennedy,' Liliana said to her in English: for my sake, I supposed. 'He's a friend of mine from England.'

I didn't correct her.

'I'm Francesca,' she said.

'Liliana told me,' I said.

Francesca leaned forward so we could kiss on each cheek.

'Pleased to meet you,' she said.

She had such a high-pitched voice I was a bit shocked. I thought that her English accent had the minimum of Italian inflection as if she'd studied or lived abroad for some time.

'Me, too,' I said, 'pleased to meet you.'

'You're coming to lunch?' Francesca asked.

'Liliana invited me,' I said.

We were out on the gravel road where the car was parked. I remember my black boots were covered with a thin film of white dust. I was fantasizing that we were in some film, maybe something by Michelangelo Antonioni, one of his early films maybe... *L'Avventura*... *L'Eclisse*... something like that...

'Are you going to a play tonight?' Liliana asked me.

I looked out across the vineyards toward the walled town.

'I don't know,' I said. 'The only thing that caught my eye so far was a version of *Medea*. But it's not on until Friday.'

'That's our company,' Francesca said.

'O Berimbao?'

'Yes, that's us,' she said in that high voice of hers, proud of herself, like a little girl.

'But that's Portuguese,' I said. *'O Berimbao.'*

'Yes, Brazilian,' she said.

'Are you Brazilian?' I asked.

'No, I'm from Argentina. Tucumán province,' she said.

We were silent for a minute. I thought that we were both dealing with images from newspapers and television. Even Liliana stayed quiet. A headline from a tabloid sprung to my mind when a British submarine sank the Argentine battleship *Belgrano*. The disgust I felt... It was not the incident itself so much... this was a war... but the crowing in the newspapers over more than three hundred Argentine dead. British troops had already landed on the islands. People were fighting and dying and being bombed and shot and burned to death while we were here in Italy about to have lunch together in the sunshine at an experimental theater festival. This stupid war about a few small islands in the South Atlantic, which Margaret Thatcher in London was milking for all the political capital she could squeeze from it. At the same time, I wouldn't want General Galtieri's dictatorship taking over any island that I was living on. I mean, would you?

If the Argentine military made their own people disappear, why wouldn't they waft away a thousand or so Falkland Islanders?

'What does it mean?' I asked.

'What?' Francesca said.

'*O Berimbao*,' I said.

'Oh,' she said. 'It's a musical instrument… made with one string and a gourd. The Indios use them. Our productions… they're very minimalist.'

'I can't wait to see the play,' I said.

'If you don't go to another play tonight, you can come to our rehearsal. Unless you want to wait until Friday to see it as it should be seen.'

'Where are you rehearsing?' I asked.

'In the basement of the Teatro Ramicelli,' Francesca said.

'You can come with me, if you want,' Liliana said.

I wasn't sure I wanted to see a rehearsal: standing around watching exercises and endless repetitions of parts of scenes. And standing there with these two women in the driveway of the church, I was all sweated up from the blazing heat. It was close to one o'clock. By three, it would be suffocating. My t-shirt was soaked through and my jeans were damp and stiff. I could feel the sun's heat through my hair and the skin on my face was tingling. I might be looking like a boiled lobster already. I couldn't imagine that I'd be very attractive to Latin women.

Liliana opened the car doors and we got in. The seat was burning and the car was like an oven. We drove up to the yellow-walled farmhouse where Liliana and Francesca were staying. We turned into the small courtyard. The ground floor of the stone building had been converted into living space. The lintels and jambs of the old stables had been filled in with stone and there were heavy double-doors of varnished chestnut.

'The owner lives downstairs,' Liliana said.

Liliana, Francesca and I climbed the steps on the outside of the building. The door to the upstairs apartment was open. I was glad to get into the cool corridor. Francesca's flat leather sandals slapped against the tiles. Liliana was ahead of us. I followed her and Francesca down the corridor and then I was in the kitchen. The window was open and Francesca went over to it and perched on the edge of the windowsill.

At the far end of the table was a tanned man, the crown of his head shiny and bald, the hair above his ears and the back of his head – prematurely white, I thought – was cropped close to his skull. He was clean shaven, his eyes behind his glasses with a slight squint. He stood up and reached out a hand.

'Gerardo,' he said, '*piacere*.'

It was not quite an Italian accent. It was rich and baritone like the voice of an actor. It would be, I supposed. We were here for a theater festival.

'Gerardo is our director,' Francesca said. 'We met in Buenos Aires.'

'You're Argentine, too,' I said.

'I'm Uruguayan,' Gerardo said. 'From Montevideo. But my theater company used to be based in Buenos Aires.'

'Now he's working with us in Rome,' Francesca said.

'I teach drama at the university,' he said.

Liliana took the lid off one of two flat white boxes on the marble countertop next to the cook stove: fat pillows of tortelloni dusted with grainy semolina flour.

'*Che belli*,' Liliana said.

'*L'insalata la faccio io*,' Francesca said.

She had a little girlish tone, that high voice. She came around the table toward the fridge and held onto my upper arm as she went around me. It was a deliberate touch. A woman in London or Dublin wouldn't touch you like that unless she was flirting with you, but this is Italy, I thought, people touch each other all the time. It's normal. She touched Gerardo on the shoulder. The affection was obvious. The white hair made him look a lot older than he was. She was in her late twenties. He seemed to me to be around forty or more.

'How long have you been in Italy?' I said.

'Five years,' he said. 'We had to get out… like a lot of people.'

'I still have relatives here,' Francesca said.

'Francesca helped me get set up here,' Gerardo said. 'I'd been living in Venezuela.'

They all spoke English incredibly well and they were speaking it for my benefit. I didn't speak Spanish and my Italian was beginner level, no more.

'So many people from South America living here,' Liliana said. 'Chile, Argentina, Uruguay, Brazil.'

'I'm lucky,' Gerardo said. 'I have a job. I can still make theater. A lot of people have no work.'

'So it's okay for you to stay in Italy?' I said.

'It's safer than staying in Buenos Aires,' Gerardo said, 'or Montevideo.'

'We both have Italian grandparents,' Francesca said. 'We can get Italian citizenship. But there are people in Italy with connections, connections with the dictatorships. We still have to be careful.'

'Argentinians?' I said.

'And Italians,' Liliana said.

'Fascisti,' Francesca said. 'MSI. P2. Ordine Nuovo… the people behind the Bologna bombings.'

I had a vague memory of the Bologna bombings. A couple of years previously, 1980, a lot of people had been killed when a bomb went off in a waiting room at the Bologna railway station. MSI I knew were fascists. Ordine Nuovo sounded fascist. But P2. I'd never heard of it.

'The fascists have connections with the South American secret services who target political activists,' Francesca said.

I could see the fear in her face; as if she could sense someone behind her in the shadows; or out in the garden, hidden among the trees. Was this just paranoia? I'd no idea what it was like to be on the run like these people, though people in the North of Ireland knew what it meant to have a midnight knock on the door. So many families in Belfast and Derry had lost relatives to the British Army, the SAS death squads, or the paramilitaries on both sides. So I wasn't completely naive about it.

'No one's been prosecuted for the bombing,' Liliana said. 'A Fascist group claimed responsibility but there are all sorts of rumors connecting it to the P2 lodge and its leader Licio Gelli. The carabinieri arrested a fascist called Roberto Fiore, but Fiore claims he's being chased to divert attention from Licio Gelli.'

'The P2 lodge?' I said.

This was getting Byzantine.

'Freemasons,' Francesca said. 'Half the government and the Mafia belong to it. They have connections in the Vatican and with the CIA. There are even rumors that some P2 members sell arms to the Red Brigades as well as the Fascists and bring heroin into Italy through Bulgaria. Licio Gelli is well known. He provided the plane for Perón to get back to Argentina from Spain.'

'Oh, come on,' I said. 'This is all a big conspiracy theory. How can you know?'

'Just read the newspapers. The government is investigating P2,' Liliana said.

'I thought the government had members in this P2,' I said.

'Some are,' Francesca said. 'Some aren't.'

'Bit by bit it's coming out,' Liliana said.

'In leftist newspapers,' I said.

'You can read it in *La Repubblica Il Messagero*,' Liliana said.

From the look on her face I could see that my skepticism wasn't appreciated.

'Hey, I'm out of my depth,' I said.

'Italy is a very complicated country,' Gerardo said.

He had the look on his face of someone in pain, personal pain; which I suppose it would be if you were in exile because you were afraid of being tortured or murdered back home; and even where you were in Italy, you were worried that some Fascist sympathizer might put a bullet in the back of your head.

I was twenty-five, and I knew that I couldn't fathom the depths of terror that these people were on the edge of… a terror I could sense in the way that Francesca held her body: the contortion of her spine, the slight twitch under her eye, the way her hand was held palm up, fingers tense, as if to ward off some evil. In the North of Ireland, we had the Special Branch and the Special Patrol Group; and I'd heard that the SAS in Ireland picked up people and tortured and murdered them; but, even then, I suspected it was nowhere near the scale that was going on all through Latin America. Later we found out that tens of thousands of people were being arrested and disappeared: Chile, Argentina, Uruguay, Paraguay, Brazil.

Liliana turned her head away. She knew more about this but didn't want to say anything else.

How did our discussion in Nepal on Buddhist philosophy fit in with all this? I thought. I suspected at this point that Liliana and her friends were all hard left. I was a bit uncomfortable. Only a few years previously, Aldo Moro had been killed by the Brigate Rosse. And I thought that I could do without problems from the law when I'd only just arrived in Italy. Were these people connected with the Red Brigades?

I'd come to Italy to escape the madness of Thatcher's Britain and I was already connected with a group of people who were involved in a political mess connected with Italian fascists and South Americans on the run, and a global conspiracy of the CIA and the Italian secret services and Pinochet and Galtieri. Or that's how they see the world, I thought. I felt like we were living in two separate dimensions. I didn't want to talk about politics any more. I was out of my depth with these people so I tried to connect to Francesca and Liliana and Gerardo with the one thing that I knew we had in common… even if they might see it as a clumsy attempt to change the subject.

'So how did you get involved with theater?' I said.

'We've always been involved in theater,' Francesca said. She turned to look at Gerardo. I was afraid for a second that they were all angry with me for being an insensitive representative of British imperialism even if I was Irish.

Francesca broke up the green leaves for the salad. Just green leaves, some of which I didn't recognize. She put the porcelain bowl down in the middle of the table. Liliana let the tortelloni slide into the boiling water.

'These take seconds to cook,' she said.

I felt a deep sense of relief when Francesca brushed her fingertips against my face as she slid past me to sit on the windowsill again.

'Would you like a glass of wine?' Francesca said. 'We have some delicious Brunello.'

'Yeah,' I said. 'I'd like that.'

We were back on safe ground for a moment... theater, lunch... but they'd left me with a lot of unanswered questions. You know what? I didn't go to the rehearsal that night. The lunch left me too tense. There was a strange chemistry in that house and I wasn't yet absorbed into it. It wasn't just the politics. They had a bond that I didn't share yet. When a group of people gets together to create something on the stage… or on film… they share a vision, a reality that doesn't let outsiders in very easily.

So that night, I had dinner alone again. I spent the rest of the evening with my sketchbook and diary, drawing from memory some of the gargoyles from the church roof that I'd seen that day. I drew late into the night and I developed a story sequence and, in one panel, I tried to capture that rapturous expression that Francesca had on her face when the priest raised the host at the consecration. I didn't think I got it right at all. I was too tired. I sketched in a profile of Bernini's *Saint Theresa in Ecstasy*. That came out pretty good. Then I left the boards strewn all around the room and I crawled into bed.

About nine thirty the next morning, there was a knock on the door. I pulled on a pair of jeans. When I opened the door of my hotel room, Francesca was standing there.

'Have you had breakfast?' she said.

'No,' I said.

'Would you like to?' she asked me.

I was a bit disoriented, and stripped to the half. I invited her in. I pulled a clean t-shirt out of the rucksack. And there was the storyboard on the floor with the half-finished drawing of Francesca. She picked it up. She was holding the board in her hands. I was holding the t-shirt in mine.

'You make *fumetti*,' she said.

I told her I liked picture stories; that I'd been working on these panels for years; that they worked like a diary in some ways.

'Do I really look like this?' she asked me.

'It will when I've finished,' I said.

'I'm a painter, too,' she said.

'You can show me your work some time,' I said, 'your paintings.'

'Yes,' she said in that strange high voice of hers, 'when we go back to Rome.'

Was that an invitation? I thought. I felt a bit jittery, then. I really wanted to go with her to Rome. I couldn't say anything for a moment. I turned away from her. I draped the t-shirt over the foot of the bed, went over to the sink, ran some water, and splashed some on my face and under my arms, and over my chest. I dried off with the hotel towel and pulled on the t-shirt. I was mad at myself for being so tongue-tied. Or maybe I was being sensible. I couldn't tell which.

She'd got the boards in her hands and she was looking at the panels where her face was surrounded by the dog-faced demons and lions with the serpent's tails and a pelican pecking at its breast to feed its chicks with its own blood.

'This is fascinating,' she said.

'You're a true believer,' I said, trying to make it sound light.

'No,' she said. 'I'm a radical believer.'

'I'm not sure what you mean,' I said.

She put down the boards and sat on the edge of the bed.

I pocketed my wallet and picked up my keys, leaned back against the sink.

'When I lived in Argentina, I became involved in the liberation theology movement,' she said.

That was the difference between me and her; I'd read about liberation theology when I was fourteen. She'd been immersed in it.

I asked her if Gerardo had been involved.

'No,' she said, 'Gerardo, no. But it *is* why he had to get out of South America. He knew me and my friends, you see, and we were in his theater group and we were involved in liberation theology… so it wasn't safe for him after some of us were questioned… were picked up. The military, they wanted names, and… and they made us give them names…'

At this moment, I felt my body temperature drop.

I was in a hotel room in Tuscany, the full morning sunshine slanting in through the shutters and leaving stripes across her back and her hair and her face, and I felt my blood had leached away from the surface of my skin. I had a sensation of dread. I had no conception at all as to what Francesca might have been through but I feared even to hear about it. I was there in Italy. I'd traveled through India and Nepal, I was a comic book artist, and an unemployed, just-qualified English teacher, and I could sense that this woman was about to reveal to me something that I knew was way beyond anything I'd ever experienced; something no one would ever want to experience.

'In Buenos Aires,' she said, 'I studied drama, of course, and I became a member of the company… But some of us were quite… concerned about how things were… the military in power… we were young... we believed in social justice… we had things we could accomplish… we knew we could. And the dictatorship had to end… the oppression… the way the CIA controlled the governments in Latin America. I'd become part of the struggle… but I didn't fit in with the communists… I *did* believe in direct action… There was a Jesuit priest, a Father Ignacio. I went to him for confession… we talked a lot about the struggle against the military dictatorship… about Christ's message that the poor gave us the opportunity for a particular way for the grace of God to manifest in the world…'

The way Francesca's face lit up then was just like that moment I saw her at the consecration in the mass… ecstatic… it seemed to me... in a kind of rapture...

'Father Ignacio was very charismatic. I was even a little in love with him. Do you know about the charismatic movement?' she asked me.

I knew enough. These were Catholics who opened themselves up to possession by the Holy Spirit. I thought, Oh no, I'm all for altered states but when you call an altered state 'possession by God Himself,' I'm a bit wary.

'I joined the Montoneros,' Francesca said. 'We were waiting for General Perón to return from Europe to take control away from the military. Father Ignacio was convinced that Perón would sweep us into power and make a just and Catholic Argentine society.'

'Okay,' I said. 'And it never happened.'

'Literally millions of Argentines were at Ezeiza airport to welcome Perón when he flew back from Spain,' Francesca said. 'I was there with Father Ignacio. All of us were waiting to hear Perón speak. Then the fascists opened fire on the Montoneros. It was the Triple A, the Argentine Anticommunist Alliance. There was a stampede. Guns going off everywhere. So many people killed. We ran into the fields and hid in a ditch. When the shooting stopped we went back to the city. We were terrified that the military would track us down and kill us, too. Perón had betrayed us. He wanted to eradicate us. What could we do but fight back?'

I could see the rapture in Francesca's eyes... I was so aware of the danger of this mad metaphysic she believed in that could lead to unimaginable violence... but you should have seen the energy that possessed and vitalized the beautiful body of this woman: the charismatic grace of God that took her over. And you know what... it was so visceral, seductive... it was dangerous... magnetizing, it drew me to her. I can still hear that little girlish voice of hers, so high, like she was a lethal little bird, twittering away in my hotel room.

'In our group,' she said, 'I fell in love with a boy called Antonio. The Montonero boys were so much more handsome than the communists. I thought all communists were just pimply kids, too intellectual.

They were so boring... all their boring dialectical arguments. Our arguments were whether it was justifiable as Catholics to kill the members of the armed forces who were oppressing the people, the poor. We decided that it was our duty. That Christ wanted us to take up arms for the oppressed.'

I think it was safe to say that she was crazy with religion.

At that point, I thought the obvious thought: Yes, of course… you can justify anything, can't you, with the Bible?

She sat on the edge of my bed with sun and shadow laying light and dark bars across her blond hair and her slightly curved back and crazy as she was, I wanted to make love to her, there and then, but I couldn't make the move. This may sound neurotic but I felt as if I just wasn't worthy of her. She'd been through so much that my experience compared to hers seemed to be pathetic. I found something terribly seductive in the way that she'd been so close to death. This woman was a mixture of sexuality, violence, mysticism, and left-wing political passion; and that, to me, was just about irresistible. I thought that if I could only make love with her perhaps I could experience that rapture; and I didn't know whether I desired her because I wanted to feel like I'd conquered her, or that I wanted to be consumed by her.

'What happened to Antonio?' I asked her.

'He was killed,' she said, 'in a raid on a country police station to get arms. He was shot.'

Jesus Christ. Had she ever killed anybody? I was afraid to ask her.

'Let's go out,' she said. 'Come on.'

She got up and kissed me on the mouth, a light kiss; and then led the way out of the room as if nothing had happened. Maybe for her nothing *had* happened, I thought. She'd had a boyfriend who'd been killed in a shoot-out with the police. I mean for romance that even beat the death of Michael Furey in that James Joyce story, *The Dead*. You know, the guy who froze himself to death for the love of his girl who was off to a convent school. You see the parallel? I did.

I have a diary from back then. It became a kind of homage to the comic book artists I discovered at that time: Hugo Pratt, Milo Manara,

Vittorio Giardino… I developed my own style… a kind of collage… I picked up a photo from a magazine, drew it in pencil, abstracted the lines… colored with aquarelle. So I made this diary in the form of a comic book. I never meant to try and publish it. I took a little poetic license with it, you understand. I didn't want to make it exactly how things happened, so I left out a couple of details here and there. Compressed a few things. But it's mostly pretty accurate. It starts off more or less as I told you about Liliana, then it goes on. A lot of strange things happened around Gerardo and Francesca. You can see for yourself in my diary. Here, you can read it.

THE FRANCESCA DIARY

A Collage

Damien Kennedy

1982

June 1982. I landed at Fiumicino Airport in Rome. Liliana Franceschini, a woman I'd met in India the previous year, had heard I was coming to Italy so she invited me to the theatre festival at the Terme di San Tommaso in Tuscany. Her theatre group was performing Elektra.

So I went to the Gregorian Mass...
About ten rows in front of us,
a woman knelt enraptured...
I knew that we were going to meet her... that she was connected with Liliana's theatre group.

And sure enough when the mass was over, Liliana brought me over to meet her. Francesca was so beautiful. Perhaps that religious ecstasy of hers connected with some charismatic rapture awakened in me by the otherworldly chant and my long buried Catholic upbringing, and it ignited that mutually idyllic psychosis that we all call being in love...
Roma
Liliana drove us to the farmhouse where they were staying. I was practically dying just being close to Francesca...
She flirted with me from the church to the farmhouse...
And it was then that I met the director of their theatre Company...

This is Gerardo... Gerardo Fischer... He's from Uruguay
Come in, we'll have some lunch together...
That's when I found out that Francesca was from Argentina...
and while we enjoyed a delicious meal in a farmhouse in Tuscany, soldiers from Britain and Argentina were killing and dying...
Falkland Islands
...and sailors drowning in the freezing South Atlantic winter.

It's such an insane war. The military junta was just crazy to invade.
It's not just the junta! All Argentines want to take back the Malvinas!
She seemed to carry that rage into her performance that night.
I thought that was the end of anything that might have been between us. But then she suggested a walk in the garden...

I have an apartment in Rome... you can come and stay with me.
You make fumetti. Can you paint scenery?
I thought Gerardo would be jealous. But it seemed that I was wrong.

Everything appeared to be perfect. While on stage, Francesca was the embodiment of tragedy. Behind the scenery...
...we became lost in each other. I couldn't possibly even think about living without her.

I found out why Francesca and Gerardo were in exile. She had been a Montonera, a Peronist guerrilla fighting against the military dictatorship. Just by knowing her, Gerardo was in danger of being picked up and made to disappear.
I'm going to a political meeting.
I was sure something was going on between them. More and more, Francesca wanted to go out alone.
I had to confront her at rehearsals, the only place I saw her now...
What the hell is going on?
I'm sorry, Damien. I can't take this any more... what we have is just consuming me... It's eating me up... I've got to go... I just need some space...

I stayed in the flat and drew our story. I imagined where she might be...
I imagined her Montonera past...
The romantic image she had of herself...
How she was picked up by the secret police...
And then I didn't imagine any more. No one should have to imagine what happened to her. No one has the right to do such things to other human beings, then or now.
When they released her after a week, no one trusted her any more.

I got a telephone call from Gerardo. He wanted me to visit him at his house on the Via Appia Antica... I thought Francesca was staying there...
But I was wrong... or he was lying...
In the garden, a cave connects to the catacombs... a labyrinth. It's been used for centuries by Christians, criminals, smugglers...
"She's been through those caves a hundred times. I think she's found something down there she doesn't want us to know about. Three days ago...
I went into the cave with her, but she deliberately lost me. She knows what she's doing. She'll come back when she wants to... Stay with us Damien. We need you..."

Liliana will take you to the Porta Magica
She'll tell you what we want you to do.
Gerardo wants to do a play based on the life of the alchemist, Francesco Bono
I was to paint a replica of the Porta Magica in Piazza Vittorio, the door through which the alchemist disappeared, leaving behind him nuggets of transmuted gold. Were they messing with my head?
Gerardo was obsessed with his new piece of writing
EIVS PENNIS
We've got to go and find her! You can't just sit there writing another play!
She'll come back in her own good time. You'll never find her by looking down there
FILIVS NOSTER
MORTVVS VIVIT
REX AB IGNI REDIT
ET CONIVGIO
GAVDET OCCVLTO
We've got to try, you madman!

I found a big flashlight on my way through the conservatory. I grabbed it and marched out of the house. The garden was completely overgrown. But I knew where the cave was. I was going to find her.
I had to find my Francesca.

I had no idea where I was going. I trusted I could find a way out. It was a labyrinth down there. I heard some Kind of singing. It echoed beneath the arches of an underground cathedral...
Who had built this... and when?

I followed the sound to a side chapel...
and there was Francesca, in ecstasy, in the middle of a charismatic mass.
When she saw me, she took fright...
and fled down a tunnel...

I'd lost her again. She might have taken any of the exits from that Piranesian chamber.

I saw a light above. Perhaps she'd gone to the surface...

I came out of the cave complex...
I was expecting a woman.
I followed a woman through the caves...
His name was Omero. He lived in the woods, eating raw food, bathing in cold streams, just about naked all the time... a hermit...
She's been translating a book for me. It's the gospels of the Essenes.
Perhaps you'd like to see it.

Omero took me to a hut in the woods
Bunches of grapes hung from the rafters
I didn't care much about the book. But maybe Francesca would appear.
The rotten fruit crawled with wasps
Above me the wasps buzzed, maleficent
Maybe the wasps knew that I was no Essene...
AAAAAGH!

Don't go! She must come soon!
I lost myself in the tunnels again.
I stumbled around until I found another way out.

I was on the lower reaches of the Via Appia where women waited for desire-driven men...
Are you looking for someone?
Her name is Francesca She haunts the tunnels
Go through these catacombs always turn to your right

I found myself in a gallery high above a Mafia chop shop
Francesca was down below putting a package into the panniers of a Harley
The other mechanics were oblivious of her. She was obviously well known here.
I'll be back within a week.

I thought that I'd lost her for sure. But she didn't get far...
They must have been waiting for her... or for the package...
The BMW clipped her rear wheel...
and she came off the bike.

They took the package
By some miracle she wasn't hurt badly
What was in it?
Don't ask... I'm dead without it.
Gerardo's house was close by...
I couldn't stand the way they gazed at each other...
I was forgotten
We have to get out. We'll leave right after we do 'The Alchemist, Bono'

Whether they'd come to enjoy the play, to scare us, or worse, a Fascist group was at the theater...
Likewise the occultist aristocrats whom Gerardo had interviewed while researching 'The Alchemist Bono'
Gerardo had told me they wouldn't take me with them, neither would they take Liliana. She and I sat in the stalls.

Gerardo's play was a hybrid of Goethe's 'Faust' and Genet's 'The Balcony'... set in early eighties Argentina or maybe Italy
Secret police...
corrupt cardinals
I was devastated.
The chemistry between Gerardo and Francesca was electric...
Liliana saw it.
Either you come through that door with me, or you stay here and burn in the Inquisition's fires

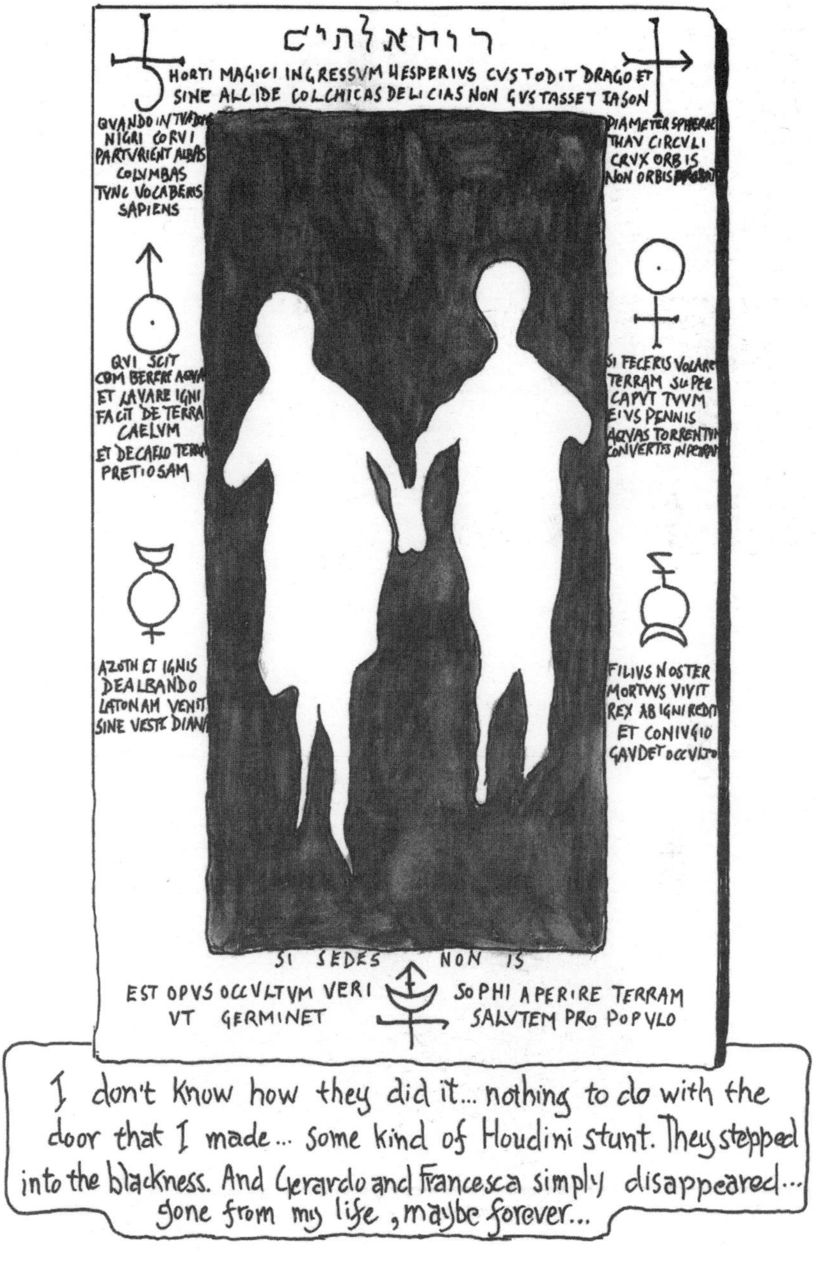
HORTI MAGICI INGRESSVM HESPERIVS CVSTODIT DRAGO ET
SINE ALCIDE COLCHICAS DELICIAS NON GVSTASSET IASON
QVANDO IN TVA
NIGRI CORVI
PARTVRIENT ALBAS
COLVMBAS
TVNC VOCABERIS
SAPIENS
DIAMETER SPHERAE
THAV CIRCVLI
CRVX ORBIS
NON ORBIS
QVI SCIT
COMBERERE AQVA
ET LAVARE IGNI
FACIT DE TERRA
CAELVM
ET DE CAELO TERRA
PRETIOSAM
SI FECERIS VOLARE
TERRAM SUPER
CAPVT TVVM
EIVS PENNIS
AQVAS TORRENTIV
CONVERTES IN PETRAM
AZOTH ET IGNIS
DEALBANDO
LATONAM VENIT
SINE VESTE DIANA
FILIVS NOSTER
MORTVVS VIVIT
REX AB IGNI REDIT
ET CONIVGIO
GAVDET OCCVLTO
SI SEDES NON IS
EST OPVS OCCVLTVM VERI
VT GERMINET
SOPHI APERIRE TERRAM
SALVTEM PRO POPVLO
I don't know how they did it... nothing to do with the door that I made... some kind of Houdini stunt. They stepped into the blackness. And Gerardo and Francesca simply disappeared... gone from my life, maybe forever...

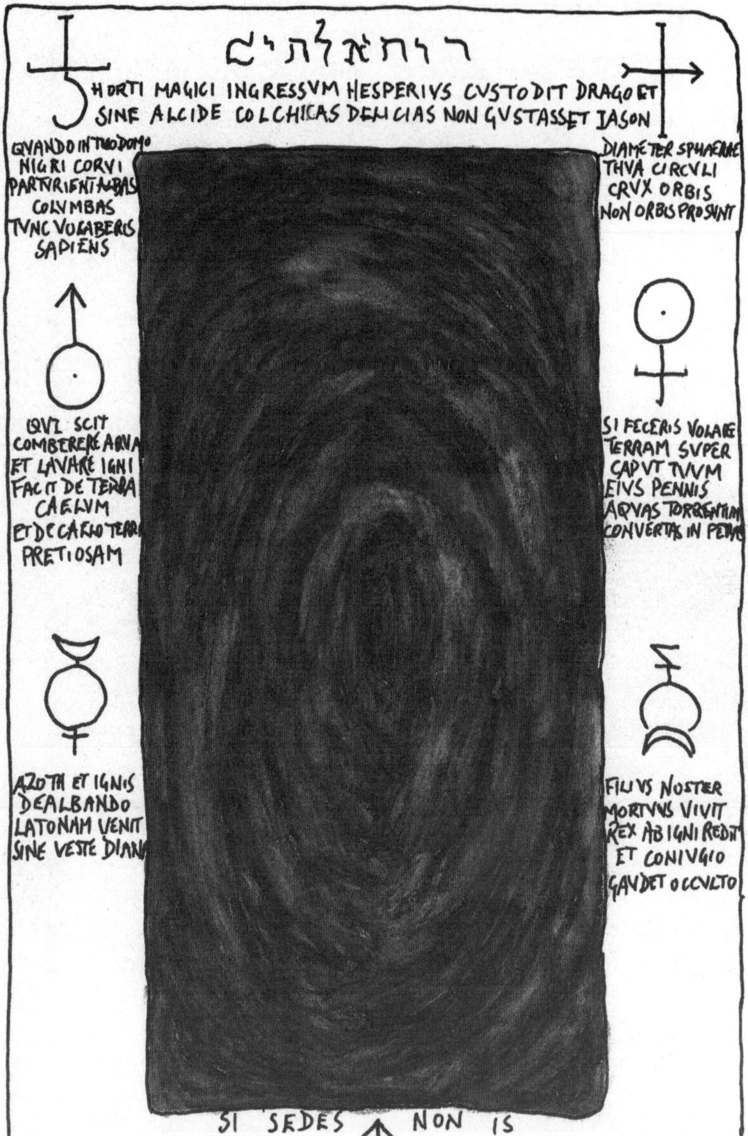
רוחאלהים
HORTI MAGICI INGRESSVM HESPERIVS CVSTODIT DRAGO ET
SINE ALCIDE COLCHICAS DELICIAS NON GVSTASSET IASON
QVANDO IN TVO DOMO NIGRI CORVI PARTVRIENT ALBAS COLVMBAS TVNC VOCABERIS SAPIENS
DIAMETER SPHAERAE THVA CIRCVLI CRVX ORBIS NON ORBIS PROSVNT
QVI SCIT COMBERERE AQVA ET LAVARE IGNI FACIT DE TERRA CAELVM ET DE CAELO TERRAM PRETIOSAM
SI FECERIS VOLARE TERRAM SVPER CAPVT TVVM EIVS PENNIS AQVAS TORRENTIVM CONVERTAS IN PETR
AZOTH ET IGNIS DEALBANDO LATONAM VENIT SINE VESTE DIANA
FILIVS NOSTER MORTVVS VIVIT REX AB IGNI REDIT ET CONIVGIO GAVDET OCCVLTO
SI SEDES NON IS
EST OPVS OCCVLTVM VERI SOPHI APERIRE TERRAM VT GERMINET SALVTEM PRO POPVLO

Extract from the casebook of Juan Manuel Pérez
January 11th 2006
Hours: 23:30 to 00:45

I closed Kennedy's comic book diary and handed it back to him.

'Thanks,' I said. 'That's a pretty strange work.'

'Those were strange times,' Kennedy said. 'Gerardo is someone special. It dawned on me later that being in the company meant so much to me… more even than the love affair that I was having with Francesca. It was shocking to think that… for Gerardo, too… the company was the focus of everything he did… more than any love affair he might have… and that he cared for every member of the company as much as, or more than, he cared for himself. You might find that difficult to believe but I believe it. The company was everything to us. And you know what? It still is. But we're all of us like that… all of us in the company… and Gerardo gave us that.'

He looked me straight in the eye as he said it. The wrinkles on his face, the slight sag of his jowls, the scruffy hair-do, didn't completely hide the similarities with the character in the panels of his comic book. It had been strange to see images of this man – and Gerardo Fischer – as they might have been twenty-five years previously.

The comic book diary was the work of a man who had lost his senses over an unstable woman; and who had been psychologically overwhelmed by his involvement in this incestuous theater group that was still headed by Gerardo Fischer. What was it about this Gerardo Fischer that made people think that they wanted to be in his theater company so much so that they would happily leave behind all that most people considered normal in the world?

'So you've no idea where he might be?'

Kennedy shook his head.

'Do you know where Francesca is now?' I said.

'She's in Buenos Aires,' he said.

'Buenos Aires: are you still in contact with her?'

'I haven't seen her for... a long time. I heard where she was from Sara. Francesca visits Sara's sister down there.'

'Do you think Gerardo might be with her?'

'How would I know?'

'Do you have a number for her?'

'For Francesca?'

'Yes.'

'No.'

'Do you think Francesca's kept in contact with Gerardo?'

'I'm sure she would have.'

'And you've kept in contact with Gerardo ever since those years in Italy?'

'On and off, yes,' Kennedy said.

'And you've been with him this time for around six months?'

'That's right.'

'Working on scenery?'

'That's what I do,' he said.

'Right here, in your... diary... the comic book... whatever you call it... Gerardo and Francesca disappeared... I mean what happened?'

'They were gone out of my life. Out of everybody else's, too. I don't blame them. Francesca was in trouble. Maybe Gerardo, too. Don't forget what was going on over here at that time... and those connections with the far right in Italy. I don't blame them at all.'

'So he's done this before, Gerardo.'

'Done what?'

'Disappeared. Maybe of his own volition.'

Kennedy shrugged. 'Well, it's always possible, but... you know... maybe the past finally caught up with him.'

'You, Damien?'

'Me?'

He laughed. I believed that he wasn't murderous or jealous enough to do something crazy with Gerardo. I had the feeling that Kennedy... maybe he hadn't exactly been lying... but... even if he loved to talk... he'd been holding something back.

'Have you any idea at all what might have happened to him? Could he be with Francesca?'

'Anything is possible with Gerardo...'

'What state was he in when you saw him last?'

'State?'

'Mental state.' I was beginning to think that most of these people were half-crazy.

'Focused,' Kennedy said, 'on the rehearsals of the present play... and preparing for the next one, his revival of *The Alchemist Bono*.'

'Would Francesca be in that?'

'Acting?'

'Yeah.'

'He hadn't got that far, not into casting. I thought maybe he'd get Ana to play the part.'

'So he gave you no hint that he might be about to take off for a while?'

'None.' Kennedy stared into the space between us as if he were looking into a kaleidoscope of all the possibilities of what Gerardo Fischer might be doing, or where he might be, or what might have happened to him.

'Do you think he took off of his own accord?'

'I have no idea,' Kennedy said.

'I'd better be going. I may need to talk with you again. Is that okay?'

'Any time.' He followed me to the door. I raised a hand in a wave and I walked back along the dirt path to the wooded copse and the rest of the colony. It was pitch dark. My eyes took a while to adjust to the lack of light. I should have brought a flashlight of my own. I took out my mobile phone and used it to light the way for a while.

Fischer could have skipped out on his own. He'd done it before, hadn't he?

It was past midnight. When I got to Ana's cabin it was all locked up. No one at home. Where could she have possibly gone at this time of night? She'd left Damien's before we could make any arrangement that I'd come back to her house but I'd assumed she'd be there after I'd talked to him. Had she gone over to Sara's house? Why hadn't she told me? Was I just a quick fling for her and now she was dropping me? I was disappointed. I wanted to be with her. Sleeping with her had changed the dynamic, hadn't it? It wasn't just a simple client relationship any more. I liked this woman. She had opened up a different world to me. I liked books and movies but she was the kind of person who actually made the things I read and saw. I thought that I'd like to know more about that from the inside. Plus I liked her body. Not just her body: that kind of dynamism that her body expressed. That's what I'd connected with when we'd made love. Is that what an actor does? Embodies something that they have inside which is what we, the audience, connect with in all its intimacy. It is an intimacy. Maybe that's what makes a great actor: the capacity to share intimacy with a whole audience. I can see why a lot of actors might crack up... so exposed, so vulnerable. Ana had gone one step further with me. But maybe it had been nothing so special for her. I'd slept with her once. I wanted to sleep with her again. It was no use getting sentimental or too romantic about it.

I waited a while. Around fifteen minutes, I guess. Maybe a half hour. She didn't show. I wasn't going to wait any longer. I walked down the path towards Sara's house. Getting involved with a client wasn't always such a good idea. Although I hadn't actually been paid. A couple of days to arrange to get American dollars in cash, that was okay. No need to get anxious. Not yet, anyway.

Sara's dogs started barking: something normal about that. The shutters were closed and there were no lights behind the windows. Why had Ana done that? Was she messing with my head already? These theater people were strange. Did I want to get involved with her? I guess I did. I kept walking up to the parking lot. Maybe Ana and Sara had gone out for dinner together. I'd made no plans with Ana before stopping at Kennedy's house. Maybe I should have. I wished that I had.

I got in the car, started the engine. I'd go to sleep in a cold bed.

It would be weird asking Ana for money after going to bed with her. I could keep the two things separate in my mind, the money and the sex. But anyway, it had been Sara I'd negotiated with for the money. I'd have to ask Sara for the cash. I would do that. But first thing in the morning, I wanted to visit Pablo Arenas again. According to Carlos Brescia, Arenas had a real motive for seeing Gerardo Fischer gone. I wanted to see Arenas's reaction when I brought that up.

Extract from the casebook of Juan Manuel Pérez
January 12th 2006
Hours: 09:30 to 11:00

Rangel was at the computer when I arrived at the office. The sun slanted through the blinds of the window on the sunny side of the building and laid a grid of shadow and light on our tiled floor. Next to Rangel's mouse pad, the crumbled and flaky remnants of the pastries that he'd had for breakfast lay in a small cardboard box. In his left hand, he held a Styrofoam cup filled with milky coffee.

'Let's go see Arenas,' I said.

'We've already seen Arenas,' Rangel said.

'New information. From Carlos Brescia, the boy who shot him.'

'About Fischer?'

'Fischer was with Carlos and Ramón when Maria Dos Santos delivered a threat to them to stop nosing around a family business.'

'Maria Dos Santos? That girl?'

'Yeah.'

'So?'

'I want to talk to Arenas again.'

'You driving?' Rangel said.

'Yeah.'

'You have a weapon?'

'Yeah.'

'Okay,' Rangel said. 'Let's go.'

When I pulled up at Arenas's house, with Rangel in the passenger seat, my car was the fifth in the driveway. Four guys in black suits and dark shirts stood smoking on the porch. I hadn't expected to see four guys in black suits and dark shirts. I'd expected to find Arenas alone.

'This wasn't such a good idea, was it?'

Rangel shook his head. 'No. It wasn't.'

I turned off the engine. My legs and back didn't want to separate from the driver's seat. My whole body felt heavy: some survival instinct that was preventing me from getting out of the car and going to meet the four men on the porch. It was as if they were in a different league of potential violence even than Arenas. To get out of the car had something of a suicidal air about it. I was conscious that to turn the car around and drive away would have been just as suicidal. It would have been to show fear. I had to lift the weight of body and get out of the safety of the car. The porch crew had seen who we were, and what car I was driving, and they could track me down and find me, and I would probably suffer if I turned around now and didn't brazen out some kind of communication with them. They might make Rangel suffer, too. Rangel said nothing. His breathing was shallow.

I opened the car door and got out. The passenger side door banged shut. Rangel shifted the shoulders of his jacket. He was sweating and he rolled his head around on his shoulders as if to ease some tension in his neck. I could have hugged him: maybe later if we weren't too battered and bruised.

When Rangel stood at my shoulder I walked along the dusty driveway toward those four flat expressions that did not change at all – not a twitch of a facial muscle, hardly the blink of an eyelid.

Rangel and I stopped at the bottom of the porch steps, which put us in a distinctly disadvantageous psychological position, vis-à-vis the four hard-faced men in suits standing on the porch about a meter and a half above us.

'Is Arenas around?' I asked. 'We were hoping to speak with him.'

'You're Pérez.'

It was the tallest and broadest of the four men who spoke. His face had a narrow roughness to it, like a piece of sheared-off limestone. You look at some people and you realize that they are capable of murder, that they feel a sense of impunity about this; that your own life is worthless to them. This was the face of a man who would probably enjoy inflicting pain. I was aware that there are many people like that in the world. Too many.

'You're the guy who hit on my woman,' the tall man said.

A prickly chill crawled across my shoulder blades and whatever had been solid in my stomach turned into some kind of dark slurry. Maybe my complexion got just that bit lighter, too. I was aware of a very deep and permanent black hole that I could easily tumble into.

'Who would that be?' I said.

'Maria Dos Santos.'

'That's not the way I see it.'

'How do *you* see it?' the boyfriend asked.

'I offered a lady a ride to town. She accepted. That's it.'

'She said you hit on her.'

'She must have misunderstood.'

'I don't think so.'

'We're looking for Arenas,' Rangel said.

The boyfriend turned his head toward Rangel.

'He doesn't want to see you,' the boyfriend said.

A scuffling sound came from inside the house.

'I do want to see him. Where's that son of a bitch?' Arenas appeared framed by the porch door. He rested his left hand on the doorjamb with the right hand leveled at me, pointing his finger. It was a little shaky. One of the dark-suited goons tried to ease him back inside the house. Arenas shook him off... despite being bent over almost double... as if he'd taken a few kicks to the ribs... and from the livid bruises around his eyes and jaw line, a few to the face, too. Who'd been beating on him? These guys? Some rival crew? Did someone else want to get hold of Fischer and think that Arenas might be able to help with some information? No one here was likely to enlighten me. I didn't want to look or feel like Arenas did.

'You know why you're still alive?' Arenas said. 'Because of the respect I have for your father. That's why. Now get the fuck out of here before I lose my memory. And do not fucking bother one second more asking me about anyone, okay?'

I assumed he meant Gerardo Fischer. He did not want me asking about Gerardo Fischer. But Fischer was not here. Of this I was certain. I was glad that Arenas had distracted the attention of Maria's boyfriend. I was glad that he told me in front of these men that he didn't want to kill me out of respect for my father. This meant that I could walk away alive and unhurt from the front of Arenas's house if I just kept my mouth shut. I glanced at Rangel. He needed no more prompting than that brief eye contact. We turned around. We walked back to the car. We got into the car without a word. I turned the ignition. The car started up right away. Through the windscreen I saw that Arenas had already gone back inside the house. Maria's boyfriend and all his dark-suited friends simply kept the hard stare on us: no, not on us, on me. Rangel might just as well not have existed.

I turned my head to look out the rear window: the welcome sight of the road, the dusty soccer field with its spindly white goalposts, and the red-tiled buildings of San Sebastian behind it. I laid an arm across my seat back. I reversed down the driveway. On the passenger seat, Rangel let out a long held breath.

'Who the fuck are those guys?' I said.

Rangel said nothing.

'Arenas is crazy,' I said. 'I can handle him and his psychotic family, but these guys are in a different class.'

Rangel said nothing. He stared straight out through the windshield up the drive toward Arenas's house. Back on the little side street, I got the car into forward gear and we moved off toward the town of San Sebastian. Rangel was having a difficult job of controlling the shakes as he plucked a cigarette from a fresh pack and place the orange tip between his lips.

'You want one?' he said.

'Yeah,' I said.

He pulled one from the pack and handed it to me. I put it between my lips and pressed the control to lower my window. Rangel leaned over with a lighter. I took in smoke.

As I pulled onto the main street it seemed that all the little old ladies doing their shopping, the kiddies on their bicycles, the taxi drivers lounging in front of their storefront office, and the young kids in replica soccer shirts, all stared into the car as I eased it toward Route 60. The sun blazed down. The paintwork on the hood was a blinding glare. The sweat that soaked my shirt was cold despite the late morning heat that prickled my skin through the auto glass. Nausea in the pit of my stomach. Rangel lowered the passenger side window. He blew out a heavy lungful of smoke that was whipped away in the hot wind.

'I didn't think we'd be getting out of there so easily,' Rangel said.

'Right.'

Whatever it was that my father had done, for or with Arenas, that debt that Arenas felt he owed to my father had saved me and Rangel from the hands of those ghouls in dark suits. Those men were capable of appalling violence. I knew this. That my father's link with Arenas – and what they had been involved in together – was the cause of my immediate salvation might well turn out to be a burden that I would have to carry for the rest of my life. But right this second I just felt a sense of relief.

Rangel took a long drag on his cigarette.

'We're going back to the office,' Rangel said.

'I'd like to talk to Maria,' I said.

'You fucking what?'

'Maria.'

'Not with me you don't.'

'I'll take you back to the office.'

'Listen, we need a little divorce work,' Rangel said. 'We've upset a lot of people looking for this Fischer guy.'

'You recognize the goon?'

'Maria's beloved?'

'Yeah.'

'Pedrito "the Hook" Matas,' Rangel said.

'The Hook?'

Rangel nodded. 'You don't want to know.'

'I do.'

'I'm not saying. It's ugly and nasty and connected with butcher shops, you understand?'

'Okay,' I said.

'He imports a lot of coke from the north. Also marijuana. Maybe heroin. He has a storefront in Ciudad Azul. Textile store run by some Lebanese guy: Ali, Mohammed... who the fuck knows what the guy's name is? Something Arab.'

'Sadiq?'

'Something like that.'

'Are you sure his name's Sadiq?'

'You said that... not me ...'

'What about weapons? Bombs?'

'I don't know shit about bombs... I do know they got a sideline in currency exchange. Maybe more. I'm sure Matas pays off the right people. You don't want to fuck with this guy.'

'Kidnapping? Murder?'

'Not beyond the bounds of possibility.'

I drove in silence for a while.

'You want I drop you off at the office?'

'I guess I do,' Rangel said. 'I don't like to interfere in family business; other than the kind where a woman wants me to find out what her husband has been doing... or vice versa. That's easy money. The hurt is all emotional... or financial... and it's between them not me... I can deal with that.'

'Okay,' I said.

My father. Arenas had brought up my father again. I hadn't heard from him about the files yet. Maria Dos Santos. I couldn't just go knocking on her door.

Arenas was relying on me to give up the investigation. He'd assume that I wouldn't want to offend my father; that I would appreciate that he, Arenas, hadn't caused me death, or severe pain. I would appreciate that he had done me a big favor because of my father. I had put Arenas away for a few years but that had been an unavoidable part of my life as a cop. Arenas could forgive me that. I was doing my job for the force. It was within his rules. Now I was not a cop. I had no right to be causing him difficulties over someone he might, or might not, have been holding for ransom. Or had killed and buried. This was interfering in his private business without my having any pressing reason. I had to keep my business out of his business. It was as simple as that. Arenas assumed I would agree with him... that I didn't need that kind of money.

Who had beaten up Arenas? Did it have any connection with Fischer? The boyfriend and his dark-suited goons were family friends of Arenas. They hadn't beaten him up... probably... unless they were taking over his business. So did some rival gang beat up Arenas to get a hold of Fischer? No one had asked for a ransom yet – as far as I knew – so how much could Fischer possibly be worth that one gang of Mafiosi would risk a war with a rival group? This didn't make sense. I thought my father might know. This was the second time that Arenas had mentioned my father. Continuing with this case meant that I might very well find out a lot more about my father that I didn't really want to know. This much I knew.

I also didn't want to have Pedrito the Hook Matas breathing heavily in my face. Nor did Rangel. I knew this. Back at the office, Rangel could take care of the easy work, the divorce work. It would probably pay more in the long run. I could talk as smart as I liked but I was too close to the business interests of people whose methods included extreme cruelty and violence – often against innocent people – and that wasn't likely to be at all entertaining or funny. And my own father might know a lot more about this than so far he'd let on. For me, this whole affair was getting to be something personal, very personal, extra personal. But I couldn't abandon this case. I couldn't just go away and forget about the whole thing. I had no right to do that, whatever it might reveal. I owed it to those people up there to find this Gerardo Fischer. Did I? I think I did.

'I'll take you to Ciudad Azul,' I said to Rangel. 'Then I'm going to look for Maria.'

'You are one crazy motherfucker,' Rangel said.

'I guess,' I said. 'You're right.'

[Extract from the casebook of Juan Manuel Pérez
January 12th 2006
Hours: 11:30 to 13:30

I dropped off Rangel at the office and cruised the main drag of Ciudad Azul to calm myself down a little. I turned off the main drag and into the streets around the lakeside: the small cafés, the boutiques, the souvenir stores, the *alfajores* cookie stores, the closed-up nightclubs. Pure blue sky over the Lago Gran Paraíso, late morning sun glinted on the ripples stirred by the mountain breeze. The sails of windsurfers ballooned in whites and yellows and oranges. Why couldn't I take a vacation like all these people down here on the lakeshore? Rangel was right. What was the point of talking to Maria?

Because she was the one who'd carried the threat to Carlos and Ramón and Fischer to lay off their digging the dirt on the Artemisia Adoption Agency.

What could I do? I could drive back to San Sebastian and look for her up there but I really didn't want to run the risk of being seen again by Matas or Arenas quite so soon after this morning's face-off. Maybe it was this sense of closeness to possible death that was conjuring up images of pure desire: last night's lovemaking with Ana mixed up with the comic book drawings of Damien Kennedy's Francesca. I wanted to see Ana again. Rangel would approve of that. Lie low. I couldn't just go knocking on the door of Maria's apartment in San Sebastian, could I? What would it get me... talking to her... really? Would it bring me any closer to finding Fischer? Gerardo's body might already be in one of those concrete struts that were being erected to carry the new overpass across town. Or neither Arenas nor Matas nor Maria had anything to do with Fischer's disappearance. There was no body and it was still just the third day he'd been gone and it was still possible that maybe Fischer had skipped out of his own accord just like he skipped out on Damien Kennedy all those years ago in Rome with some Houdini trick through a magic door because it had all got too hot for him.

I pulled over in the parking lot of a lakeside supermarket. I flipped open my cell phone and called Ana.

'Hi,' she said.

'Can I come by?' I said.

'We're having a meeting,' she said.

'Who?'

'Temenos: the people of the colony.'

'What about?'

'Gerardo. What we should do next. I think you should come. I should have called you. The meeting's at half past twelve.'

'I'll be there. I can just about make it.'

'Good.'

'You been thinking about me?'

'No,' she said. 'Maybe a little.'

'I been thinking about you.'

'So you should.'

'I'll see you soon.'

I hung up.

I was just about to start the car when I saw Maria in the rearview mirror. I stared at her reflection. She was walking with a slight limp. Even at this distance, the dark glasses didn't hide the redness and bruising on her face. Her hips moved awkwardly under her loose fitting white cotton smock. Maybe whoever had done Arenas had done her the same way. Matas? I opened the car door and got out. I went around the back of the car. When Maria saw me step onto the sidewalk, she glanced around in a panic, the straw basket in her hand swung around against her knee.

'Maria,' I called.

She couldn't just run across the road because of the traffic. She looked back the way she'd come and then she gave up trying to avoid me. I walked toward her.

'Please, I don't need to talk to you,' she said.

'Who did this to you?'

'None of your business,' she said.

'You don't have to take this. Maybe I can help you.'

I couldn't see her eyes but her mouth twisted in a wry smile of utter contempt.

'You can't even help yourself,' she said.

'Did Matas do this to you?'

'You've caused enough trouble in my life, you and your kind, now leave me alone or I'll tell Pedrito you tried to hit on me again.'

'Is that why he did this?'

'Fuck off.'

'Is that why he did this?'

'He saw me get out of your fucking car and he didn't like it. You're lucky to be alive. Now go away and leave me alone.'

She held a hand up toward me. My knees felt a little shaky. I didn't know what to do. I wanted to be gallant and take her to a café to buy her a drink and offer to help her deal with Matas but I knew that was stupid and would very likely get her another beating and me maybe worse. Cop instinct. The words 'domestic violence' came to mind; but for a man like Matas those words were wholly inadequate, and I knew that any interference from me would make things worse for her. I knew the way her family connections would operate to keep her from permanent damage, but her life, if it hadn't become so already, would be colored by seven shades of hell. I wasn't helping her at all by stopping her in the middle of a busy street in Ciudad Azul. Maybe Arenas had done something gallant for once in his life and tried to protect her and he'd got that beating for his troubles. But who am I to speculate about family business?

I waved a palm, turned around and walked back to my car. I got in. I lit a cigarette. I could still see her in the rearview mirror. She stood on the sidewalk like a shell-shocked bag lady. I still had time to make that meeting with the Temenos theater group. It seemed like Ana and those artists belonged to another world. Somehow, it had intersected with that of Arenas and Matas and Maria to nobody's advantage. I started the car and eased it into the traffic. I hated to leave Maria standing on the sidewalk like that. I wanted to get Matas.

Where the fuck was Fischer?

I drove between the concrete struts of the new overpass with the soundtrack a rattle of heavy plant, and truck engines, and the creak of cranes and the shouts of men in hard hats. I aimed the Ford's black hood at Highway 60.

I met Ana in the Temenos parking lot. I was still shaken by the meeting with Matas and Maria. I bent down to exchange a simple cheek kiss. The ropes of Ana's dreadlocks scraped against my face.

'Come on,' Ana said, 'we don't want to be late.'

'What's with the meeting?'

'We have to decide what we do about the performance in Buenos Aires next week,' Ana said.

'The performance?'

'Yes, the one we were rehearsing before Gerardo disappeared.'

I nodded. I guess Temenos was a kind of commune. Maybe they had meetings all the time. I guess all of the people up here were dedicated to some kind of ideal: writing or painting or music; or – like Ana – for the theater group. Gerardo Fischer had been a charismatic focus for her dedication to that ideal. Why hadn't they just stuck to theater and kept out of politics or crime? I guess that's unfair. Crime had come to them in the form of Arenas, and politics had always been an integral part of Arenas's criminal career. Maybe Fischer's, too.

Ana and I followed the path from the parking lot down through the pines towards the meeting hall. She didn't hold my arm, or my hand, and we might have been two strangers, or a client and an investigations consultant on our way to a meeting, which we were.

On the hillside paths from the cabins, other residents of the colony were headed toward the same place. Down near a small wooden bridge over the tree-shaded creek, cigarette smoke rose above the heads of two women and a man. Out of politeness I guess, they were keeping away from the main gathering of people in front of the hall. I raised a hand in greeting.

'Hi,' I called.

One of the women, about forty years old, had a halo of thick black hair, a thick waist, clothes stained with paint.

'You're the investigator,' she said.

Ana kept on walking as if she hardly knew me.

'That's right,' I said.

I lit another cigarette to calm myself down some more. All these images in my head: flat-faced Matas, bruises on Maria's face, Ana's face framed by dreadlocks that fanned in ropes across her pillow.

'Thanks for coming,' the dark woman said.

'What? Oh, yes.' I dragged some smoke into my lungs.

The male was wearing a brown sports coat that had seen better days. He was unshaven, a bit jowly. Either he ate badly or too much. The other woman had her hair cropped short and dyed a bright red, big eyes and cheekbones, a slash of bright red lipstick.

'We should go inside,' the redhead said.

'Sure.' I stubbed out my cigarette in a sand bucket with other butts.

Ana was with Sara, framed by the doorway of the meeting hall. Everyone started to drift into the meeting. When I got to the door, Ana took me by the arm.

'You sit next to me,' she said. I was glad of that.

Inside the meeting hall, the shutters had been folded back from the windows so that the theater space was flooded with light. The walls were black: ceiling and floor, too. Bleachers were bolted to heavy alloy scaffolding. It seemed to me that most of the colony's residents were gathered in the hall.

Sara stayed at the front of the auditorium, facing the bleachers. Ana and I sat midway up the bleachers just off the aisle. I kept imagining the faces of Matas and Maria. I just didn't want anyone else getting hurt. My nerves were raw.

'Who's in the actual theater company?' I leaned toward Ana. 'You've got a lot of people in here.'

'Right now the company is made up of three Argentines – myself, Justo and Enrique – then we have an American, two Australians, a Frenchwoman, and the Irish set painter, Damien, the guy you met last night. The others who live here are painters, potters, writers… I'll tell you their names as they speak.'

A gray-haired biker type limped into the auditorium.

'That's Dean Mills,' Ana said, 'an American writer.'

Mills was leaning on his cane, a black cane with medals from AA or NA dangling off it. It was the right leg that was stiff. The pain of it gave him a sour expression and it seemed he was in a mood to match. He sat down on one of the wooden folding chairs against the wall below the bleachers. Damien Kennedy, his gray blond hair hanging over the big features of his face, was the last to arrive.

'Sorry I'm late,' Kennedy said to Sara. Mills nodded to the Irishman and Kennedy sat down on a chair next to him. Kennedy pressed his palms together and brought his rough thumbs up to the level of his mouth, stared at the floor in front of him.

'Can we start?' Sara said.

Sara pointed me out on the bleachers.

'This is Juan Manuel Pérez,' Sara said. 'He helped us all out when Melissa, Miriam, Carlos and Ramón were robbed some time ago. He isn't with the police any more. We've engaged him privately to help us find Gerardo.'

I was shocked that Sara had started the meeting off by introducing me. It felt as if I was on stage, not in the bleachers. The edge of my seat dug into my legs just behind the knees. I needed to piss really. Right away, one of the foreign guys said: 'So what happened exactly? We just heard rumors... do you know?'

I leaned forward on the bench.

'That's Paul,' Ana said. 'He's from Australia.'

I nodded.

'I'm sure Sara and Ana will have told you all we know at the moment,' I said. 'Three days ago, Gerardo Fischer disappeared from his house. There was no sign of violence. No clue as to where he might be or how he might have disappeared. It's been reported to the police. For them, so far, it's a simple missing person case. For sure, they'll investigate fully but you have to understand, he's only been gone a little more than seventy-two hours. For the police, statistically speaking, he could turn up any minute having just skipped out to meet someone. Ana and Sara are worried about him. They asked me to help find Gerardo. I'll do everything I can to find him.'

'Gerardo could be anywhere. He might have just taken off.'

That was a deep voice from the front of the room.

'That's Patrick,' Ana whispered to me. 'He's Australian, too.'

His Argentine accent was quite passable. He must have been here for quite some time. It was because of Gerardo Fischer that all these theater-group gringos had come here to this place. They believed in him. Just like Ana. And Damien Kennedy. Believed that he could take them further than they had ever been before in their lives. Not just in the way they made theater, but how they lived their lives making theater. Temenos. Sacred space. I wished I had a belief like that in my life. It might help me deal with the violence that was Matas, was Arenas, and all the violence of the past. I was trying to find the man who transformed these people's lives, who gave them this motivation, almost like a religion.

'Yes,' I said, 'it's possible he'll turn up. The police will assume there's a simple explanation unless he stays missing. And I hope they're right. But I'll do everything I can to find out one way or another.'

'So what can we do?' Carine the Frenchwoman said.

'I'm going to get me a Doberman,' Dean Mills said.

'Why don't you get a gun, Dean?' Carine said.

'Because I'm not an Argentine citizen and I'd get put away for murder if I shot someone,' Dean said. 'Even in self defense.'

'Look,' Patrick said. 'We just don't know where he is... that's all. Maybe he'll just turn up.'

'I'd like to come around and talk to some of you,' I said. 'Anything you can think of, anything that might be helpful. Sooner or later, the real cops will be involved. I know some of them. I can work with them, too.'

I intertwined my fingers and gripped them tight between my knees. It was sinking in deep now how much I really missed being a cop and how proud my father had been of me when I got out of training, and how quickly I was drafted in to work with the violent crime squad. He must have been desperately disappointed when I left the force. I could always sense it in his body when we sat around the table in his garden, to drink *mate*.

A French accent cut into my thoughts.

'Gerardo has missed six rehearsals with us so far,' Carine said. 'He's been up here for months rehearsing with us. Every day the same routine. He's meticulous about that. That's what's so strange: that he'd say nothing and just not show up for rehearsals when the show is so close.'

'Nobody saw any strangers around here?' I said.

Total silence.

'Look,' I said. 'If someone can think of something desperately important right away, tell me now. Otherwise I'll come around and talk to you all one by one. Does anyone object if Sara gives me your residence details and phone numbers?'

No one said anything. A lot of head shaking. No public objections.

'Thank you,' I said. 'I'll be in touch with you.'

I didn't like being the center of an audience's attention.

'Okay, but we've all still got a problem,' Patrick said. 'We're supposed to perform in Buenos Aires starting next Wednesday for two weeks. Do we call it off?'

'No, we go ahead,' Carine said.

'With no director?' Paul said.

'We've been rehearsing for six weeks already,' Patrick said. 'We're close.'

'But with Gerardo missing...' Paul said.

'He'd want us to go ahead no matter what,' Carine said.

Ana's voice, right beside me: 'I think we should go ahead,' she said.

Outside the first dry thunder rumbled. It would pour with rain soon.

'Do want to vote on it?'

Ana leaned over and she whispered to me. 'That's Justo. He's Argentine, too.'

'It's not about a vote,' Carine said.

'Carine's right... either we all want to do it... or we don't do it,' Paul said.

'I want to do it,' Patrick said.

'Me, too,' Carine said.

'I'll say yes,' Ana said.

And then they all agreed. I found it kind of funny that they had this kind of 'show-must-go-on' attitude. There was a kind of childish innocence to it. Something I didn't have. But that was really none of my business. A squall of rain rattled on the straw thatch of the roof. Everyone began to fidget.

'Okay,' Sara said. 'Anybody have anything else to say?'

Nobody did. I guess they weren't communists or we might have been there for hours.

'Let's close the meeting,' Sara said.

Ana held onto me as we left our seats and went down the steps of the bleachers. My cell phone rang. It was my father. I opened the phone.

'Hello, Juanma,' he said.

'Pa, what can I do for you?'

'There are no files on Arenas or Fischer in the police department.'

'No files?'

'No files,' he said.

'That's impossible,' I said.

'That's the way it is.'

'That's what they're telling you.'

'No, that's the way it is. They're not there any more.'

'Who's got them?'

'Come around later this afternoon,' he said, 'we'll go for a ride together in the mountains.'

Extract from the casebook of Juan Manuel Pérez
January 12th 2006
Hours: 16:00 to 17:30

When I pushed through the entrance to my father's garden, he was sitting on the low gate that opened onto the stream and its steppingstones. He was relaxed, smoking a cigarette. A *mate* gourd in his left hand rested on his knee. Next to his right riding boot was a metal thermos flask. In the paddock across the stream, both of the bays had been saddled. Costanza brushed at the haunches of one of them. The reins of the other were looped over the branch of a pine tree. At first I thought that she and Pa were about to go riding, or had been riding, but Costanza was wearing rubber flip-flops and tight shorts. If they were to go out riding together, she would always dress in britches and boots. She always dressed for the occasion. Pa put down the gourd and stubbed out his cigarette on the gatepost. When he kissed me on the cheek he had that reek of nicotine on his breath and on his clothes that was particularly fresh – or particularly stale – depending on how you wanted to see it.

'Let's go for a ride,' Pa said.

I held my arms open. I was wearing slacks and loafers and a linen jacket. And the .45 was hooked on my belt.

'Leave your jacket with Costanza,' he said.

I took off the jacket but I left the weapon on my belt. Pa held the gate open for me. He was making an effort to show his paternal affection. I walked through the gate and crossed the stream. In the paddock, Costanza kissed me on the cheek. I handed my jacket to her and slid the hip holster back a little. I took the horse's reins from Costanza. I adjusted the tooled leather stirrup, got a foot into it, and swung up onto the horse. The saddle was padded with sheepskin, and a quilted blanket. I enjoyed the sensation of sitting up straight on a horse again. The bay tossed her head for a second, twitched her ears. I leaned forward and stroked her neck and she relaxed under my touch. Costanza brought Pa the reins of the other bay. He pulled himself up into the saddle, turned the horse around and we moved up the slope toward the gate that led out onto the hillside. Pa leaned over and unlatched the top gate, drew it open, let me through, and pulled it shut behind him without needing to dismount. We got out into the broom and scrub above the paddock and then we took a trail that led up towards some high granite rocks on the ridge. From up here we could see down into the village of San Pedro, across the valleys with their ranch houses among woods and paddocks, and – just above Pa's property – the whitewashed shrine to the Virgin. The sunlight picked out the borders of its walls, edged with yellow and gold paint that glittered.

The hooves of the horses kicked up puffs of dust and sent mica skittering off trailside as we eased into a canter. When we reached the highest point of the ridge Pa sat his horse and allowed it to crop at some sweet grass in the shade of one of the big boulders. Granite glittered where the boulder's facets reflected the bright afternoon sun. Lizards flitted across the rock surface and back into the shadows.

'Arenas speaks very highly of you,' I said.

'Stay away from Arenas,' Pa said.

'That's what he said.'

My bay's head lifted and her ears twitched and I laid a palm on her neck to quiet her down.

'A lot of people are looking for this guy Fischer,' Pa said.

I looked at Pa. He wasn't generally in the habit of sharing this kind of information, even with me. But he had bothered to go to his friends in the police department… only to find out that Fischer's file was missing. And Arenas's, too.

'Some people want to drag up the past again,' Pa said. 'They're looking to get people arrested and prosecuted for what happened about thirty years ago. And they've come very close to some interfering with the business interests of some very powerful people. This is not good for anybody.'

'Some of this I know.'

'Look, Juanma, this Fischer knows a lot of people… including these two queer guys who got robbed. And these queers have been asking a lot of questions around town and it seems they can contact any number of people who might be willing to talk and implicate a certain number of other people in activities who don't want to be implicated in anything. And not just about the past. About things that have happened since… and things that are happening now. Do you understand? This guy is not good news.'

'And somebody took the files on Arenas and Fischer away to study them?'

'I don't know who took the files away, or why, and I don't care.' He looked across at me as if asking me not to judge him. He'd found out a lot in the past twenty-four hours. And he was letting me in on some of that. Not all. I didn't want to judge him. He was my father and I didn't want to see him go to jail. Whatever he had done in the past he was still my father and whatever he might have done to others, he had treated me with love and support as I grew up. He was a cop and he told me stories of cops who stood against what he called those who would take too much advantage of decent people who had worked very hard to be in the positions they were in. He also stood up against those he considered would undermine the fabric of what he deemed a decent society. My father even went to church, every Sunday when I was a child, and pretty often now. His churchgoing didn't stop him from divorcing my mother and taking up with Costanza but that was in the realm of human frailty and could be confessed to God who would understand and forgive him; even if the Church wouldn't recognize his divorce, or his new marriage, and would consider that he and Costanza were living in sin. Pa may also have taken the odd bribe to turn his head the other way in the case of some questionable business deal but that, too, was normal and was how business was conducted in order that society benefited those who had initiative and took care of their families. One of the main duties of a policeman, as he saw it, was not to interfere in business matters where there were venial sins involved. He had no doubt that movements for what was called social justice were entirely suspect and he feared such movements would undermine the fabric of a society that honored the family, the fatherland, and God, whom he honored in that order. In his own way. With a certain degree of ruthlessness. I may not share any of his beliefs on that front, but that's the way he thought.

'So you found something out about his disappearance?' I said.

'I didn't say that,' Pa said. 'This Fischer that you've been contracted to look for is a man whom a lot of people would prefer wasn't around... and a lot of them for opposing reasons. Any one of those groups may have found him... worried cops or ex-cops, Triple A, someone else with a particular business interest... And now we have politicians who want to show that the police force is different, is capable of prosecuting former members who were acting under different rules in the past. So maybe some of them are looking for Fischer, too, and maybe someone in the police department found this out, and asked someone to fix it so that Internal Affairs didn't find any files on Gerardo Fischer or anyone else with whom the police had dealings to take care of some maybe... extra-curricular activities.'

'Like Arenas.'

'Arenas has done his time,' Pa said. 'You don't need to put him away again. And you can't... you're not a cop any more.'

My father pulled the bay's head up from where it was still nipping at the green shoots below the granite boulder. He leaned across its mane.

'Listen,' he said. 'If this Fischer is out of the way maybe it's the best for everybody… best for you… best for me… you understand? Do you really need to find this guy… if he's still alive? If he's skipped out, he's a smart guy. But fuck him. If he's dead, what's the point?'

Those hard blue eyes on me. He wasn't trying to intimidate me consciously but it was all I could do not to turn my gaze away from him. His stare reminded me of Matas, that flat stony stare. I continued to look straight back at him but my thoughts were sparking like pinwheels.

'People have called me up, Juanma,' he said, 'people of respect. I said I'd have a word.'

Respect. Was my father involved with this disappearance? My father had found out enough now through his connections that he needed to warn me off. And somehow Fischer's involvement in politics or business might implicate my father in some way. I didn't know anything about my father's current business interests. He might well have a reason to be happy that Fischer was gone, if Fischer, Carlos and Ramón had dug up something to which he was connected. So where did that leave me? If my father had taken on a private case… as I had done… that might result in me doing time… what would he do? I knew what he'd do: he'd drop it. He'd never keep on with anything that might allow outsiders to hurt his family. He had hurt my mother by divorcing her and marrying Costanza… but that was inside-the-family business. My father had brought me out here to show me in private why I should give up the case. I would do nothing to have my father jailed. I would not call the cops on my father. This I knew. But I'd been hired to find Gerardo Fischer. To me, it didn't seem like Fischer was such a bad guy. He may well have been an indiscreet guy. But unless I found out something about Fischer that made me think he wasn't worth finding, I was going to discover what had happened to him. My father knew that. And he didn't like it. But also he did expect me to have filial piety… and just lay off on his say-so.

I kept looking into those blue eyes in the deeply tanned face of a man that I genuinely loved and I didn't have to say a word to him. What I wouldn't do is call the cops directly about anything Pa might have done, or might be doing, that I might discover while looking for Fischer. The cops had their job to do. And I had mine. Mine was to find Fischer, that's all. Pa knew I wasn't going to give up my case. He must have known that from the start; but because he loved me, he was asking me in a dignified way to walk away from it.

'Some very dangerous people have become very annoyed with you. And they won't let me stand in their way for long.' he said. 'Think it over.'

And he knew I would. He knew I would think a lot about this. I suspected that he knew Matas was involved as well as Arenas. Pa really wanted me to just give up the case altogether. I knew it would hurt him if I kept on. It would hurt him like he hurt my mother over Costanza. He'd been well aware of how much the divorce would hurt my mother… and his remarrying Costanza… and he'd gone ahead anyway. Like I was going ahead in the hunt for Fischer. My father was a stubborn old bastard. I guess I'd inherited that stubbornness from him, too. He was also well aware of how men like Matas and Arenas might hurt me severely.

Damn… I'd rushed out here to talk to my old man and I hadn't collected my money from Sara. I wasn't going back to Temenos right now after this little chat. First thing in the morning, I'd go get paid.

Pa turned his bay horse and set off down the trail at a canter, back toward his ranch house, and his new wife. Now that he'd warned me off, I had a strong sense of nausea: if I got into deep trouble searching for Fischer, Pa would let whatever consequences there might be for me take what course they may, without any help, or interference from him. Pa had his own hard streak. He could be mean and vindictive, too. I'd seen that over my mother and the divorce. But I wasn't giving up any search, was I? That's a fact. I think he knew it.

Extract from the casebook of Juan Manuel Pérez
January 12th 2006
Hours: 18:30 to 20:30

I took it easy on the drive back to Ciudad Azul. My father's warning had stirred up old resentments that I still harbored over him divorcing my mother. I had my own theories about why he'd left and it wasn't that he'd just fallen in love with a sexier younger woman.

My father didn't sleep so well at nights. After dark, he lived in a world of nightmare. Around the time I'd been born, he'd waded into the mire of politics and crime at a time of terror and confusion... and for a long time he couldn't help but relive the images of horror that came back to haunt him: the broken bodies of the dead, the broken minds of the survivors... these men and women with whom my father's mind maintained a disturbed psychic connection... hardwired into his consciousness by the horrific and relentless suffering to which these prisoners had been subjected under my father's direction; or under the operation of his own hands.

And he'd told my mother what he'd done when the icy lid on his memory shifted to let his demons out. My mother had only sought to relieve his guilt. As far as she was concerned, Pa had been protecting the fatherland from the godless reds. I think Pa left Ma because he'd poured all his guilt into her and the way he saw to expiate it was to push her off the cliff of divorce. Or am I being too biblical? He'd unloaded his guilt on my mother and dumped her, and he believed that with Costanza, he could make a fresh start. I guess that's why I've always hated Costanza. It stops me hating him.

I knew of my father's insomnia. Of course I did. But when I was a child, I'd never suspected the reason. He had never once mentioned his night horrors to me. Years later – post-divorce – that was when I found out, just after Pa announced to Ma that he was going to marry Costanza, I'd gotten a call from my mother at about three in the morning. She'd sounded terribly drunk and asked me to come to her apartment right away. She'd been distraught. When I reached the apartment house, Ma was slumped in an armchair. The whisky bottle on the coffee table in front of her was more than half empty. She had a full tumbler in her hand that spilled over each time she swirled the ice around. Some awful late night soap opera was on the television and she talked at me over the noise of the melodrama. She recounted a long and detailed compendium of my father's recurring night visions: bare bed-frames, cattle prods, blowtorches, and the contorted faces of the often innocent victims.

'And I know he kept a lot back from me,' she said. 'That's the kind of man your father was.'

And then she had broken down completely: her eyes puffed up red, streaming tears, her mouth twisted, the sobs that racked her body. This hadn't been the picture of my mother that I'd always carried around with me in my head. She had always been strong and beautiful, dark and sexy, to me. Now she was a frail old woman with a shattered self-image who was taking solace from her mental anguish and abandonment through the booze and cigarettes that were ravaging her looks and mental stability even more. I never really forgave my father for reducing her to that... How bizarre that the suffering that he'd caused my mother affected me more than the knowledge of the terrible suffering he'd inflicted on others... while at home I'd grown up in comfort and ignorance.

In the present time, we're dealing with a different kind of evil: a callous kind of evil that isn't driven by any other ideology than self gain. Money. Power. I guess that isn't much different than the old days. Except there are people like me, from families like mine, and people like Ana from groups like Temenos who can now talk to each other. Help one another. Even make love together. This was unthinkable thirty years ago.

At that moment when I watched my mother break down, I became aware of all the little corrupt acts to which I'd been a party when I'd served as a policeman. The way I didn't see some things: like a long-term lowlife thief getting a beating; a little pay-off you take from a drug dealer, or a pimp, because these are small things; and your job is the need to take care of far bigger crimes and more terrible violence from which to protect the ordinary citizens of this country. That's what I'd believed when I'd been a cop.

All of those stories that I heard about my father, that night, from my mother, I'd always tried to keep shut up in the darkness myself, out of memory, just as she had for so many years. Now, I could feel them wanting to surface from a deep and fearful place inside of me. How would I have reacted if I'd been a cop back in that time of total political turmoil? Hadn't Pa's genes formed my body? Hadn't his DNA shaped my mind? Of what might I be capable right now?

Like him?

I knew what I wanted to believe. But I had no way of knowing.

Driving back to town, I wanted to make sure that my mother was okay. I'd had enough of seeing my father just fine with Costanza. When I reached Ciudad Azul, the sun was close to setting. I pulled up outside Ma's apartment house, just at the western end of town, not far from the lake.

I rang the buzzer on the gate.

'Who is it?' Her voice crackled in the speakerphone. She buzzed me in both doors when she recognized my voice. I took the elevator to her floor. She'd left the apartment door open. It was dark inside. The shutters were down and the air was stale with smoke. She was standing in the living room, the flickering of the muted television illuminating the walls and the gaunt stick frame of her. Her dark dress covered her arms and fell below her knees, elegant, as if she was in mourning. I went to her and she lifted up her head to give me a kiss on the cheek.

'Juanma, so nice to see you.' Her voice was gravelly with whisky and cigarettes. Her hair was stiff in a new dyed permanent, and her eyes dark with shadow, her lipstick a reddish brown. 'You want a little whisky, Juanma?'

'Yeah, go ahead... Christ, open the shutters, Ma... Get some air in here.'

She waved me toward the windows with a dismissive hand: wrinkles, liver spots, not like Costanza. I yanked on the canvas tape and the shutters clattered up. I opened the glass doors to the balcony. The last rays of the sun glinted on the lake. It was cooler this evening. The stale air drifted out. Cool lake air drifted in.

Ma freshened her glass with the scotch and poured me a liberal one. She put the bottle back down on the sideboard where she kept her framed photographs, none of my father, obviously, but four of me: one as a baby in her arms – I guess I must have been about seven months old; me in the cassock and surplice of an altar boy, about nine years old – a picture I'd found embarrassing as a teenager; my high school graduation photograph – a boy with an already receding hairline; and my graduation photograph from the Police Academy – head shaved, goatee and looking tough. Behind the pictures was the trophy I'd won for marksmanship in my last year at the academy. I don't know why she kept it there. I didn't want it.

Ma sat on the sofa and I slumped into the armchair opposite her. On the coffee table was an old newspaper, the one with the report on the weapons heist from the airbase in Córdoba; and a playbill from a production that had been on at the Theater Colón that was nothing to do with the Temenos people.

'What brings you to see your old mother?' she said.

'I just thought we could have a little drink together,' I lied.

I really wanted to ask my mother more about Pa's involvement with the political right and if she'd heard of Arenas – or if she knew anything about him from the old days – but for the moment, I couldn't bring myself to form the words.

This visit wasn't helping me to find Gerardo Fischer. And her squeezing my hand with such affection didn't endear me any more toward my old man. So I said it. 'Hey, Ma, what do you know about Pa and Pablo Arenas?'

Her hand shook as she lifted the glass to her lips. She took a large swallow. When she lowered the glass her eyes were two little balls of ebony. She had a wry smile that told me what she was going to say before she said it.

'I don't know anything about any Pablo Arenas. Who's he?'

I knew right then that she wasn't going to say another word no matter how much I pressed on it; on Arenas, or anything to do with my father in the far or the not so distant past. If I had pressed her, this little affectionate visit would all end up badly. I knew that.

'Forget it,' I said. 'He's just some guy.'

[Extract from the casebook of Juan Manuel Pérez
January 13th 2006
Hours: 08:00 to 10:30]

I guess it was inevitable that I would have a particularly vivid dream that night. I was in a city on the coast of Chile, not in Argentina, and a powerful storm in the distance had obscured the Andes with dark cloud. The coastal ranges hid the full impact from my view so I climbed up a steep street and by the time I reached the top of a hill above the city, the blizzard seemed to have blown itself out. In the distance, Aconcagua and the peaks around it were completely white with new snow that gleamed in the bright sunlight. Bright beams cut through the clearing mists and clouds and they evaporated into an empty blue sky. A broad canal with barges docked at its wharves ran the length of the plain between the coast range and the Andes. With what looked like a huge snowplow on the bow, a gigantic icebreaker ship broke up ice floes that had formed on the canal's surface during the storm.

I was now a bodiless point of consciousness observing the unfolding dream vision. I became aware of a large mansion behind me. In the house, a young boy, about seven or eight years old, was being held captive by a large family that included a husband, a wife and four or five of their children. The family seemed to be in a momentary state of suspended animation, as if they were aware of what was going on in the house but were unable to move. The disembodied state of consciousness in which I found myself was somehow responsible for this. The captive boy realized that he had a chance to make a run for freedom. I urged him to climb out of the window while the family was still in a state of paralysis. I followed him onto the street to make sure that he got away safely… and then I was wide awake.

I didn't think I needed to analyze anything. The dream was mysterious and beautiful and had left me in a good mood. I got up. I showered. I shaved. I sat on the balcony of my apartment that overlooked the lake and I sipped at a cup of coffee with milk. My cell phone rang. It was Ana.

'I'd like you to come and meet someone,' Ana said. 'She wants to help with the investigation.'

'And this is?'

'Clara Luz Weissman. She's the producer for Gerardo's theater company.'

'The producer?'

I had another moment of doubt as to whether it had been such a good idea to sleep with Ana. Did it come from guilt? Or was it a baseless anxiety? She was so different from me. Younger for sure… but why should that be an obstacle? The dreadlocks, the tattoos, the oriental symbols on her arms, and me an ex-cop, in white shirt, black pants and penny loafers. I was a digger in the dirt of human lives. But wasn't that what she aspired to as an actress? We must have that in common, right? We were both interested in extremes of what people did. I was also interested in getting paid. Had that made me anxious? I needed the money and I'd complicated collecting it by having sex with the client. I wanted to be with Ana some more, I was sure of this, but I also wanted to get paid for doing my job. How much would she want to be with me? I might have just been a one-night stand for her, some fun, a little fling.

'She drove all the way up here from Buenos Aires,' Ana said. 'She knows more about Gerardo's movements in the past few years than any of us.'

'And she wants to help?'

'Yes...'

Ana paused.

I waited.

'She has the archives of the company, everything Gerardo has done...'

Had this Clara Luz Weissman seen the folder that I'd found in the kitchen drawer of Gerardo's house? Maybe she could shed some light on the people in the photographs, the signatures on the postcards.

'Can you come to the house and meet her?' Ana said.

'Sure, right away.' I pocketed the cell phone.

Me, an ex-cop, Ana, a dreadlock actress – signs and wonders – I was a bit in love with her, wasn't I? I wanted what we'd had to be more than a one-night stand. And I'd ask Sara about the money. I'd been working for three days and I hadn't seen a cent.

I finished my coffee. I hooked the .45 onto my belt. I grabbed the folder of postcards and photographs. I locked my apartment and got the elevator to the basement garage of the apartment block. I was nervous in the dim light and the deep shadows, my nerve ends grating with the day's first coffee. My car was in its parking space some twenty meters away from the elevator shaft. The bodywork of the black Ford Executive gleamed. Somehow that was a pleasant surprise to me. I'd half expected the car to be vandalized with some slogan painted on it... yet another warning for me to lay off the Fischer case.

I tossed the folder on the passenger seat. I hesitated before I turned the key in the ignition. The image of Maria Dos Santos's boyfriend was sharp and clear in my mind. I was too nervous. I turned the key and the car started. It didn't explode.

I reversed the Executive out of its parking space. I drove up the ramp from the garage, turned onto the street, and drove out on Route 60 to the Artists Colony.

My father would be hoping that after I'd slept on our discussion,

I would awake with the clear light of reason and make a sensible decision to go back to divorce cases and forget all about Fischer. But I was choosing these Temenos people – artists, actors, psychologists – over my father, the ex-cop, despite the fact that these were privileged people who had hardly ever done a day's real work in their lives.

After a leisurely drive down Route 60, and a bumpy ride down the long dirt road, I turned in through the gates of the Artists Colony. A dark red Dodge Ram was parked in the driveway of Sara Suarez's house, just behind Fischer's white Fiat van. I stopped beside the Ram. I got out of my car. The Ram was a pretty expensive pick up truck. It was dust covered. On the passenger side of the bench seat was a pile of files, papers, books. I assumed that this truck belonged to the theater producer, Clara Luz Weissman. If so, she had access to more money than I would have thought for someone in her line of business. Maybe she was very successful at it. Maybe she was just from a rich family, or had a rich husband to bankroll her.

I walked up the pathway toward Sara Suarez's house. The dogs were barking inside the house. I took a slow pace up to the front door to give Sara Suarez time to lock the dogs away… if they hadn't already been corralled when the Dodge Ram driver had arrived. Security. Insecurity: it's a constant issue in people's lives.

Sara opened the door just as I reached the terrace.

'Come in,' she said.

I followed her into the living room.

A dark-haired woman, slim, mid to late thirties, I thought, with big dark eyes stood next to Ana by the front window. She was taller than Ana by a lot but she still didn't look how I imagined the driver of a Dodge Ram to be.

'This is Clara,' Sara said.

'Pleased to meet you,' I said. 'Juan Manuel…'

'The investigator,' Clara said.

We exchanged a cheek kiss.

All these people in the theater company had a quality of being hyper-real. I felt as if I was part of an audience witnessing them on a brightly lit stage. This whole investigation seemed so unreal all of a sudden, as if any one of these actors might disappear without trace as Gerardo Fischer had done. Come back as another character. Like a dream. It was disconcerting. Clara and I sat down opposite each other on the armchairs at either end of the sofa. Sara and Ana sat on the sofa.

'Clara knows more about the history of the company than anyone else,' Sara said. 'She's booked just about all of the performances…'

'All over the world,' Ana said. 'She's great.'

The marks under Ana's eyes were darker, her dreadlocks a total mess. I guess she wasn't sleeping… thinking about Gerardo? That's the way the mind works for people when someone close to them disappears. They stare at the clock. They listen for the ring on the telephone that never comes.

'Just how long *have* you been the producer?' I said to Clara.

'Seven years.'

'So you know everywhere Gerardo has been since then.'

'Pretty much.'

'And Clara's putting together an archive of everything that Gerardo has done over the past forty years,' Sara said.

'It's a bit daunting,' Clara said. 'It's so fragmented. But it's like the history of the company.'

'You keep it up here in the Sierras?' I asked.

She shook her head.

'All of the raw material, you know, like the playbills, reviews, his writings, I have in Buenos Aires,' she said. 'But I've transcribed a few things and I've scanned a lot that's now on my computer…'

'Maybe I should see this.'

'What have you found out here?' Clara said.

'So far, very little.' This was a small lie.

'I think we need to be more active in the search.'

'Oh… What did you have in mind?' I couldn't keep the sarcasm out of my voice. Clara gave me the hard stare. Then she reached down to the briefcase at the side of her chair. She flipped open the leather flap and pulled out a sheaf of printed notices.

'I thought we should post these all over the area.'

She handed me one of the papers.

HAVE YOU SEEN THIS MAN?

There was a rather poor photograph.

GERARDO FISCHER IS MISSING
IF YOU HAVE ANY IDEA AS TO HIS WHEREABOUTS
PLEASE CONTACT CLARA LUZ WEISSMAN

There was a phone number and an email address below it.

'I'm going to set up a website, too,' Clara said, 'where people can post messages.'

I nodded. I was happy that my phone number wasn't on the flyers. I would not have to answer any bogus calls of false sightings or fake information from people looking for a reward. Also, it wouldn't draw anyone's attention to the fact that I was still involved with the case. My father and Arenas might even think that I'd given it up. What was sure is that with all these posters plastered over the region, some newspaperman would certainly want to pick up on the story. 'Theater Director Disappears.' And then the police would be asked some questions. Someone from the police department would then have to come and investigate. This was sure. They would eventually have got around to this missing person case anyway but I imagined that they would be more focused on bigger things that were missing like the cases of small arms taken from the military base in Córdoba. But then again, if some cops saw an opportunity to use Gerardo Fischer as a means for advancement through the ranks... because now, as my father said, it was politically expedient to show that the police force was cleaning itself up... these cops would declare to the press just how much was being done to find Fischer's whereabouts, and they would start to ask questions about why he had disappeared. They might put it down to a simple ransom case... but really, based on what my father had told me, I'd say it had all the potential to blow up into a major media event with every political, criminal and commercial interest in the province and beyond, trying to make some kind of capital out of it. And Fischer might end up dead because he'd have become too much of a liability to keep hidden in the event of a major kidnapping manhunt.

'I'm going to coordinate the campaign,' Clara said. 'I'll pass on any information I get to you, and you can do the same for me.'

'Okay,' I said.

You're going to coordinate the campaign? I thought. Fine. If this was a simple kidnapping, and the kidnappers didn't know who to ask for a ransom, they'd have a name and a phone number and an email address now, provided by Clara Luz Weissman. Whoever else was looking for Gerardo Fischer would be alerted to the fact that these people, at least, had no idea of where Fischer might be. If my father or Arenas's or Matas's goons should ask, I could say with all honesty that this leaflet campaign had nothing to do with me.

'Is that it?' I said. 'Would you prefer that I drop the case, now; let you get on with it?'

Ana's eyes hardened on me.

'Please, no,' Clara said. 'We just want to be involved in the search. We can all help, can't we?'

'I guess,' I said.

The silence was a little uncomfortable. I looked at Sara.

'I hate to bring this up right now,' I said. 'Would it be possible to get the first payment out of the way?'

Sara looked a little shocked.

'Yes, yes of course,' she said. 'I have the money right here.'

Extract from the casebook of Juan Manuel Pérez
January 13th 2006
Hours: 10:30 to 11:30

With a thousand US dollars in cash in my wallet, I felt a lot less nervous.

Of course I could work with Clara. I sat close to her as she opened up her laptop. She had an electronic folder on the desktop that was simply entitled Gerardo. When she opened that up, there seemed to be around thirty subfolders. She double-clicked on the first.

'I've grouped all the reviews I could find into these PDF files,' she said. 'It's a huge job of scanning.'

I wasn't interested in his reviews. They weren't going to help me find Gerardo Fischer. Clara clicked on the next folder, ran the mouse down a set of documents.

'These are articles about his work. The pros are grouped by number, like this, 01, 02 etc, and the cons are grouped by date. People either like Gerardo a lot, or they hate him. I don't think anyone in the theater world would hate him enough to kidnap him or to... no... that's impossible.'

I pointed to a folder marked letters.

'What have you got in here?'

She double clicked on the icon.

'These are letters that Gerardo sent and kept copies of on his own computer. We have scans of some of his original letters that were kept by friends. And some of the letters and postcards that Gerardo kept in his journals or in folders.'

'I found a folder with a notebook and some postcards and pictures in the house he rented,' I said.

'You did?'

'Yeah. I brought it with me.'

'Can I see it?'

'Of course,' I said. 'It's his, not mine.'

'We'll need to scan it,' Clara said.

'The postcards come from Israel, Italy, Iguazu, Bariloche.'

'Bariloche?' Clara said.

'This Priebke business. He was involved with that, wasn't he?'

'It came out of what was going on in the eighties in Italy,' Clara said. 'It was before my time with the company obviously, but some things I know connected with the plays he developed back then.'

'Damien Kennedy told me something about that time,' I said, 'up to the end of the story with Francesca Damiani. Kennedy said he lost touch with Fischer after that until very recently. Is there any way that Kennedy might know something that he'd be reluctant to tell me?'

'Damien came back a few months ago. It's true he blamed Gerardo for his losing Francesca Damiani, that's kind of a legend in the company, but really... I can't see Damien doing anything to Gerardo over that. Damien's one of us.'

'There's a big gap in what I know about Gerardo between Francesca's disappearance and Damien's reappearance.'

'It was just after he did the play on Francesco Bono, the Alchemist,' Clara said.

'Damien mentioned this,' I said.

'When he was researching the play, Gerardo came across a whole network of occultists who were happy to talk to him about Bono, alchemy and the Porta Magica. Crazy people. Right wing Italians, aristocrats, rich people. During the Second World

War they'd been cosseted by the Nazis. Some of them had made connections with Himmler's special SS groups; the ones that met in Bavarian castles. The ones who practiced rituals to contact Secret Masters that they thought could be brought to this dimension through esoteric doorways that had been discovered by alchemists during the time of the Renaissance. In the late seventies and early eighties there'd been a resurgence in interest in the occult. So it wasn't so difficult to find people who were still involved in this kind of thing.'

'Gerardo believed in all this?' I asked.

'Gerardo didn't ridicule the idea. These people were a source of information for him about the play. He wanted them to trust him, be sympathetic to him and his work. Gerardo would say anything to ingratiate himself with a subject, no matter how bald the lie. Whether these people had the power to contact some weird occult forces or not, the earthly forces they'd contacted in the past were manifestly evil. If they'd been in contact with some kinds of spirits, I don't think they'd be so benevolent either. One of these doorways between dimensions, according to the occultists, was the Porta Magica. It's been reconstructed on Piazza Vittorio in the center of Rome.'

'This I know about from Damien,' I said.

'Another portal was supposedly in the chapel of Sansevero in Naples,' Ana said, 'where medical experiments were said to have been carried out on slaves belonging to a certain Raimondo de Sangro in the eighteenth century. In some perverse way, these occultist Nazis believed they were the heirs of Raimondo, using inferior human beings to carry out their medical experiments.'

I nodded. There wasn't anything to say to that.

'Some of these Italian aristocrats,' Clara said, 'who still hold positions of influence with the government, and maybe the Vatican, helped Nazis to escape from Europe after the war. This is well documented. A number of these people still have contacts with postwar fascist groups like Ordine Nuovo and P2.'

'Yes, Kennedy told me some of this.'

That sense of theatricality that had begun when I walked into the room intensified: the edges of the table and chairs were sharper, Clara's lipstick and eye shadow garish; Ana's dreadlocks alive, the darkness below her eyes a deeper shade of green; Sara's cheeks red-veined. The skittering of the dogs' claws in the next room sensitized the hairs above the vertebrae in my neck.

'Gerardo lived close to the Fosse Ardeatine,' Clara said. 'I know he went there. He'd heard stories that Priebke, the officer responsible for the massacre there, had gone to Argentina. And Gerardo knew about the Nazis in Bariloche through Miriam and Dieter. You know Miriam, right?'

I nodded. 'She told me in some detail about the mass executions.'

'The thing is,' Clara said, 'in the seventies and early eighties, even in Argentina, not many people knew the real identities of these people in Bariloche. They all had assumed names, false papers. And no one wanted to find out about them. And even if you did know about them as Dieter and Miriam did, and so Gerardo, too, what could you do? These ex-Nazis all supported the military dictatorships. They were vehemently anti-communist so they were obvious allies for the military against the godless revolutionaries. Even Isabelita, the president of Argentina, and her secretary, Jose Lopez Rega, were occultists, too, remember. This is common knowledge. They consulted astrologers about every decision, God knows what else. Whether Isabelita, and the Nazis, and the Triple A, had anything to do with the powers of darkness or not, what they were doing was patently evil: they killed and tortured their enemies... and a lot of innocent people, too. But nothing changed for the Nazis in Bariloche when Isabelita was thrown out. Videla and Galtieri and the rest of the generals in power during the Dirty War saw them as allies, too.'

The image that arose in my mind... of my mother on the night of her breakdown... was as real to me then as Clara's face in front of mine. Clara was talking about a chain of command that began with people like Arenas and my father and continued up to heads of state. Arenas and my father were the foot soldiers. Maybe Arenas, maybe my father, got some kudos in being buddies with ex-SS men.

'I suppose,' Clara said, 'the occultists who were talking to Gerardo in Italy thought that he was sympathetic to their cause. He was spending time with them. He was interested in their occult ideas. He was Argentine. Francesca was very seductive. She was a Christian esotericist, an Argentine nationalist. They felt free to talk about the colony in Bariloche, and the *unfortunate* incident at the Fosse Ardeatine where the SS had killed those three hundred Italians that they called subversives and communists.'

'But Gerardo already knew about Priebke,' I said, 'through Dieter and Miriam.'

'Yes,' Clara said. 'But Gerardo said nothing. He was an exile from the dictatorships. He was powerless to do anything in Italy at that time. With the fall of the dictatorships, and the restoration of democracy in the late eighties, Gerardo recognized that there might be an opportunity to flush out the Nazis. The democracy was still fragile. What guarantee was there that it was going to last? Gerardo was in Rome. He had his theater company. He was working. Then in 1992, Hizbullah, a Shiite terrorist group backed by Iran, bombed the Israeli embassy in Buenos Aires...'

'You know it was Hizbullah?' I said.

'Look,' Clara said, 'it was a truck bomb, Lebanese style; twenty-nine dead, two hundred wounded, including children from a school nearby. And in this letter from Sara's sister, Isabel...' Clara clicked on a document. 'She says that she's sure that the killers had help from right wing Peronists, some of them inside the police force and the military; Nazi sympathizers who hated Jews and who wanted a way to strike against the new democracy while the direct finger of accusation obviously pointed at Hizbullah.'

I read the letter.

'Gerardo,' Clara said, 'thought that there was nothing to be gained by going back to Argentina. If the responsibility for the bombing was being covered up, what could he do to identify the killers, or to expose their Argentine allies if he'd lived in exile for so long. But if nothing else, Gerardo had a sense of theater. Isabel, in Israel, had contacts in New York. That's when Gerardo came to the United States. That's where I met him.'

Witness Deposition: Clara Luz Weissman

I first met Gerardo Fischer in New York City in 1995. This was when Gerardo was close to fifty years old. Very charismatic. Head shaved, dark eyes behind rimless glasses, curved nose, square jaw. He wasn't a tall man but he was in great shape. I was twenty-six and doing a masters in Theater Arts at Columbia. Gerardo was going to give a series of workshops on site-specific theater. And the places that Gerardo Fischer chose for his theater performances, I mean, no one else would have gone to.

I'd heard about Gerardo from Angela Farini, one of the professors who'd worked with him in Rome. Gerardo had done plays at the Fosse Ardeatine caves; and another performance he'd done in the catacombs down on the Via Appia Antica.

I suppose I shouldn't have been surprised when Gerardo decided that we Columbia students should put on a performance under the arches below the Riverside Drive viaduct, above 125th Street. Surprised? No. But terrified? Yes. We all were. We had four student actors, Nora Jane Wills, Betsy Carrington, Paolo Cassini, Hank Adamson, and a lighting tech, Gary Bounds. Imagine this, six students and Gerardo, we came out of Dodge Hall on 115th Street and walked up Broadway toward Harlem. The four actors, two men and two women, were dressed in early twentieth century formal suits, tailcoats and top hats. Gerardo had written a play based on Fernando Pessoa's *A Little Larger than the Entire Universe*, and the four actors had the parts of Pessoa's heteronyms, four invented personalities each of whom wrote in a completely different style. All the actors stayed in character. Gary carried the portable lighting rig. He had the battery in a kind of canvas satchel slung over his shoulder.

At 125th Street, we turned left under the elevated rail tracks and made our way toward the river. It was late, about eleven p.m. Across the river, the lights of Jersey twinkled in the darkness. We turned right onto 12th Avenue going north.

Back then we had to step over pools of blood on sidewalks outside the wholesale meat warehouses. There were a couple of music clubs up there but I would have been afraid to go into them. We kept on, past the Fairway Store, toward 138th Street. In a couple of blocks we were in a kind of no man's land under the Henry Hudson Parkway: steel and stone arches, human shapes in the shadows, behind the walls, in stone niches. Eyes turned up to look at us out of hunched bodies wrapped in blankets and sleeping bags, the sudden flare of a lighter illuminating two faces, one gaunt and unshaven, the other puffy with a kind of unhealthy sheen, both bent over a homemade crack pipe.

A tall stooped black guy with thick curly gray hair and strangely well-trimmed beard waited for us at the first of the derelict warehouses.

'Hola, Virgil,' Gerardo called.

I thought that was a joke. But no. He was our guide.

'Gerardo, *que pasa*?' Virgil said.

Gerardo had already been down there. Virgil had set up Gerardo making a performance for his friends and acquaintances, for the lonesome, the loose and the mad. He'd guaranteed Gerardo safe conduct for us. And Gerardo trusted him. I trusted Virgil. But here, beneath the arches, what were we going to find?

The iron door to the back of the warehouse had long since been forced. Old newspaper pages stuck to the damp stones in front of it, Styrofoam boxes and dead coffee cups, a scattering of crack vials.

Virgil pushed against the rusty metal and motioned for us to pass him.

Gary struggled with the portable lamp. He turned sideways to get the battery satchel through the gap between metal and stone. I followed him in. He turned on the lamp. The dank inner walls were a tumble of tags and obscene scrawls, magical symbols like some shadow world voodoo signs.

Virgil eased past us into the brightness cast by Gary's lamp.

Then he reached up to help me keep my balance on the trash underfoot.

Gerardo turned on a big black Mag light. The arches above us lit up.

The beam of Gerardo's flashlight held me like a shaky stage spot. Nora Jane came up behind me, her face pale in the lamplight, her narrow chin framed by the white wing collar of her shirt and the black lapels of her frock coat.

'Jesus, Clara,' she said. 'What are we doing here?'

I didn't answer.

Gary arrived next, also lit by the beam of Gerardo's flashlight.

Then Gary turned the big lamp on again to illuminate the cavernous brickwork. We were in an etching by Piranesi. Curved stone arches, rusted metal walkways. Muffled human forms emerged from black doorways at the back of the warehouse space.

'Hey, the play guy's here!' Virgil called out.

Framed by rickety jambs, backlit by dim lamplight, the people of this dark disused-warehouse world stared out at us, thin and ragged. Behind them, the interiors of their underground lean-tos were furnished with chairs and cabinets that must have been scavenged from the roll-off dumpsters on the street.

'Hey, Virgil!'

I couldn't tell if the voice was a man's or a woman's.

Beneath the gleam of our flashlights, dogs barked. Tethered in makeshift pens, they bared their teeth. They snapped at us. I was terrified. Could they be rabid? They lived here among the rats and bats and vermin of this hidden village within the city. The dogs strained against the cords that held them.

Here we all were, the privileged from the mansions on Riverside Drive and these feral creatures, desperate homesteaders, with their dogs to protect them from the deranged and the predatory and the ever present rats that would scratch at whatever food chests they must have in here, competition for the scraps these warehouse people salvaged from the day's garbage in the outer world. Then flame. A roar. A blue flickering light played over piled firewood: chopped up palette boxes, the crackle of dry leaves on sparking branches. The reek of the smoke was abominable. But it rolled upward and seemed to be sucked away by some bizarre microclimate managed by unseen ventilation shafts.

Nora, Betsy, Paolo, and Hank stumbled into a row of white, upended, joint compound buckets that the lean-to villagers, far more men than women, used as seating for our theater space. Gary set the lamp on a tripod.

I slid my arm into Gerardo's.

The stunned faces of Virgil's people stared at the four actors lit up by the fire and Gary's lamp.

'Sit down here,' Virgil said. And the six of us, puzzled, sat down on the six joint compound buckets in the front row, aware of the eyes of the dark-dwellers just behind our shoulders. We were in the seats of honor in the front row. Gerardo had turned us into the audience but we were still on the stage for the warehouse people.

'This is our space,' Virgil said. 'We do the performing in here.'

Virgil stepped aside and a tall black man with a shaved head and dark goatee stepped forward into the brightness of Gary's lamp.

'Okay,' Gerardo said. 'Now we begin.'

Extract from the casebook of Juan Manuel Pérez
January 13th 2006
Hours: 11:30 to 16:00

'Gerardo's performances were attracting interest in the press,' Clara said. 'After the late night show below the bridge arches of Riverside Drive, we did another on Randall Island, under the expressway, right next to the mental hospital. Gerardo became a name in a fringe, cult kind of way. *Village Voice* did an interview with him, the *New York Observer*. In Manhattan, Gerardo got to meet people who recognized a good news story. He knew how to work the press for himself, for the company, and for his private projects. He dropped hints that, back in Argentina, he might be able to identify the hiding places of former Nazi war criminals who were on the run. He knew that in New York, he'd have sympathetic listeners to that story. Somehow, word of Priebke's presence in Bariloche got to ABC television's *Primetime* current affairs program.'

'Through Isabel?' I said. 'She was with an American in Bariloche some time in the early nineties.'

'Anything's possible with Isabel,' Clara said. 'What we do know for sure is that Sam Donaldson, ABC's news anchor, actually went to Argentina. He managed to get an interview with Erich Priebke, himself. Maybe Priebke thought he was immune by then, nearly fifty years after the massacre at the Fosse Ardeatine. But when that interview aired on American television, the program put the wheels in motion for Priebke's eventual extradition in 1995.'

'But what did this have to do with the bombings in Buenos Aires?'

'Isabel, in Israel, was convinced that the same political groups responsible for keeping Priebke safe had a hand in the organization of the bombings of Jewish targets in Buenos Aires,' Clara said.

'But I thought she put the blame for the bombings on Hizbullah.'

'They had to have had some help from inside Argentina.'

'And you think Gerardo helped finger Priebke in Bariloche?'

'I can't be sure, of course, but everything about the extradition, the bombings, and who was involved in what, is still very murky and convoluted. Even now, local involvement in the bombing is still being investigated through the Buenos Aires courts; and you know that in Italy Priebke still isn't in jail. He's under some kind of house arrest.'

'Okay. But why should anyone have wanted Gerardo out of the way now?'

'Something is going on with Isabel, I'm sure, but they're all very secretive about it. Isabel comes and goes between Israel and Buenos Aires. She has some kind of position working for the Israeli government, a trade envoy...'

'I thought she was a peace activist.'

'Sure. But she's been in Israel for years. I don't know how that might have affected her politics over fourteen years. You'd have to ask her.'

'And Carlos and Ramón are in Buenos Aires.'

'That's right. Gerardo and Isabel have always been very close. The boys have been spending a lot of time with him, too...'

'I spoke with Carlos.'

'When?'

'Two nights ago, by telephone.'

'And?'

'I don't know. I spoke with Damien Kennedy, too.'

'He was with Gerardo in Italy.'

'And this Francesca?'

Clara blushed for some reason. 'Yeah, she's there, too, in Buenos Aires.'

'Could she be involved in some way?'

'In the disappearance?'

'Whatever.'

'She's... well... I'd say a little unstable,' Clara said. 'But I haven't seen her together with Gerardo lately.'

I opened the folder and took out the packet of postcards and photographs. 'There's a card here from Bariloche and some more from Iguazu. Do you recognize either of these names: Araujo or Sadiq?'

Clara shook her head.

'How about this guy?'

I brought out the photograph of the gray-haired man in fatigues that Isabel had written that she'd met at the lake. Clara shook her head.

'I'd like to scan all these things,' Clara said. 'May I?'

I looked into her deep brown eyes. I'm trying to find the guy who's disappeared and she wants to archive his collection of photographs.

'I'd like to keep all this for now. I'll turn it over to you, later. Or to Gerardo when I find him... and you can ask him directly, okay?'

'Do you know who that man is?' Clara said.

'Which man?'

'The one in the picture by the lake.'

'No, I don't. On the back of the card from Bariloche, Isabel mentions a well-connected gentleman. I thought maybe it was this guy...'

'Isabel might know,' Sara said.

'She's back from Israel tonight, right?' I said.

'You could call her tomorrow.' Sara wrote down Isabel's number for me.

'One more thing,' I said. 'Damien Kennedy told me that Gerardo and Francesca pulled a disappearing act one time in Rome. Do you think he's done the same thing now? Because we're wasting a lot of people's time if he has.'

Clara and Sara looked at each other. It had obviously crossed their minds.

'Not this time,' Clara said. 'I don't think so. Gerardo can be very unpredictable, I know. But he's been missing four days without anyone hearing from him. He would have turned up by now, or called us, I'm sure, if he'd been able.'

'All right,' I said, 'maybe that's enough for now. Keep me posted how the flyers work out, okay?'

'I will,' Clara said.

'Call me if you hear anything at all. You've been really helpful.'

'Likewise.'

My hand brushed against my pants pocket where my wallet lay in safety. I kissed Clara, Sara and then Ana on the cheek. I made for the door, my car.

Had Ana told Sara that she'd slept with me? I didn't think so.

I waved to them when I opened the car door. I dropped the folder on the passenger seat. When Rangel and I had first gone to Arenas's house, Rangel had recognized Priebke's photograph right away. This other character in the photograph was connected with Priebke and Fischer and Sara's sister, Isabel. What were the chances that Rangel would recognize this white-haired guy with the shades and fatigues, too? Slim to none. But it was close to lunchtime. I figured Rangel would be in the office. I could catch him before he left to eat. Slim isn't none.

I called Rangel. 'I need to talk to you.'

'Not about that case.'

'Afraid so.'

'You remember what that goon looked like on Arenas's porch?' Rangel said.

'Sure.'

'I don't want to meet him again.'

'I want you to look at a photograph. That's all.'

'A photograph?'

'Right.'

'I'm at the office.'

'See you there,' I said.

He hung up.

I was at the office in thirty-five minutes, just past noon and the dry heat must have been close to forty degrees. I parked on the street. Looked around at all the tourists and locals on the sidewalks and I didn't see anybody hanging out on the corner who looked as if they wanted to beat me with a baseball bat. I went up the stairway on the shady south side of the building. Rangel was at his desk. A pall of smoke hung in layers above his head, an ashtray full of crushed butts next to his cola can. His jacket hung over the back of his chair and his considerable bulk was draped in a white cotton shirt with sweat marks under his armpits. His tie was loose.

'You hungry?' I said.

'Show me the picture,' he said.

I showed him the picture.

The wry twist of his lips and the tilt of his head showed me that he recognized the image. 'Man, you should forget these people.'

'Who is it?'

'Sandro Casares,' Rangel said. 'This guy is international. Much bigger than Arenas. Major Triple A. And a friend to very big fish. Used to be close to Lopez Vega after Perón's death. He's a legal fixer for ex-generals who don't want to be brought to trial for crimes against humanity.'

'How the fuck do you know all this? And I don't.'

'You worked for the Feds back in the day. On a need to know basis. You didn't need to know what this guy was doing, did you?'

'And you did need to know what he was doing?'

'This guy ran everything in Ciudad Azul from high-class whores to high-class drugs for industrialists, bent government people and suspicious militaries. I've always been in private work. You need to know these people to stay out of their way.'

'Where do I find him?'

'For fuck's sake, Juanma, you don't find him.'

'Is he still here?'

'He comes and goes. Regularly. But listen, he's retired. Forget him. He has a house in Mendoza. I hear he has a vineyard that produces fine wines. Leave the man in peace.'

'Bariloche connections?'

'Who knows?' Rangel said.

'You know.'

'I don't know.'

'Why would Fischer have a photograph of this guy?'

'Fischer had a photograph of this guy?'

'Yeah.'

'No wonder the son of a bitch disappeared.'

'It might be connected, you think.'

'How's your math?'

'Where's that storefront?'

'What storefront?'

'The textile store that Pedrito the Hook Matas rents to some Arab who maybe has the name Sadiq.'

'Don't be going there,' Rangel said. 'Definitely don't be going there and asking questions about this guy.'

'I won't, I promise. Where is it?'

'You're a stubborn son of a bitch.'

'Where is it?'

'Opposite the Adidas Sports Store.'

I pocketed the photograph.

'How was your father?' Rangel said.

'He told me to lay off this case.'

'He's taking care of his beloved son.'

'I'm going for a drive,' I said.

'Why don't you take a vacation?' Rangel said.

I parked the Ford Executive on the street beside the sports supply store. All the stores on the main drag were closing for lunch. I went into a café and got a window seat in the air-conditioned interior. Two middle-aged men sat at an outside table on the other side of the plate glass from mine and blocked any view of my table from the street. I ordered a coffee and a *Milanesa* steak sandwich. The waiter brought the sandwich just as a tall Arab guy came out of Pedrito's textile store and started pulling down the steel roller blinds. I bit into the sandwich and let bits of tomato fall into my plate. I chewed quickly. A dark blue Volkswagen Passat pulled up outside the store and Pedrito the Hook Matas emerged from the driver's side door. He went into his textile store. Maybe Pedrito and the Arab guy were going to have lunch together. Still, I'd finished my sandwich before Pedrito and the Arab came out of the store again.

The Arab pulled down the steel blinds over the doorway and locked them with a padlock at sidewalk level. Pedrito walked away from the store, west, toward the bridge over one of the rivers that feeds the lake. The Arab came around to the driver's side of the Volkswagen Passat. Why was the Arab taking Pedrito's car? And where was he taking it? Was there something in it? I gulped down my coffee, waved a ten-peso bill at the waiter, dropped it next to my plate and made for my car. The Arab had the Passat in gear and was trying to pull into the lunchtime traffic but nobody was giving him much room to move from the curb. I got into the black Ford and started it up. I edged onto the street, blocked the moving traffic on my side of the street which caused a lot of car horns to blast but I forced my way into the flow on the other side about five cars behind the Arab in the Passat who was now headed toward 60.

Lunchtime traffic. This was no car chase. All I had to do was to make sure I got through the same sets of lights behind the Passat. We followed the direction that Pedrito had taken on foot. The flow got quicker as we approached the bridge and then I saw Pedrito and Maria sitting at a table in a café at the end of the main drag, close to the bridge. I saw the Arab raise a hand as he drove by. Pedrito gave me the hard stare. Maria, in big black shades, turned her bruised face away. I nodded to Pedrito. I couldn't pretend I hadn't seen them, or that I didn't know who they were. They had to think of this as a coincidence: their man, the Arab, five cars ahead of me, quite by chance, as we all make our merry way to lunch on a normal working day in Ciudad Azul.

Would Pedrito call the Arab on his cell phone?

I pulled a hard right on the other side of the bridge and hoped that Pedrito would see me turn off the main drag and not go the same way as their Arab buddy in the Passat. I headed up the side streets in the direction of the baroque town clock. If the Arab was going up Route 60, maybe I could still catch up with him. I made the clock tower, pulled out left at a green light, and crossed three lanes onto the main highway east. The Arab would be well ahead of me now if he was driving down 60. Why did I care to follow him? The car switch, Pedrito, the direction the Passat was taking. I was on the hill going out of town past the nightclubs and hotels. I got stuck behind a truck that had all kinds of metal junk teetering and dangling over the edges of the rickety plywood box that was jerry-rigged onto the flatbed. If the Passat was on this road, I was a long way behind it. It could turn off anywhere.

I managed to get by the truck and after a few kilometers reached the broad junction of 60 and 16. I swung onto 16 just because it was a smaller road and it wasn't going to San Sebastian where Arenas lived. It was the road to San Pedro, the direction of my father's house. I believe in intuition. Sometimes it worked. Near to El Arroyo there was a towable roadside snack bar with a gaudy sausage sign fixed to its roof. Pedrito's Passat was parked next to it and a white GM truck with a closed cab and matching white box behind was parked parallel to the blue VW. The Arab was at the counter chatting to the sausage man and maybe the truck driver. He might have been an Arab, too. He wasn't eating and nobody was looking my way. I kept my foot on the gas and kept the two Arabs in sight out of the sliver of an eye as I passed and then again in the rearview mirrors. A few kilometers down the road, I swung off left onto a dirt road and turned the car around in the driveway of a farm property so that the nose of the Ford was pointed back toward 16 again. The dust settled around the car. The sun blazed on the hood. I kept the a/c on and hoped the engine wouldn't overheat. I waited. I waited for fifteen minutes; and then the Passat, followed by the white truck, went by on 16. I got the Ford in gear and pulled out onto the road. Not a lot of traffic. Lunchtime: siesta time. I could see the truck and the Passat on the slope that went down again toward the lakeside hotels and nightclubs and casinos at the northeast end of the lake. I kept a sensible distance behind the vehicles and one eye on the rearview mirror in case Pedrito, or one of his goons, should appear behind me.

The Passat and the truck kept on going past the end of the lake and out into the rolling hills toward San Pedro. Thirteen kilometers into the hills, very close to my father's house, they turned off right. I slowed the Ford to a stop at the junction and then waited for a few minutes for them to get well ahead of me. Then I turned onto the dirt road. It was full of ruts and rocks and washboard cambers and I made slow progress. I figured that the truck would have to make slow progress, too. I breasted a rise and caught sight of the two vehicles just as they turned down a dirt driveway toward a small property perched on a terrace on the hillside below.

I pulled up behind a granite outcrop, did a k-turn to get the Ford aiming out of there, then pulled over onto the dry grass next to the dirt road. I turned off my cell phone. I got out of the car. This was stupid and dangerous. I could hear Rangel's voice in my ear. The still air must have been well above forty degrees by now. I went around to the passenger side and opened the glove compartment. I pocketed a small set of binoculars. I shifted the hip holster and my .45 caliber Colt automatic to the back of my belt.

I climbed up onto the hot granite boulders, the mica glistening in the bright sunlight. I peeked over the top of the rough rock and brought up the binoculars. There were two buildings on the property: an old thatched-roof *quincé* structure that might have sheltered animals at one time; next to it was a modern storage shed made up of an open girder frame with a corrugated roof. Three black SUVs were on the dirt parking lot with a number of Pedrito's goons in attendance. Pedrito's Passat was parked close to the old thatched barn. The driver of the white GM truck was reversing his rig under the corrugated-roofed garage. Maybe they had Fischer in the back of the white truck. Already in the open-sided garage, there was a big flatbed truck with a canvas awning. Two men wearing sporty tracksuits were leaning against one of the framing pillars. One of the men was Pablo Arenas. The other was his young nephew from the robbery all those years ago. Two weapons, assault rifles, were propped against the pillars beside them.

The two Arabs got out of the white truck and two of the goons joined them and Arenas and his nephew in the shade. They all lit up cigarettes, chatted and laughed together. The two Arabs came out of the garage after about ten minutes. They got in the Passat.

I slid down off the granite. If Pedrito had called the Arab on a cell phone and warned him to look out for a black Ford, it would be better that I should make myself scarce. Which I did. I got back in the car, tossed the binoculars onto the passenger seat, got the car in gear and tore down the dirt track back toward Route 60, raising a lot of dust bucking over washboard ruts and sliding by boulders. I had enough distance between me and the Arabs so that I could get over rises and dips and between rocky outcrops and tree stands to keep well out of their sight if they drove at a sensible speed for the road they were on. I wasn't driving at such a sensible speed. I reached the junction with 16 and – just about head on – another black SUV pulled into the dirt road. I hit the brakes. My Ford fishtailed through the dust. I turned into the skid, went sideways across the road and fetched up to a stop parallel to the big black Dodge with tinted windows. The driver's side window on the SUV slid down. It was impossible to see who was in the passenger seat through the tinted windshield and because of the height and angle of the Dodge cab relative to my Ford.

My hand was shaking. I pressed on my own window button.

I looked up into the lenses of mirror shades poised below perfectly styled white hair which offset the tanned and smooth complexion that comes from deep relaxation beside swimming pools surrounded by beautiful women, all of whom would be more than happy, I was sure, to give Sandro Casares a deeply satisfying massage. That's what I imagined.

'You should drive a little slower, my friend,' Casares said. 'It's dangerous to drive these country roads like that.'

'I'm sorry,' I said. 'I'm in a hurry. My wife's in labor.'

'Wish her the best for me,' Casares said. 'And your new child.'

'Thanks,' I said. 'I appreciate it.'

The tinted window slid back up.

I restarted the Ford and eased past the Dodge.

I stopped at the junction with Route 16 and in my rearview mirror I watched the black rear end of the Dodge disappear over a ridge toward the property with the white van and the flatbed truck and the SUVs and the heavily armed heavies. I was still shaking. I have to admit that.

Casares wouldn't know me from Adam, would he? And if those guys had Gerardo Fischer... it didn't bear thinking about... my job was done. Maybe it really was time to fly to Miami. Maybe I should be listening to Rangel. And my father.

I thought: Well, a sensible man would drive back to Ciudad Azul. Because yes, right now, I know, I'm in a world of shit. But what I did was to pull onto 16 and take a right toward San Pedro assuming that the Passat, which was going to be right behind me any second, would head back left toward Ciudad Azul. I put my foot on the gas and drove for a kilometer or so, pulled off the blacktop at the next dirt road and waited. I waited half an hour. The Passat didn't pass by. I drove back down 16 to the little country road. A few kilometers up this dirt was the property where all those SUVs were parked, and one of them belonged to Sandro Casares, the man in the picture that was in the folder that belonged to Gerardo Fischer.

Most of the way over the bumps and the rocks and the ruts I prayed that none of the goons up there would be coming to meet me on this very narrow dirt road. And especially not Sandro Casares. This was a stupid and foolish thing to do but I honestly believed that I couldn't leave Gerardo Fischer out there with those men if indeed he was out there with those men, which I didn't know. I reached the point on the dirt road where I had to hide the Ford. I left it relatively well hidden behind a stand of pines. I grabbed the binoculars again, locked my jacket in the car, eased the safety off the .45, and made my way through the shady stand of pines and back toward the property. I ran across the road and climbed in among the granite rocks again. It was quiet down there. Only two of Pedrito's goons were on watch. The rest of the crew must have been keeping to the shade. Maybe Mr Casares was having a quiet chat with them. I could make out movement beneath the corrugated roof. Whatever was in the white GM truck, they were unloading and putting the boxes into the rear compartments of the black SUVs. At least it wasn't Fischer. Maybe this was some kind of dope deal. Silly me. What was I doing interfering in this? And when it seemed that all of the dope, or whatever it was, had been transferred from the white truck into the SUVs, the goons began to unload long wooden cases from the big flatbed truck. It took two men to carry each case to the back of the white truck. I didn't really want to know what was in the wooden boxes. I was witnessing a simple exchange of merchandise and risking my life for nothing. Gerardo Fischer was not here.

Then my father walked out from under the thatched roof. He was arm in arm with Sandro Casares. Fuck. This was definitely very bad news. Maybe it was the kind of news you're supposed to get on Friday 13th. I wished that I wasn't witnessing this. Sandro Casares steered my father under the corrugated shelter. Casares said something to Arenas, who then said something to his nephew who then opened up one of the wooden boxes that was on the ground next to the white GM truck. Casares bent over and took an assault rifle out of the open case. A few more words from Arenas and his nephew went over to the cab of the flatbed truck and came back with a curved magazine that Casares slotted into the assault rifle.

Down on the terrace, in front of the garage, Casares lifted the assault rifle to his shoulder and fired off a series of single rounds towards the hillside. A dog began to bark. Casares seemed to be amused by this. He and Pa laughed together. Casares adjusted the rifle and let off three bursts of automatic fire that tore up a bush on the hillside between them and me. The dog's barking turned furious.

It was then that I caught sight of the two goons who were patrolling the hillside. One of them had the stock of a pump-action, twelve-gauge shotgun propped on his hip as he struggled to control a black and tan Doberman on its short leash. He yelled at the dog and it quieted down. It was obviously a well-bred animal. It was obedient.

But maybe the wind changed at that moment. The dog began to strain at the leash and bark again. It seemed to want to drag its handler in my direction. The Doberman was all muscle and bone. The other goon looked up toward the rocks where I was lying down with the binoculars to my eyes. He lifted an Uzi up with a casual hand that had been hanging down by his thigh and cradled it lovingly in front of his belly. I slipped backwards off the surface of the boulder, turned away from the rocks and ran toward the little stand of pines. It was cooler running through the trees. I stumbled over the twisted roots but I kept my feet long enough to reach my car.

I started the engine. The air conditioning whirred into life. I hit the gas and peeled out. I have an aversion to dogs. The big

Ford lurched forward onto the dirt road and I gunned it hard and bounced it down the slope back toward Route 16. I guess it didn't really matter whether the goons had seen the Ford or not. Casares had seen it, and my face, and so had my old man if he'd been behind the tinted windows in the passenger side of the black SUV. I wasn't exactly sure where that left me with regard to my options for the next few days. Rangel's idea to make myself scarce made a lot of sense. I was thankful for the cloud of dust rolling up behind the rear tires. I drove hard and fast for Ciudad Azul. I didn't think it would be a good idea to go home, or to the office, in the next few days.

I could, I suppose, have called the police and told them that I had witnessed what might have been a deal with weapons that could have been connected with the heist from the military airbase that had happened a few days back. Maybe the same day that Gerardo Fischer had gone missing. Perhaps that would have been a sensible option; except it would have been very definitely turning my father in to the law. I couldn't do that. Not directly. Not even I could stoop to that. What had this weapons deal to do with my investigation into Gerardo Fischer's disappearance?

As I tooled down the highway back toward Ciudad Azul, I got out my cell phone and turned it on again. I called the number of the Hotel Cristal in Córdoba. I could use a hotel room as a base of operations while I considered my options. I glanced in the rearview mirror. No one was following me. Maybe they didn't care. I'd seen some kind of deal go down. So what? If I kept my nose out of this, Casares and my father would likely forget all about it. Maybe. But I couldn't be sure. I got reception. I booked a room for a week. I figured I could claim for it on my expenses for the Fischer job. I needn't stay there all the time but I thought that I'd be relatively safe at the Hotel Cristal. I'd be safe as long as it wasn't owned or under the protection of Sandro Casares. I turned my cell phone off. My old man knew my number. It might be a way for Casares and his friends to track me down. I kept driving south. I needed to keep myself off the map.

[Extract from the casebook of Juan Manuel Pérez
January 14th 2006
Hours: 14:30 to 21:00

I woke in my hotel room after a fitful night obsessed with the idea that my father was involved with Arenas, Matas and Casares. And I'd been seen. I was sure that if Arenas, Matas and Casares considered me a problem, which no doubt they would, they'd want to resolve it by ensuring my silence. I spent an unquiet morning at the Hotel Cristal, doing nothing but worrying, showering, shaving, and trying to distract myself with bad movies on cable TV. I waited until after lunch before I called Enrique Sandino from the hotel telephone booths. He was at his nightclub, the Dark Moon.

'I want to come by,' I said.

'To what do I owe the honor?'

'Maybe you can help me out.'

'I can?' Sandino said.

'I want to go away for a few days to relax. Maybe you can give me some advice.'

'What kind of advice?'

'Advice I can pay for. Substantial advice. Something to alter my mood, relax me.'

'Juanma... come around. I'm in the office.'

It took me a half hour to get from the hotel in Córdoba to the outskirts of Ciudad Azul. The roads were quiet. Siesta time. Bright sunlight. I got off the highway and threaded my way through the road works and down onto the underpass that brought me onto the lakeshore. The sun sparkled on the flat water. This end of the lake is surrounded by high-rise hotels, time-share condos, beach bars, and dance clubs. They'd attract some action as people got up from their siestas but they wouldn't come alive until after sunset. Long after sunset. The Dark Moon was prime property on the water; cinderblock structure, concrete stucco to make it look like adobe, and black light neon sign that would come on around midnight. The straw-roofed terrace bar on the verandah was deserted. I eased the black Ford onto a narrow side street and parked it in the shade. I knocked on the featureless metal door at the side of the club. One of Clara's flyers had been taped to the flat surface: the blurred features of Gerardo Fischer, and her appeal, and the phone number that wasn't mine. One of Sandino's bouncers, dressed in traditional black, unlocked the door. He stood aside for me. I was obviously expected. The concrete corridor stank of stale smoke and cleaning fluid. Sandino's office door was open. He sat at his desk, his wire-framed glasses on the end of his nose, his sleek hair oiled back against his brown and balding skull.

'Juan Manuel,' he said.

He got up, removed his glasses, and we exchanged a cheek kiss.

'So... why here, why now?' Sandino said.

'If I was to throw a party and I wanted something special for my guests what could I find in town?'

'What kind of question is this?'

'It's a curious question.'

'Are you throwing a party?'

'No.'

'Then why bother your head?'

'It's personal business.'

'How personal?'

'It's about my father.'

'What's your father got to do with anything?' Sandino said.

'This is what I want to know,' I said.

'I don't follow,' Sandino said.

'I'm not sure... This is upsetting... I worry about what he might be getting himself into.'

'I don't get this,' Sandino said.

'Sandino, listen, I've done you favors in the past. I hate to bring this up. I need to know something. Is my father dealing heroin or coke?'

Sandino's stunned stare and the way his mouth dropped open made it obvious he didn't want to be having this conversation.

'That's a very indiscreet question, Juan Manuel.'

'So what am I going to do with this information? Bust you?'

Sandino regained his composure. His lips pressed together in a straight line. Silence.

'It's just like a weather report,' I said. 'What's blowing through? That's all. I find out. I go away. I'm not interested in a drug bust. I'm not a cop any more. But if my father is dealing heroin or coke, I'm going to fuck him up.'

'I don't get this... You've become a concerned citizen all of a sudden.'

'I'm a family man.'

'You're worried that your father is leading young children into a life of perdition and addiction,' Sandino said. 'I don't buy this, Juanma. Even you're not that squeaky clean.'

I colored up now, worked up a rage inside.

'Listen... there are some things... maybe more than a few things... I can't stomach. Especially not from my own father. You know this. I know this. That's why I want to know if he's involved in coke or heroin.'

'Are you serious?'

'I'm serious.'

Sandino's stare was simply incredulous.

'Juanma, this is bullshit. I don't know why you asked me this.'

He shook his head.

'It's a simple question,' I said.

'Juanma, sit down... please.'

I sat down. The office chairs were upholstered in green plastic over a steel-molded frame. He walked over to the office door and closed it. He sat back down behind his desk. He had a decent chair. I made a conscious effort to relax.

'You're overwrought,' Sandino said.

'You're right. I've got to get away for a few days.'

'You don't worry about your father getting involved in any of that kind of shit, okay?'

'He's involved in something,' I said.

'Rest your weary mind.'

'I can't.'

'Okay, let me tell you. You're going away. And I have a special present for you... very special... Everybody wants to get their hands on this. Something very rare these days. Very smooth, very mellow. Hashish to mellow your brain, my friend. Legendary hashish. You been a cop... you know this hash... you smoked this hash... I know... you know... Lebanese Red. Can you believe this? Wonderful. The stuff of legend... Arabian Nights, my friend. Showed up about a month ago; rumors of more on the way. Everybody's waiting for more.'

'Lebanese Red,' I said.

'If your father's involved in this... and I say *if*... then he's doing the world a favor. It's not crack, it's not coke, it's not heroin, no harm to anyone. Just a very mellow smoke... chill everyone out... Put your mind at rest.'

'Okay.'

'This what you want to ask me?' Sandino said.

'Yeah.'

'You want to take a little smoke with you. I'll give you a little smoke... my personal stash. You'll see I'm not lying.'

'Okay,' I said.

Sandino knew I had a weakness. A little weakness. But I hadn't smoked any hash in years. Well, at least... not since I gave up being a cop. Not since my buddies in the drug squad stopped popping in on my office to drop off little presents for me. Sandino went over to his filing cabinet, opened the top drawer and took out a round cake of hashish wrapped in pale muslin. It must have weighed about half a kilo. That was worth a lot of fucking money. If he kept it in the drawer, he wasn't afraid of any raid. Maybe he bought it from my father. Or maybe Sandino was paying someone off. He'd paid me off in the past and I'd got him out of a little trouble. Okay, like he said, I'm not so squeaky clean myself.

The muslin that covered the cake of hashish was scorched where it had been cut with a hot knife. It also had a design printed on it, some letters, some Arabic, some Latin script. I'd seen large muslin-wrapped blocks of hashish from Lebanon at various times in my cop career. All of it came with the distinguishing marks in purple or blue ink of some Middle Eastern guerrilla group: Christian militia, Shia militia, PLO and this one, Hizbullah.

Sandino picked up a jackknife off his desk, opened the blade, dipped a hand into his pocket and clicked a flame from his gold lighter. He heated the blade, set the cake of hashish on the desk and pressed the blade into muslin and through the reddish brown resin. A pungent blue smoke curled up from the blackened blade. That was good fucking hash. Sandino carved off a large block that I reckoned was about twenty-five grams. The edge of it crumbled a little. Sandino took a plastic bag from his desk drawer. He dropped the lump of hash into the bag, sealed it shut.

'You always treated me well, Juanma,' Sandino said. 'And your father's a decent guy, too. You don't need to fuck him up, okay? Now just go somewhere and fucking relax, okay? And don't come back here and ask me any more indiscreet questions, okay. I always liked you.'

I stood up. Sandino dangled the plastic bag of hash and I held out my palm. He dropped the bag into my hand. I slipped it into my jacket pocket.

'I said nothing,' Sandino said. 'I know nothing.'

'Of course,' I said. 'Thanks. I owe you one.'

'No, you don't. You owe me nothing. I never saw you here.'

And by implication, he owed me nothing more. I'd called in a debt. He'd paid, and now I had to get out of there and never ask him a favor like this ever again. It was a cheap pay off: a little information and twenty-five grams of hash, no matter how good it was. I left Sandino's office. The bouncer let me out. The air had cooled a little. Very little. It was still brutally hot.

Lebanese Red. My father and Lebanese Red: Lebanese Red comes into the province in one direction; boxes of small arms go back the other. What were the odds? With that truck up there, pretty good, I guess: automatic rifles, maybe a few pistols, some larger items. Who knows what the fuck Arenas had got his hands on? How was my father involved? He seemed to be very close to Casares. Had Fischer found out about this when he was nosing around with Carlos and Ramón? And that's why he disappeared.

I'd take very short odds that Sandino would be having a word with my father very soon. It would concern my nosing around about him and his interest in drug deals. Thus it would get back to Casares and Matas and Arenas. Happy days. Hizbullah, Gerardo Fischer, Sara Suarez, Isabel Suarez, Israel, synagogue bombings, AMIA bombings, Jose Arenas, Sandro Casares, Lebanese Red, Argentine military rogue traders... my father was in very deep. What was his role in all this? Had Casares, Arenas and Matas pulled him into the deal just to close me down?

Maybe Fischer had been some kind of problem to them, too. He'd disappeared the same day as the heist of a shipment of arms from the military base at Córdoba. What the fuck did I know? I was stumbling around in the dark making a nuisance of myself for some very nasty people.

I walked down to the lakefront. Out in the distance a lone speedboat tore up the lake surface and made wavy wakes. Taped to the stanchion of the streetlight was another of Clara's leaflets with

Gerardo Fischer's face in among the notices about bands, clubs, and bars. And yet more leaflets decorated the brick pillars of the lakeside fence. I went back up the shady side street and got into my car. The cops would be at the colony very soon, at the latest tomorrow, if the leaflets had got all around town, which they probably had.

I ought to talk to Isabel Suarez in Buenos Aires about Gerardo Fischer. Why didn't I have much heart for it? Because my father was in this now. Still, that was no guarantee that I was safe any more. I *had* been safe just after the horse ride with the old man... right up until I decided to follow Pedrito's Arab buddy up into the hills. Now I wasn't. My life might or might not be in danger but I didn't want Casares or Pedrito Matas or Arenas or anyone else to come looking for me in Ciudad Azul or Córdoba. A few days in Buenos Aires pursuing a possible line of investigation might help to clear my head and keep me out of their thoughts.

I drove back to the office. I drove around the block twice to make sure there weren't any black SUVs or blue VW Passats. There weren't. I parked the car and walked up the stairs. Rangel was at his computer. I tossed the heavy bag of dope to him. It clattered on the desk next to his keyboard.

'What's this?' he said.

'Lebanese Red,' I said. 'It's a present from my father.'

He lifted the bag to eye level.

'You fucking with me?'

'I gave it up long ago,' I said.

'You know,' Rangel said, 'a guy came around early this morning asking to see you.'

'Oh yeah,' I said.

'Yeah... Pedrito Matas.'

I nodded. Matas was here in the office. That was not good news.

'He brought a message from Mr Casares. Mr Casares says that you don't need to worry. He's talked with your father about you. Casares has got a file he'd like you to see. You can see it any time you want. Matas left this phone number. "Make an appointment," he said.'

Rangel handed me a card: Casares's name and number.

An appointment to see this file: what file? Arenas or Fischer? Not Arenas, must be Fischer; or an appointment with a bullet in the back of the neck? That wasn't a phone call I needed to make. Not now. Maybe if I got desperate.

'I'll call them later,' I said. 'I'm going out of town for a few days.'

'Good idea,' Rangel said. 'Don't tell me when you're coming back.'

I parked my car between Fischer's white Fiat and Clara's Dodge Ram. I walked across the hillside to Ana's house. She wasn't home. I walked back across the property to Sara's house. Clara opened the door to me.

'Is Ana here?' I said.

'She and Sara went for a walk down by the river,' Clara said.

'I'd like to talk to them.'

'Let's go down there. I'll come with you.'

'Sure.'

'Are you okay?' Clara said to me. 'You look terrible.'

'Thanks,' I said.

From the porch I looked back toward my parked car. All quiet on the road to the colony. I walked down the hill with Clara. Some thunderheads were gathering over the Sierras. The sky beneath them was a deep orange.

'I saw your notices by the lake.'

'They're all over town.'

'I guess.'

'Do you think the police will ever show up?' she said.

'They will now,' I said.

'You don't think it's a good idea, do you?'

I shrugged. 'I don't know. Honestly…'

We passed by Fischer's house that was all shuttered up. As we walked along with the orchard wall on our right, I glanced across toward the plum trees. Ana was lying in the hammock. Sara was sitting on a garden chair on the terrace above us.

'I thought they'd gone to the river,' Clara said. 'I'm sorry.'

I opened the orchard gate. Ana appeared to be asleep, her tattooed arm was flung across her breast and her other arm across her face. Her head twitched for a moment as if something was troubling her. She was lost in that world of sound and image that exists somewhere inside our skulls into which we cross every time we fall asleep. I'd slept with her once and I wanted to sleep with her again. I still didn't know enough about her or her about me to know if we could go much further than that. Except that I was being drawn more and more into this theater world. It was phantasmagoric in a lot of ways. But how much more illusory was this world than the world that I'd been used to: the world of cops, and thieves and killers. The muscles of her face were so relaxed, framed by the dreadlocks that pillowed her head on the hammock. She looked so young. I touched her shoulder.

'Oh,' Ana said. 'I drifted off.'

She had dark rings under her eyes. They were puffy.

'I had a dream about Gerardo,' she said. 'He was standing beside the hammock in the shade of the plum trees. It seemed so normal. I reached out to touch him but then he stepped back into the light and I couldn't see him any more.'

'It was just a dream,' I said.

'He was standing right here,' Ana said. 'I just reached out to touch him, and he stepped back into the light and then he was gone.'

She slid off the hammock and stood next to me. Maybe Ana had just come up with the answer. So easy. Fischer had stepped out of this dimension and disappeared into another. He was fine. He was okay. He'd let us know through Ana having a dream about him.

Maybe you had to be dead to be able to communicate like that.

'Come on,' Ana said. 'I've got to drink some *mate*.'

Clara was above us on the terrace with Sara.

'What are you doing down here?'

'We miss him,' Ana said.

Fischer. This Fischer was so important to them. These Temenos actors were decent people. But what had made Fischer become so important to me? I'd never even met him. This guy that these people cared so much about, who'd been with them for so many years, he must be worth finding, right? I hoped that he wouldn't turn out to be just a normal, egocentric son of a bitch, like most of us. If he turned up at all.

Ana and I climbed up the steps to the terrace.

'I'd like to visit your sister, Isabel, in Buenos Aires,' I said to Sara. 'You said she should be back from Israel... maybe last night... Will you call her for me?'

'Didn't I give you her number?' Sara said.

'Something's come up,' I said. 'I'm not sure it's so smart to use my phone.'

'Let's go up to the house,' Sara said. 'There's no signal down here anyway.'

In Sara's living room, Clara took the gourd from Ana and filled it again from the thermos. She handed it to me. I sucked on the silver tube.

'When you talk to Isabel,' I said, 'please... just find out if she's going to be in Buenos Aires for the next few days. I think it's better that way.'

'But you said you wanted to talk to her?'

'There,' I said, 'face-to-face, in Buenos Aires. Don't even mention my name, right now, if you don't mind.'

Sara stared at me. Her mouth twisted.

'What?'

'Please,' I said. 'I have my reasons.'

She punched the buttons of Isabel's number into her cell phone.

'Isa, is that you? Yes... how was Israel?... Right... Wait a minute.'

Sara went into her study to talk to her sister. She closed the door behind her. Maybe she wanted privacy for such an intimate call. We drank another round from the gourd among the three of us again before Sara came out of the study. Her face was wan.

'She's tired. She plans on staying in Buenos Aires at least for the next few weeks,' Sara said.

'She already knew about Gerardo's disappearance by email,' I said.

'That's right.'

'When you gave her the news, how did she take it?'

Sara shook her head.

'I can't judge my sister's emotions. She spent so many years in the Middle East. That's hardened Isabel. It's difficult to judge her emotions at all, but especially in an email.'

'Can you give me her address?'

Sara picked up a slip of paper and a pen and wrote down Isabel's address for me. I put it in my wallet right next to Casares's business card that Matas had left for me at the office. The one thousand dollars was still in there, too.

'Thanks,' I said. 'I'll see you when I get back.'

Ana followed me down to the car. It's not that I didn't want to spend the night with her, it's just that I didn't want Matas or Casares's goons to find out I was up here and arrive in the middle of the night when I might be asleep like a baby in Ana's arms.

'How long will you be away?' she said.

'I don't know. Not long.'

'We'll be in Buenos Aires in a few days to put on the theater piece.'

'I'll come see it if I'm still there.'

'I'll call you,' Ana said.

'Don't call me for a couple of days. Someone might want to trace my phone.'

'You're frightening me,' Ana said.

'Your friend Gerardo did you a favor. Kept you out of it.'

'Am I going to see you again?'

I couldn't help but smile.

'I hope so.'

I kissed her on the lips. I didn't care who saw.

I got in my car and reversed it out of the parking lot. She stood and looked at me while she could. I got into a forward gear and took off down the dirt road. Yeah, I really did want to see her again.

I drove to Córdoba. I would keep my discreet hotel for a few nights so that I could leave the car in the underground garage, but in the morning I'd fly to Buenos Aires and search out Isabel.

I checked into my room at the Hotel Cristal. I used the hotel phone booth again to make a call.

'Hello, Ma, it's Juan Manuel.'

'Oh, Jesus, how are you?'

'Are you okay, Ma?'

'Your father came around here, today, Juan Manuel. He was so mad. What have you done to him?'

'What did he want?'

'He said, "You tell that boy of yours to give up this stupid investigation he's involved in. Tell him to stop digging up the past. He'll be sorry if he keeps on." He was so mad, Juanma.'

'Are you okay, Ma?'

Her words were slurred. She'd been drinking... a lot of whiskey. What the fuck was my father doing showing up at my mother's apartment? He hadn't spoken to her in years. When he'd left, she'd been on the verge of a nervous breakdown. She was still pretty fragile. And the whiskey on top of the medication didn't help.

'Please, Juanma, do as he says, it'll be better for all of us. You don't know what he's capable of.'

Maybe that wasn't strictly true.

'Did he hurt you, Ma?'

'No, no, he didn't lay a finger on me. I swear. He came to talk about you.'

'Why's he talking to *you* about *me*?'

'He said he talked to you already and you wouldn't listen. And he wasn't going to talk to you again. He told me to make you see sense, Juanma. Or we'd all be sorry...'

'Don't worry about me, Ma,' I said. 'I'll be okay.'

'Juanma, I beg of you. Do as he says, or something awful is going to happen, I know this. Believe your mother. I love you.'

'Okay, Ma,' I said. 'Don't worry. I'm going away for a couple of days. Everything will be fine. Don't worry.'

That was an obvious lie, the last part anyway.

'I'll see you as soon as I get back,' I said.

'Please, Juanma, I beg of you.'

'Okay, Ma, okay, I'm going to hang up, now. I'll see you when I get back, okay? Bye now.'

She didn't say anything. I hung up.

I went back up to my room. I jumped when the telephone rang. It was the receptionist. He'd called to say that he had my air ticket for Buenos Aires.

[Extract from the casebook of Juan Manuel Pérez
January 15th 2006
Hours: 09:30 to 21:00

My flight from Córdoba to Buenos Aires was at 10:30 am. From the way that the clouds had started to build up I feared that a thunderstorm would keep the plane on the ground. Air chaos in the summer is so normal that I almost wished that I'd taken the overnight sleeper bus. I had no wish to drive. I also had to worry about the weather over Aereoparque in Buenos Aires. Maybe I was in a worrying mood. I was particularly worried that Casares, Matas and Arenas might appear and want to force me into the back of a car and make my life not worth living... or simply end it after a short ride; something that might have happened to Fischer. But maybe Fischer had done what I was doing: close down all communication by cell phone or computer and get out of town. Except that I had to talk to people whereas Fischer did not. In the departure lounge, I checked in for my flight and walked over to the *locutorio*. I got a phone booth. I called Isabel's number. She picked up.

'My name's Pérez. Your sister, Sara, hired me to help her locate Gerardo Fischer. I got your number from her.'

'Yes,' Isabel said. 'What can I do to help you?'

'I'm on my way to Buenos Aires. I'd like to talk to you... this evening if possible.'

'This evening?'

Surprise in her voice.

'Yes,' I said. 'I'm sorry for the short notice.'

'Do you have my address?' she said.

'Yes.'

'How about seven o'clock?'

'Perfect.'

I hung up. I called a cab company in Buenos Aires, told them my arrival time and gave them a false name to write on a card for me.

The call for my flight came over the public address system. I made for security. I had no gun. I dangled a hold-all with a few changes of clothes. I threw it onto the conveyor belt to be X-rayed. I went through the metal detector and on to the departure lounge. The flight was delayed for forty minutes. I had a coffee and tried to read *La Nación* but it was difficult to concentrate on the news stories. I thought I might call my mother to see if she was okay but it was too early and I knew that she'd only be nursing a hangover. They called my flight for boarding.

I went through the ticket check and out through the glass doors onto the tarmac. After a short ride across the tarmac on an air-conditioned bus, I climbed up the stairs of the plane. The middle-aged woman in the window seat next to me was a bottle-blond with a bright red, sharply cut business suit. She had good legs in sheer nylons and black patent leather shoes. She wasn't in the mood to talk to a wild-eyed, disheveled private dick.

I opened *La Nación* again. I turned to the sports pages. I read the build up to the big game: Boca Juniors versus River. I had a feeling that Boca would just about edge it. The report kept me distracted for a while but my mind kept straying back to the file that Matas had said Casares was willing to show me. Or was using as bait to get me into their hands. I still didn't want to talk to him. But a file missing from the police archives? Fischer's? How had Casares got a hold of it? What other file could it be? Well, if Arenas had managed to steal cases of weapons from a high security military base in Córdoba, what should be difficult about a big-time fixer like

Casares getting one little file from friends among the cops? I couldn't imagine that Casares' willingness to share any information with me was a positive turn of events. 'He'd talked to my father.' That was Casares way of showing me that he could just about own me, if he wanted to.

Aereoparque close to 1:30 pm. I steered my way through the chaos of the arrivals area and the taxi ranks. This is a busy time of year: people taking summer vacations, flying in or out to see their families. Just before I left the terminal building, I went into another *locutorio* and called Andrés, an old friend of Rangel. I always stay at an apartment he owns in the Federal Capital when it's available. I arranged to meet him to pick up the keys.

Outside the terminal building, a balding man waited for me. What gray hair he had was slicked back with oil. The mustache was sparse. His little pot-belly pushed his white shirt out over the belt of his gray suit pants. He held a card with the word *Llamas* written on it. I nodded to him and he led me to his battered red Datsun. He eased the car out onto the coast road and we headed downtown. The River Plate, gray under the low thunderclouds, glinted metallic where the sun's rays slanted through the threatening sky. Container ships at anchor on the horizon waited for their turn to come into dock. A squall of rain hit the windshield as the taxi reached the port. We rode between canyons of stacked truck containers, and under gigantic cranes, their gears and cables enclosed in spread-legged gantries: urban sculpture, beautiful. Just beyond the port, the cab driver maneuvered through the snarl of traffic around Retiro station and the English Clock and down past the embarkation point for the Buquebus ferry that took passengers to Montevideo, Gerardo Fischer's natal city. I don't like beaches, I'm from the mountains, but I do love the sea and ships and docks. Maybe it would be smart to get on that big Buquebus catamaran and power across the water to Uruguay. What would I do over there? Maybe I'd find Gerardo Fischer.

Just before the renovated warehouses of the Dique, we swung

west onto Avenida Córdoba, crossed Nueve de Julio and made a left onto Talcahuano. We crossed Corrientes and pulled up on the corner with Bartolemé Mitre. Andrés was already there, a youngish-looking forty-year-old with neatly cut brown hair, a stylish blue windcheater over a yellow polo shirt and dark blue, sharply pressed cotton slacks. I paid the cab driver.

'Come on up,' Andrés said. 'You can get a shower in the flat.'

I guess I looked rough.

He handed me the keys. I opened the main door with its steel scrolled bars and we took the elevator to the top floor. Andrés showed me the usual things in the kitchen that I was welcome to use, the bucket under the leaky pipe in the bathroom ceiling, and the new double bed.

'If you bring any girls up here,' he said, 'try not to stain the mattress. It's new.'

'Where's the iron?' I said. 'My clothes are all rumpled.'

He showed me and then he left.

I took a shower, trimmed my goatee, shaved and flopped out on the clean sheets of the new bed. For the first time in about a week, I felt safe. It felt good. I fell asleep to the grating noise of a horrible *Cumbia Villera* tune that sawed out of the apartments opposite.

At six thirty in the evening, I walked down Talcahuano to Rivadavia, crossed the road and took the subway, Line A, west. I was on one of those old cars with the polished wooden seats and panels and the mirrors beside the doors. The train passed through the tunnels below Rivadavia: Congress and Miserere and Loria, and I came out at Medrano. I crossed back over to the north side of the street again.

Facing me like a vision from a film set was Las Violetas, the pastry shop and restaurant where Ana had said she'd met Gerardo Fischer for the first time. Fischer must have brought Ana here and gone on to Isabel's house, which was very close by. Through its big plate glass windows, the café was resplendent with pillars and mirrors and gold leaf and crystal, even if it was pretty much empty at this time of the evening. I wished that Ana were here now so we could have a coffee together. I looked at the empty tables half expecting to see her and Fischer appear from the ethers as if in a dream. But the café stayed empty.

I walked on up Medrano on the other side of the street from Las Violetas. Angel Peluffo was a small side street just off Medrano. Isabel's house was halfway up the street on the right, white stucco and an imposing armored door with elaborate paneling. I rang the bell. It took a while for all the locks to be opened.

Carlos Brescia stood framed in the doorway.

'Good to see you again,' he said.

His being at Isabel's didn't completely surprise me. He had that clean-shaven, well-oiled build of a gym rat, body taut under a tight white t-shirt and black jeans. His dark hair was tied back in a ponytail. I was glad that I'd ironed my shirt and pants up at Andrés's apartment. I didn't want to be looked down on by a strutting muscle freak.

We shook hands and leaned in to kiss on the cheek. Behind him, Ramón waited to greet me; big-boned blond German stock with a trimmed goatee. He'd put on weight since I'd last seen him, mostly on his pecs and shoulders. His Hawaiian shirt hung loose over linen pants. Carlos and Ramón had the air of a pair of rugby players at the peak of their fitness. I was sure that they'd enjoy hard physical contact.

Two women were in the back of the living room, a raised area close to the kitchen off to my right. They stood in front of the plate glass doors that opened out onto a paved terrace and a small garden that was framed by fig trees and latticed red brick walls. They were both in their late fifties. One was short and dark, the other blond and slim, and a little taller. They both used a good hairdresser. Isabel – I was sure that the smaller and darker one was Isabel – wore a finely tailored black blouse and skirt. A touch of eye shadow and blush brought out the high cheekbones. The blond woman had a few crow's feet near the corners of her eyes and those spidery lines at the corners of her mouth that some women get when they smoke all their lives. She was smoking now. The skin on her neck had lost a little tone, as if her cheeks had been fuller once and she'd recently lost weight. She stared into the space above my head.

'Juan Manuel, welcome,' the dark woman said. 'I'm Isabel.'

'A pleasure,' I said.

I detected a faint hint of tobacco under her expensive perfume as I leaned over and kissed her on the cheek. The blackest, sharpest eyes looked into mine as she drew back from me. She waved a hand back toward the blond woman.

'This is Francesca,' Isabel said.

'Francesca?'

'Yes,' Isabel said. 'Francesca Damiani.'

Francesca came toward me and kissed me on the cheek.

'I've heard about you,' I said.

Her head pulled back, her eyes wide for an instant.

'How come?' Francesca said.

'Your colleague in the theater, Damien Kennedy.'

'How is Damien?' The tone was a sudden deadpan.

'Last I saw him he was fine.'

Then Isabel eased between us.

'Please. Sit down.' Isabel waved toward the burgundy velvet sofa up against the wall and the two matching easy chairs. Francesca's birdlike head shifted with quick movements, glancing here and there in the room as if my knowing about her caused her neurons to jerk. I sat down in an armchair that kept the walled garden in front of me. Francesca sat in the armchair opposite me. Her blond head swiveled right, left, right again. Isabel sat on the sofa flanked by Carlos and Ramón. She reminded me of Ava Gardner in *Night of the Iguana*.

'You're looking for Gerardo,' Isabel said.

'I am. I still have no idea where he might be. He might be in hiding. I do know he came to the attention of some individuals who have reputations for operating outside the law. I've talked to some of them. They are definitely aware of Gerardo. And Carlos and Ramón, as I'm sure you know.'

Isabel nodded. Francesca's face was agitated. On the sofa, Carlos clasped his hands between his knees. Ramón slid his hands under his thighs.

'I found a folder with a notebook, and some postcards from the time when Gerardo Fischer was in Italy and you were in Israel, and then later back in Argentina,' I said. 'Among the photographs and postcards from you are some from Bariloche and Iguazu...'

I pulled out the photograph of Casares.

'You mentioned a helpful German,' I said, 'but it seems that you were referring to this photograph. This man's name is Sandro Casares. He's Argentine. How come you said he was German?'

Francesca lifted her cigarette to her lips, drew on it, her eyes on Isabel.

'Our amateur attempt at secrecy,' Isabel said. 'We tried to send messages that were ambiguous in case we were under surveillance because we were part of a Jewish legal organization trying to get information about the bombings of AMIA and the Israeli embassy.'

'Casares was part of the bombings?' I said.

'Casares is a fixer for a number of far right groups,' Isabel said. 'He coordinated legal immunity deals for military personnel who were implicated in the Dirty War. He was in Bariloche to help Priebke avoid extradition after his discovery. We don't think he had any direct contact, but he may have helped those who provided some support for the bombers. Like Pablo Arenas.'

'Why Arenas?' I said.

'Look, after the restoration of democracy, Arenas was out of work. Here in Buenos Aires, Arenas did what he knew best: armed robberies, gun supplies, dope deals and kidnappings for ransom. He had connections with Nazis, ex-Nazis, neo-Nazis, anti-Zionists. He could set up safe houses, organize routes into and out of the country, and supply materials and weapons. He had all the expertise to help set up the team that bombed AMIA and the Israeli Embassy. He's also done a lot of footwork… and enforcement for Sandro Casares in Bariloche, in Buenos Aires and around Córdoba,'

'And you found this out…' I said.

'Through a Jewish legal group that tracks these things,' Isabel said.

Francesca leaned forward to stub out her cigarette in the glass ashtray on the coffee table. She sat back and let her hands flop into her lap.

'I saw Arenas's police file when I got him put away,' I said. 'There was no mention that he might have had anything to do with these bombings.'

'If there was nothing in your police file about AMIA and the embassy bombings, it was kept out for a reason. Our legal group got information from the Israeli government. I don't know how they came by it. I'm sure they have their means. Especially in the wake of the bombings.'

'You were involved with the peace movement in Israel,' I said.

'That doesn't mean I support Nazis or Hizbullah,' Isabel said.

'Of course not.'

'After the second bombing in Buenos Aires,' Isabel said, 'things got hot for Arenas. The police were rounding up suspects of far right groups. Casares got Arenas out of Buenos Aires. Arenas had family connections in the Sierras…'

'A cousin of his ran the Artemisia Adoption Agency,' Carlos said.

'So Casares set Arenas up in Ciudad Azul. Arenas began supplying narcotics to the club scene around the lake,' Isabel said. 'He kept a low profile for years. But maybe he missed the excitement of armed robbery.'

'And that's how he met you two guys,' I said to Carlos and Ramón.

'We all fit the kind of profile he would be happy to target. Maybe he needed a little spending money, or just a little perverse fun,' Ramón said.

'And you took off a finger and piece of his ear,' I said to Carlos.

'I didn't have any choice,' Carlos said.

'And the reason that Arenas might have to wanted to get at Gerardo is because you two guys had been snooping around looking for dirt?' I said.

'Carlos told you about Artemisia,' Ramón said. 'Arenas was serving his time for the robbery but he was due out. Arenas's cousin ran Artemisia. We thought that if we could find the agency's records there might be something concrete to implicate Arenas with supplying children to the agency whose parents had died in custody, and that Artemisia sold on to other adoption agencies... sometimes in other countries.'

'We found out where the records were kept and had a lawyer serve an injunction to the current owners of the agency to give up the records,' Carlos said. 'The records are still in existence. They're being held in a storage facility. We've had them sealed and impounded while the adoption agency... with Casares's help... fights a legal battle against the human rights group to stop the files being used in an investigation. The agency claims it's a client privacy issue. We're afraid that some of the more incriminating records might have been destroyed already.'

'In the meantime, Carlos and I kept on asking around about Arenas,' Ramón said.

'Which is when Maria Dos Santos spoke to you, Carlos and Gerardo,' I said, 'and you decided to make yourselves scarce.'

'That's right,' Carlos said,

'We wanted Gerardo to come to Buenos Aires with us,' Ramón said.

'When we asked all those questions around town and we know it upset a few people,' Carlos said.

'You have to be careful who you upset,' I said.

'We weren't,' Ramón said.

I guess I hadn't been that careful myself.

'We found out a lot about Arenas,' Carlos said. 'He's got a hand in everything: drugs, guns and women. But he's just a foot soldier. Those trades are all controlled by bigger business interests.'

'Casares?' I said.

'Sure,' Carlos said, 'then again, Arenas and a local hood called Pedrito Matas made a connection in Ciudad Azul with a Lebanese guy who has Shia connections. It opened up a new line of supply of specialist goods from the Middle East. We thought Arenas might have been introduced to him through previous connections...'

'Connected with AMIA and the embassy bombings,' I said.

'It's possible,' Carlos said.

I had a mental picture of Casares holding my father by the elbow.

'Would you like a drink?' Isabel said to Francesca.

She nodded.

'Juan Manuel?' Isabel said.

'A cognac?'

'Sure,' Isabel said. 'Everyone?'

Mutual assent it seemed.

I turned back to Carlos and Ramón. Isabel tinkled five balloon glasses out of a kitchen cupboard. She uncorked a bottle of Martell VSOP and poured.

'Casares and Arenas have upped the ante on the dope scene,' I said. 'I think they're trading stolen military weapons for dope and money. I witnessed what looked like an exchange of goods up in the hills.'

'We know this,' Isabel said.

'You what?'

'Kirchner has purged a lot of military from the armed forces because of their involvement in the Dirty War,' Isabel said. 'Casares organizes business for ex-militaries; and, with the help of Arenas and Matas, and through that Lebanese guy – his name is Sadiq

Hussein – they've opened a two-way route for a flow of merchandise that comes and goes through the three borders region at Iguazu.'

'How did you get this information?'

Over at the kitchen counter, Isabel shrugged.

Isabel carried the tray with five glasses of cognac to the table. She handed the first glass to Francesca, the next to me.

'Casares has a shipment of weapons about to leave right now,' I said. 'Or it's left by now… it's on its way. Casares and his crew did the military airport heist.'

'It hasn't left for Iguazu yet,' Isabel said. 'We believe that it will leave Ciudad Azul early tomorrow afternoon.'

'You know this?'

Isabel handed a glass each to Carlos and Ramón.

'You can stop this shipment,' I said.

'No,' Isabel said. 'I can't.'

'Why not?'

Francesca had a smile on her face. She sipped at the cognac. Then she rummaged in her purse for another cigarette.

'Nobody wants to stop it,' Isabel said, 'not the police, nor the military, nor the Secret Service; and neither do the Americans, nor the Israelis. Or they would stop it. All these law enforcement and anti-terrorist groups want to track the route the shipment takes from here to the Lebanon after it leaves Iguazu. It's possible Casares, Matas and Arenas know this, too. They may be in on it. If so, they know that no one will touch them. It's low risk, easy profit.'

'But these are weapons that will kill people,' I said. 'Maybe innocent people.'

'Pardon me if I say so, Juan Manuel, but you seem to be a little naïve,' Isabel said. 'In Ciudad Azul, a few Shiite Lebanese organize a small shipment of arms through Casares, and in return, they sell a little dope to Arenas and Matas to support the cause back home. Meanwhile, everything is under surveillance by the Federal police, the Secret Service, the CIA, and probably Mossad. It's a little transaction that could lead to catching bigger fish.'

This woman got her Jewish legal group information directly from Mossad, the Israeli secret service, didn't she?

'But these are weapons that are on their way to kill Jewish people in Israel,' I said. 'Don't you want to stop that?'

'When I was in Metullah, in 1982,' Isabel said, 'Israel invaded Lebanon with the aim to crush the PLO. And it did. In the years that followed, Hizbullah filled the vacuum and made their power base there. And now, they're regularly firing rockets into Israel and engaging the Israeli forces on the border. It's only a matter of time before Israel invades Lebanon again in order to crush Hizbullah, just like they did with the PLO. It's coming. All it needs is a trigger. And Hizbullah is sure to pull the trigger at some point. The Israeli army are just waiting for that.'

'And then?'

'And then the Israeli armed forces will bomb Beirut... and Tyre... and Sidon... and across the whole of Southern Lebanon; and along with the men who launch Hizbullah's rockets, a lot of innocent men, women and children will die along with the guilty,' Isabel said.

She'd written on her postcard, the last one with the picture of Masada... *The truth is that it's in no one's interest to have peace in the Middle East...*

'And you don't want to stop this?'

'Of course I want to stop this,' Isabel said. 'What am I supposed to do? Call the police? Any one of at least four federal or international agencies can stop that arms deal anywhere along the line. The Israeli Navy might still stop the ship when it sails on into the Mediterranean. And then all the people involved can be arrested.'

Including my father, I thought. Should I warn him to get out? He'd tried to warn me off, hadn't he?

'Nobody wants to know, you understand?' Isabel said.

'Arenas and Casares are a long way down the food chain,' Carlos said.

And we're lower still, I thought.

'Okay, but this still doesn't find us Fischer,' I said.

'No,' Isabel said. 'It doesn't find us Gerardo.'

'He's just a nosy writer to them,' I said.

'To whom?' Isabel said.

Her hands shook as she reached for her purse on the coffee table. She took a long cigarette out of a velvet-covered case.

'To Arenas, Casares, the police, Hizbullah and the fucking Israelis,' I said.

She was bristling.

'We love Gerardo,' Isabel said. 'Find him for us.'

'You mean you don't know where he is? You know everything else.'

'Not this... no... I don't.'

'We tried to persuade him to come with us,' Ramón said. 'But he wouldn't.'

The flame wavered as Isabel lit a cigarette with her gold lighter. She blew out smoke. Was Rangel smoking that large block of Lebanese hashish right now... courtesy of Sandino and Hizbullah?

'Gerardo was afraid that he was under surveillance,' Carlos said.

'Well, that's a surprise,' I said. 'Everyone else seems to be.'

'Gerardo deliberately rented that house below Temenos because it was out of cell phone range,' Carlos said. 'He refused to communicate by email because he said any fourteen-year-old hacker could probably get into his emails. And if anyone with a grudge against him decided to monitor him he was a very easy target. That's one reason why he gave his entire archive over to Clara.'

'He wanted his legacy preserved,' Isabel said.

'But he also wanted it in a safe place away from his house,' Ramón said.

Maybe Gerardo had left me that folder to find.

'So why didn't he leave for Buenos Aires with you two?' I said.

'He wanted to finish rehearsals with Ana and the theater

group,' Ramón said. 'And to work with Damien Kennedy.'

'But they didn't see him after you left,' I said.

'No,' Carlos said. 'We know that now.'

'Then the only hope we've got is that he's skipped out of his own accord,' I said, 'because he thought that things were getting too hot for him.'

'I hope that's true,' Isabel said.

'When did you see Gerardo last?' I said to Francesca.

'I haven't seen Gerardo for a long time.' From Francesca's flat affect I wondered if she was on some kind of medication, tranquilizers, anti depressants. But then again, wasn't she an actress?

'How long might that be?' I said.

'Oh, a few months,' she said.

'Where?'

'Here. In Buenos Aires.'

She lit another cigarette and blew smoke downward and toward me.

'Socially?' I said.

Francesca smiled. 'We've always been good friends.' She posed, a hand in the air, head tilted slightly.

'Did he give you any indication that he might be in trouble, or going off on a trip somewhere?'

She shook her head. It was a languid movement. She kept eye contact with me.

'No, nothing like that.'

I got up. It was irrational, I know, but I'd just about had enough of these people who knew so much and did so little. Maybe, they were being realistic. But something rankled with me about them. They'd told me a lot but they were holding something back. We all hold something back, don't we?

Fischer... Gerardo Fischer... Casares, Matas and Arenas would be very glad to get rid of him. To them he had been an irritation like Carlos and Ramón. But Fischer had a history: he'd escaped from the military in the seventies and gone into exile in Italy; he'd skipped out on Damien Kennedy when Fischer and Francesca had made it too hot for themselves with Mafiosi, fascists and occultists in Rome back in the eighties; who took New York graduate students into Crack City and mental hospitals to make their theater real; who may have had a hand in fingering Erich Priebke; who, Damien Kennedy said, delighted in stripping away people's masks.

If Fischer *had* skipped out wouldn't he have done exactly what I was doing now: no cell phone, no computer, and crucially no information to anyone who might know where he was going so that they couldn't advertently, or inadvertently, let slip – even under physical duress – where he might be? And my running around like a blowfly on speed, employed as a private dick, by these people who were all concerned about him, would show Casares, Matas and Arenas that Ana and Sara, the theater group, the artists at Temenos, Isabel, Carlos and Ramón, also had no idea where Fischer might be. I would be the fall guy for Fischer's disappearance. I made his disappearance a genuine mystery because neither his friends nor enemies could possibly know where he was. And I was the proof of that.

Was I being paranoid?

I knocked back my cognac.

'Okay, thanks for your time.'

'You're going already?' Isabel said. 'I thought you might have dinner with us.'

'Thanks for the kind offer. I'll stay in touch. Do you mind if I call on you again?'

'No, not at all,' Isabel said.

It was all very warm.

The four of them got up to kiss me on the cheek.

Carlos took me to the door. He turned the keys on the three locks that drew multiple steel bars out of the reinforced concrete doorjambs, lintel and threshold. The night air was fresh. The friendly street security guy lifted a hand to wave at Carlos in the doorway behind me. I walked down Angel Peluffo to Medrano, crossed the street to Las Violetas, went in through the glass door, sat at a window seat and ordered a large cognac from a waiter in a stiff black waistcoat and a white shirt.

All the waiters wore stiff black waistcoats and white shirts.

When the waiter came back with the cognac, I asked to see a menu. Early dinner, why not? I chose a rare steak, with asparagus and sautéed potatoes. And a green salad. I had a good view of the street where Angel Peluffo joined Medrano. Every time anyone came out of Angel Peluffo, my head jerked up to see who it was. I couldn't help it. It might well have given me indigestion.

Fischer had skipped out? Was that true?

And my father, did he know that the whole arms and drug deal was under surveillance? I wasn't going to talk about this over the phone either.

Strange night. I'd met Francesca Damiani, a comic book character come to life. After all she'd been through, that she should really be in a fragmented mental state shouldn't be any surprise to me. Perhaps I was being callous, but that flat affect would be a handy front to hide behind. For what? She didn't live at Isabel's house. At some point she would go home. Where was her home? I was sure that she wouldn't tell me. Was Gerardo hiding there? Not if my theory of total disappearance was correct. And around 9 pm, there she was. Francesca Damiani. She came out of Angel Peluffo and made a left on Medrano just as the starch-shirt waiter peeled my change out of his billfold. I finished the last sip of my coffee.

Francesca had the collar turned up on her lightweight, dark colored raincoat and the beret on her head reminded me of a frame of Damien Kennedy's comic book diary... that, and the hold-all that she dangled from her left hand. She headed away from Rivadavia. I saluted the waiter at Las Violetas and left a six-peso tip next to my coffee cup. When I came out of the café, Francesca was on the corner with Avenida Bartolomé Mitre. A man stepped out of a shop doorway. Francesca kissed him on the cheek. I could see him from the back. Thick set, with grayish blond hair, a heavy denim jacket.

Kennedy. It was Kennedy. I was sure that it was Damien Kennedy from the artists' colony and when he turned in profile, there was no doubt in my mind. The big-featured, unshaven face was unmistakable. Both of them had made out to me that they hadn't seen each other in thirty years or so, and here they were on the street together in Buenos Aires.

Francesca lifted her hand and a taxi pulled up. She and Kennedy got in. The taxi took off downtown. I hurried toward the corner. I flagged the next cab.

'Follow that one in front,' I said. 'Ten dollars if you don't lose it.'

Extract from the casebook of Juan Manuel Pérez
January 15th 2006
Hours: 21:00 to 22:00

My cab driver pulled out into the downtown traffic.

Why had they lied to me? Or had they lied to me? Maybe this was the first time they'd seen each other in thirty years and I was about to spoil a poignant reunion. What business was it of mine? They were Fischer's oldest friends – apart from Miriam maybe – and now they were meeting up and this might, or might not, have something to do with Gerardo Fischer's disappearance. Maybe their mutual grief about Fischer – or just being in the same country – had finally brought them together again.

Their cab went straight down Mitre; crossed Avenida Nueve de Julio, still going east, got to Parque Colón, turned left down Rosales to Madero and at the end of the Dique, it swung right into the Buquebus terminal. The light changed before my cab could cut across the road, too. A swath of trucks, buses, coaches, and cabs poured out of the terminal area and left me in a cab stranded in the middle of the multi-lane highway. Should I pay the driver and get out? No way could I get across that intersection through eight lanes of port traffic.

But I could see the glass front of the Buquebus building and Francesca and Damien getting out of their cab. Why hadn't Damien come into Isabel's house? Why were they keeping their meeting secret? Just to avoid gossip? Everybody keeps their meetings secret. Hadn't Ana and I kept a low profile? Where was she now? At Sara's?

Francesca and Damien disappeared into the departure lounge.

'I'm sorry,' the driver said. 'The lights.'

'Don't worry.'

The lights finally changed. The cab driver swung us into the terminal. He slid in close to the curb where the other cab had stopped. I paid the meter fare and pulled out ten US dollars from the back of my wallet.

Damien and Francesca were at the check-in counter. Francesca fidgeted with her purse. The guy at the counter handed over two boarding passes to Damien. Damien and Francesca hurried toward the stair that led to the boarding area. They would just make it for the last ferry to La Colonia. I ran across the departure lounge. Francesca and Damien were at the top of the stair. I had no ticket to follow them into the boarding area, but two at a time I took the stairs that led to a balcony overlooking the whole concourse.

Francesca and Damien were already at the immigration/emigration desk with their boarding cards and passports in hand. The woman at the desk stamped the boarding cards and passports and gave them those annoying slips of paper that the immigration authorities insist you keep and never lose and give back to them when you return from Uruguay to Argentina.

Francesca and Damien went through the barrier.

I ran along the balcony and pulled up short, being without passport, ticket or boarding pass.

'Can I help you, sir?' the lady immigration officer said.

'I was just wanting to see someone off. The couple that just went through.'

'I'm afraid you're too late, sir.'

I craned my neck and caught a glimpse of them at the little coffee bar in the boarding area. The line of people that had been waiting to board had already begun to move forward toward the gate.

'I'm sorry, sir, but if you don't have a ticket you'll have to go back down stairs now. Security.'

'Just one second, please. Maybe if I wave.'

I began to wave. Through a gap in the crowd I could see them again. Francesca and Damien. Someone else was talking with them. He had his collar up and a wide brimmed fedora pulled down so that his face was half hidden. He was clean-shaven. This much I could see. His skin was pale. As he turned his head away from me light flashed on the lenses of his glasses. He was a lot taller than Francesca and a little taller than Damien, too. Was that Fischer? No. It couldn't be. They couldn't be going to Montevideo with Gerardo Fischer. That would be too easy. Why would they do that without telling anybody? So nobody knew, so nobody could tell Arenas or Matas or Casares no matter what the pressure? No. Impossible. Arenas, Matas and Casares would be content to have scared him off, the same way they'd scared off Carlos and Ramón.

'Hey! Hey!' I called out.

The immigration officer took my arm.

'Excuse me, sir.'

'Francesca! Damien!'

They were alone for a moment as they faced each other, documents in hand. They turned to face me. I was sure that they recognized me but they turned their backs on me. A middle-aged, well-dressed couple now stood between them and me.

'This way, sir,' the immigration officer said.

Damien and Francesca together, going to La Colonia, maybe on to Montevideo. Was Isabel in on this? Did she know that Francesca was going to meet Damien and go to Uruguay? Could it have anything to do with Fischer?

'Okay, I'm sorry. They've gone now.'

I backtracked across the balcony.

I turned on my phone. Could I risk a call to Isabel?

Three messages from Rangel.

Call me. Urgent.

Call me. Urgent.

Call me. Urgent.

I called Isabel's number. Carlos answered.

'Did you know that Francesca was going to Montevideo?' I said.

A long pause.

'I had no idea,' Carlos said.

'Or that she was meeting Damien Kennedy?'

'Damien?'

Carlos sounded genuinely surprised.

'What is it?' Carlos said.

'Nothing,' I said.

I hung up.

I had no passport but I did have my DNI card. If I wanted to get that ferry to Uruguay I could. I could see where Francesca and Damien were going and get back to Buenos Aires the next day. I hurried down the steps to the lobby. The ticket staff was packing up. The ferry embarkation was closed. I ran toward the desk. If you have enough money you can get anything.

It was then that my cell phone rang. It was still in my hand. I hadn't turned it off again. The call was from Rangel. I hit the green button.

'Yeah?'

'Juanma, where've you been? I've been trying to get you all day.'

'Incognito.'

A pause.

'Juanma, listen, I got some bad news for you.'

'Is that news? You always got bad news.'

'No, I mean it. Just listen, will you? Just a minute, now.'

I stopped in front of the ticket desk. I motioned to the Buquebus clerk to come over. He shook his head. I waved him towards me again. I could see him blow, tilt his head. He started in my direction.

'What's up?' I said to Rangel.

'Pedrito Matas turned up again,' he said.

'Yeah?'

'He said that if you don't contact Casares by noon tomorrow, Matas is going to pay a visit to your mother that you'd rather he didn't.'

'My mother? What the fuck is this?'

'I don't know,' Rangel said.

The phone call from my mother just before I left... *He told me to make you see sense, Juanma. Or we'd all be sorry... Do as he says, or something awful is going to happen, I know this. Believe your mother.*

What the fuck could they do to my mother? My stomach turned over. I didn't know what was going on but some instinct kicked in that made me capable of murder. And my father was involved in this. He'd been to her apartment to threaten her. I'd kill the bastard if he hurt her.

The Hook: It's ugly and nasty and connected with butcher shops.

Jesus Christ. My old man was involved in this with Casares... if anything happened to my mother I would fucking eviscerate him and Matas together. And Casares. If I got to live that long.

The Buquebus clerk reached the desk. He had a sour look on his face. As if he wanted to go home.

'I'll call Casares,' I said.

I hung up.

I stared into the space of the ferry terminal. I had to get back to Ciudad Azul. My father was prepared to let Matas loose on my mother to get my attention for Casares.

'It's okay,' I said to the clerk. 'I can't go anyway.'

He nodded and joined a cute clerk with long dark hair.

I'd seen what Matas had done to Maria.

I hit the speed dial for my father. No answer. I left a voicemail message.

'I want to see you, you son of a bitch. What's all this about Matas and Ma?'

I tried four times. He wasn't picking up.

Okay, I called Casares.

I dialed the number that Rangel had given me.

I don't know who answered the phone but he asked me my name and he asked me to wait and then he put Casares on the line.

'So Juan Manuel, you're ready to meet,' Casares said.

'My office at noon tomorrow.'

'That's fine,' he said. 'Let's make this a private affair, okay?'

'I might have some friend around for insurance,' I said. 'I'm sure you'll understand.'

'It's a meeting to talk, Juan Manuel, I assure you, nothing more.'

'All the same.'

'Don't worry,' he said.

'Will my father be there?'

'He's out of town.'

'Where?'

'I can't tell you that.'

'You let him know that if anything happens to my mother because of you or anyone else, anything at all, he's fucking dead.'

'I'll give him your message.'

'And you, too, you son of a bitch.'

'Juan Manuel, there's no need for these kinds of threats. We just need to talk... to clear the air.'

'I'll be there.'

'You know...?' Casares said.

'What?'

'Juan Manuel Senior is very disappointed in you.'

'What the fuck is that supposed to mean?'

'Times have changed, Juan Manuel. This disappearance case that has you so obsessed... it's best left to the police now. And we need to make sure you don't talk about some other matters, too. You understand?'

'What the fuck do I care about your business deals?'

'Maybe a little.'

'I'll see you at noon.'

I hung up.

About now, the ferry would be leaving with Francesca and Damien on it. I'd lost them. So what? Francesca and Damien – a couple of ancient lovebirds – what had that got to do with me? What did it have to do with Fischer? Why did I want these people messing with my head? I didn't need it. I came out of the ferry building. Sure enough the big catamaran was easing its way out of the dock. I got in a cab.

'Talcahuano,' I said.

I called Isabel's place.

'Yes.' Isabel's voice.

'Do you know anybody in La Colonia who would recognize Gerardo Fischer?'

'La Colonia? No,' Isabel said. 'Why?'

'Oh, I don't know. It's probably nothing.'

'Is this to do with Damien and Francesca?'

'Yes, yes, exactly.'

'And they've gone there?'

'To La Colonia, yes... maybe on to Montevideo.'

There was a long pause.

'Maybe if someone you know meets the ferry... and the transfer bus to Montevideo, if they take it... fuck... Look, I really can't do anything about this now. I'll call soon.'

I hung up.

I stared at the city through the glass of the cab window.

Too late to get a plane, tonight, I could get a night bus to Córdoba. It was early enough for that. First thing in the morning, I'd pass by the Hotel Cristal and pick up my gun.

Extract from the casebook of Juan Manuel Pérez
January 16th 2006
Hours: 06:30 to 11:30

I had an expensive full-bed booking on the night bus from Retiro to Córdoba but I couldn't sleep at all. From the bus station, I took a cab to the Hotel Cristal. I had a shower and packed my clothes. I got my .45 from the hotel safe. I hooked it on my belt. I checked out of the hotel. I got in my car and drove to Ciudad Azul and on to San Pedro. At my father's house, I pushed through the gate and into the garden. The house was locked and shuttered up. The horses stared at me across the stream from the hillside paddock. I couldn't do anything to hurt the horses.

I drove back to Ciudad Azul. I was tired. So fucking tired. I hadn't slept all night. I kind of hoped that one or more of Casares's goons would be waiting for me at my apartment. None of them was. I let myself in. Turned on the air conditioning. Poured myself a whiskey. I lit a cigarette. Nine a.m. These might be my last few hours on earth. I was going to meet Casares. What was to stop him taking me somewhere quiet? I'm sure it had happened to other people. My father had washed his hands of me. He was prepared to threaten hurt on my mother. I don't believe in any God, but for some perverse reason, I do believe that consciousness continues in some way after death. Some other worlds out there. Other dimensions. Like some Borges story: *The Secret Miracle; Tlön, Uqbar, Orbis Tertius; The Circular Ruins*;

death like a big sleep where we dream other worlds into being and share that world with other consciousnesses that are dreaming the same thing as we are. I thought: if you get a bullet in the neck, would you dream yourself into a nightmare? If I could believe that death brings oblivion, it would be easier. The idea of oblivion doesn't frighten me at all. I enjoy sleep. It's restful. There's no pain. What frightens me is the actual process of death. The suffering that I'm sure it entails. What might come after if you fuck that up; what kind of vision your consciousness is going to dream up for you: heaven, hell or something entirely unknown and marvelous; or something nightmarish. But oblivion doesn't frighten me at all.

I drifted off. No sleep on the night bus, and then the whiskey. I dreamed that a rat had got into the apartment. It was a white and red-haired rat. Like a pet rat. Somehow, it didn't bother me that a rat was running around free in my apartment. I got a rind of blue cheese off the kitchen countertop and I crumbled bits of it that the rat caught in its front paws and then ate while standing on its hind legs. I kept on feeding the rat. After it had finished eating, it used its front paws to brush away the crumbs on the carpet as if it was clearing up after itself. I woke up.

What a fucking ridiculous dream. Is that what was waiting for me after death?

I got up and showered. It was 10.30 am.

I called Ana on my cell phone. I got her voicemail.

'Call me,' I said.

I called Clara Luz Weissman.

'What news?' I said.

'It's going well,' Clara said. 'A friend of yours, from the police force, he came by today. He said he'd mobilize the provincial police and send a report to the Federal police, too. He's promised to do everything he can to find Gerardo.'

'Who's the cop?'

'Martín Vallejo.'

'That's good. He's a good guy.'

'How did it go with Isabel?' Clara said.

'No leads... Is Ana there?'

'The company decided to leave for Buenos Aires early this morning... so they could concentrate on rehearsals. They left me to deal with the media about the disappearance. Since the flyers appeared, *La Voz del Interior* has agreed to run a feature. They're coming up to Temenos at about eleven. It should run tomorrow. We've had requests for interviews from *Clarín*, *La Prensa* and the TV news. The company decided to go and rehearse in Buenos Aires... that it would be the best thing. I'll join them there later. I'm going to drive down to Buenos Aires today, right after I've been to the TV studios in Córdoba. I have to be there by about one o'clock.'

'I won't see you?'

'We'll all be in Buenos Aires.'

Why hadn't Ana called me? Shit. My fault. I'd told her not to call, hadn't I?

'Okay,' I said.

'Take care,' Clara said.

'You, too,' I said.

I called the office. Rangel picked up.

'You okay?' I said.

'Sure,' he said.

'I'm on my way to the office. I've got a meeting with Casares at noon.'

'I'll be here.'

'You don't need to.'

'I know.'

'Thanks,' I said.

'See you soon,' Rangel said. And he hung up.

Extract from the casebook of Juan Manuel Pérez
January 16th 2006
Hours: 11:30 to 14:00

Rangel got up from his desk when I arrived at the office.

He embraced me. Genuine warmth.

'Casares and his goons should be here in half an hour,' I said.

Rangel didn't alter his expression.

'Do you have a weapon?' I said.

'Yeah,' he said.

We went into our small meeting room at the back of the premises. The white Formica-topped table gleamed and the room was full of a synthetic odor of pine. I guess the cleaner had been in. We had six chairs in there, blue tubular steel frames with polished wooden seats and backrests. Rangel and I smoked cigarettes, drank coffee and watched the hands of the clock drag along in slow motion. Smoke hung in layers above the table. Noon came and no one showed.

But hey, who arrives on time?

We heard footsteps on the stairs at 12:15.

I went into the main office to meet and greet. Rangel stayed behind the long white table. Casares, Matas and Maria Dos Santos walked in through the front door. No sign of my father or Arenas. Maria was still in her dark glasses. Her chin was up, her eyes hidden by the blank lenses, and traces of the bruising still on her face. She had a kind of beige, low cut, macramé top and a khaki skirt. Her straw bag dangled from her hand.

Casares, a short man, his skin glowing behind the dark glasses, the pale hair neatly trimmed, was obviously the man in command. He wore a light green cotton shirt with pockets and epaulettes, and pale khaki slacks over light leather shoes. The clothes gave him a casual military air. He nodded to me. I nodded back. The presence of Pedrito Matas, oiled hair slicked back, shades, charcoal gray suit and shirt, kept the whole affair on the dark side of shady.

'Juan Manuel,' Casares said.

I thought for a moment he was about to approach me to kiss me on the cheek. He didn't.

'We can talk inside,' I said.

I led the way into the meeting room where Rangel was behind the white Formica table below the strata of smoke.

'You know my partner,' I said.

'We've already had the pleasure,' Casares said.

Rangel didn't stand up.

'Have a seat,' Rangel said.

Matas reached for the door handle.

'Leave the door open,' I said.

Matas shrugged. He leaned a shoulder against the doorjamb. I joined Rangel on the other side of the table and sat down. Casares and Maria sat down opposite me and Rangel. She took out a cigarette and lit it and the cloud above the table shifted as she blew more smoke into it. She didn't take off the shades.

Why had they brought her here?

'Have you made any progress in your search for Fischer?' Casares said.

I shook my head.

'You must be patient, Juan Manuel,' Casares said. 'How long have you been looking for Fischer? A week? I've had a word with your friend, Martín Vallejo. The police are taking this disappearance very seriously, now. He assures me he'll do all he can to track down this Gerardo Fischer. The police will help you.'

Martín? Had they corrupted him, too? I always thought of him as a clean cop. Casares was going to some length to make me doubt that he knew anything about Fischer's whereabouts.

'Maria has a file for you to see,' Casares said.

Maria leaned over and took a green cardboard file from her straw basket. The file had a flower pattern on it and the words Artemisia Adoption Agency.

Why should she show me this?

She slid the file across the white tabletop toward me. I was reflected in the lenses of her shades. She leaned back and took a deep drag on her cigarette so that her cheeks hollowed. The yellow and red bruising mottled on her grayish skin, the background for the red spider webs of her broken blood vessels.

What did she see in that bastard Matas?

I opened the gaily-decorated cover. In a clear plastic pocket at the front of the file was a birth certificate from Buenos Aires, section 20, in the name of Javier Alejandro Hernández, son of Don Guillermo Hernández and Doña Filomena Martínez Aramburu.

The baby, Javier Alejandro Hernández, was born on August 21st 1976, my birthday.

On the next page was a Photostat of a police identification form for Guillermo Hernández. He'd been picked up on an anti-subversive operation in the Palermo quarter of Buenos Aires on September 8th 1976. His photograph showed a young man in his mid-twenties with wavy hair swept back from his face, covering his ears and curling over the collar of his floral shirt. Hernández was a member of the E.R.P. He'd been handed over to military personnel at the Naval Mechanics School in Buenos Aires. He'd died of a heart attack, it said, while in custody. The following page was a police identification form for Filomena Martínez Aramburu who was arrested in Ciudad Azul on October 16th 1976. She was the wife of Guillermo Hernández and a suspected accomplice in a cell of the leftist E.R.P. being set up in the Province of Córdoba.

The photograph showed a woman with rather straggly dark hair that fell to her shoulders. She had dark rings below her eyes, gaunt cheeks, rather thin lips. Her baby had been about two months old at that time. She'd given the baby up for adoption, it said. Nothing on what had happened to her.

The next page was a form from the Artemisia Adoption Agency of Ciudad Azul with the date of birth, which was my date of birth, and the name of the child on the birth certificate: Javier Alejandro Hernández, parents defunct. So Filomena had died in prison, too.

I could hear the words that my mother – my mother? – had said to me on the phone: *He told me to make you see sense, Juan Manuel. Or we'd all be sorry… Juan Manuel, I beg of you. Do as he says, or something awful is going to happen, I know this. Believe your mother. I love you.*

A kind of hollow breeze whispered through the cavity of my skull.

Juan Manuel, is that my name?

It's his name.

Juan Manuel Senior is very disappointed in you.

His picture was on the next page: the child's adoptive father, Juan Manuel Pérez, police officer, Province of Córdoba. He was in his thirties then, about my age, handsome, the square jaw, bald already, his pale eyes that stared directly into the camera. His wife – the woman I'd always called my mother – was on the next page, her photograph showing her full face, the tumble of curly dark hair, a beaming smile: Inmaculada Concepción Guzmán Pérez. A medical note at the bottom of the page indicated that she couldn't have children; this woman who had taken care of me through my whole life, fed me, clothed me, even loved me; at whose breast I'd always believed I'd suckled.

I flipped back to the page with Filomena's picture. I seemed to be looking into another dimension, a parallel time. What had they done to her? What had he done to her? Had he been involved in this Filomena's interrogation? This Filomena? What did I mean by that? My mother? The woman in this picture was my mother, my birth mother.

Nausea. The room was tilted. The blank face of Matas over by the door. Maria Dos Santos, with her head bent, stared down at the file in my hands. Smoke curled from the tip of the cigarette between the fingers of her right hand that was now flat on the table. Maria Dos Santos glanced up at Casares. His complexion was like something out of a glossy magazine. She looked over her shoulder toward Matas, then at Rangel, not at me, but back at the file. Rangel's breath was a steady rasp in his throat. His head was close to mine. He was looking over my shoulder at the file.

'Juanma?' Rangel said.

Whose fucking name was that?

'It's okay,' I said.

It wasn't, of course.

My father? – my father must have told my mother that if I didn't keep my mouth shut and give up the case, he was going to show me the file. This file. Told her that he was going to tell me that I wasn't his son; that I wasn't her son.

It would destroy the last vestiges of the world she had constructed based on a normal family life with him, with me... whatever that was.

He knew what it would do to her.

But he needed to punish me.

And what better way to do it than to disown me and destroy my entire identity. I'd betrayed him: by looking for Fischer, by going to Isabel in Buenos Aires, by bringing his business deal with Sandro Casares to light. By defying him when he told me to lay off the case. Juan Manuel Senior – I couldn't say Pa – had known nothing about Fischer when I'd first talked to him but he'd found out from Arenas and Casares. And Juan Manuel Senior cared more about his son shaming him in front of the big man, Casares, than he did about me, or my mother. And why not? She wasn't his wife any more. And I had reverted to type. Juan Manuel Senior had been in Casares's SUV and when he'd seen me on the road where the drug and gun deal was going down, he knew that he'd failed to stop me looking for Fischer. I had corrupt DNA. The subversive genes that he'd brought into the bosom of his own family and nurtured, no doubt at his wife's insistence, had betrayed him. Maybe he was right. There was something genetic about it.

Inmaculada Concepción, his wife, wasn't my real mother.

This woman, Filomena – my real mother, right? – stared at me from the photograph: already the terror in her eyes for what she'd been through, and what she knew she was going to go through away from the momentary respite of having her picture taken. Did she suffer at the hands of the man who would steal her child and become my adoptive father? Did she know that she was about to lose her baby son to this man? What horror was that?

I closed the file.

'This Gerardo Fischer has caused a lot of trouble,' Casares said.

I'd never been who I had always thought I was. How about that? Juan Manuel Senior was not my father. Inmaculada Concepción was not my mother. But she'd brought me up with real love, hadn't she?

'I don't care about what went on up on the mountain,' I said. 'That's none of my business. But I'll still keep looking for Fischer.'

'You're a stubborn man, Juan Manuel,' Casares said.

'If my mother's hurt, I'll kill you,' I said.

'Your mother's already dead,' Casares said. 'No one's going to touch the woman who adopted you. She's one of us.'

That hit me like a punch in the gut and he knew it. He stood up. This Casares with his permanent tan, his confident smile. This was his way of showing me that I wasn't even worth killing. That he had no fear of me or the law or the press. He was showing me that he knew more about me than I'd known about myself. He'd just wiped away my whole identity. I still had no idea if Casares or Matas or Arenas had made Fischer disappear. Me, the not-cop. I didn't even know who I was any more. And if Casares hadn't had Fischer killed already, I might be doing Casares a favor by finding him.

Maria took a slow drag on her cigarette, shifted sideways on the chair and stubbed it out in the half-full ashtray on the Formica-topped table.

'Why don't you all get the fuck out of here?' I said. 'Just get out.'

'The police have everything under control,' Casares said.

Meaning that he was Teflon. But he fucking wasn't, I was sure.

Meanwhile, everything is under surveillance, Isabel had said… It's a little transaction that could lead to catching bigger fish. I could only hope that Casares was one of the fish they wanted to catch; that he wasn't in with the fishermen.

My job was still to find Gerardo Fischer.

And maybe to find out just who the fuck I am.

Maria reached for the adoption file.

I snatched it back.

'What are you doing?' Maria's mouth gaped open.

I pulled out the picture of my real father, and my real mother.

'You don't need these,' I said. 'Or this.'

I pulled out my birth certificate with my real name on it.

'That's company property,' Maria said.

'This is my property,' I said.

What Maria meant was that this file could get a lot of her family in trouble. She knew this and so did Matas and he would risk violence to get it back. Matas moved toward the table.

Rangel was on his feet.

'Wait,' Casares said. 'Let him keep the pictures.'

I tossed the folder back at Maria.

'I just want the photographs and the birth certificate,' I said. 'That's all. You can keep the hard evidence, I don't give a fuck.'

Matas looked confused. I guess he wasn't too bright. He glanced at Maria, at Rangel, at Casares and back to me.

'Take your file and get out of here,' I said.

'Take the file, Maria,' Casares said. 'Juan Manuel has everything he needs now. I'm sure he won't cause any more problems for us.'

Maria lifted the file and dropped it back into her basket.

Casares drifted toward the door.

I wished that I could trust that Carlos and Ramón's human rights group would take care of the Artemisia Adoption Agency and all the impounded records. But nothing was certain on that front. Not with a bastard like Casares who had so much legal and illegal influence to bring to bear on the courts and the cops.

Matas kept the flat lenses of his mirror shades on me until Casares and Maria Dos Santos were out the door of the office and onto the fire escape; then he followed them out and closed the door behind him.

'Juanma?' Rangel said.

'Whose name is that?'

'Take it easy, man.'

Rangel tried to put an arm around me but I shook him off.

'I'm okay,' I said. 'I'm okay.'

I didn't want anyone touching me.

'I'm sorry,' I said.

I held the two photographs side by side: my father, and my mother. I put the father behind the mother, and then shuffled them so that the mother was behind the father, and then the mother in front again. I put the photographs in the inside pocket of my jacket.

'I'm going for a drive.'

'You want me to come with you?' Rangel said.

'No. I'm okay.'

I stepped out of the door. The sun baked the stubble on my skull. No sign of Matas, Casares, or Maria Dos Santos down below on the street.

A cop car, black and white, was parked on the corner. In the rear side-window was a poster of Fischer; on the passenger side of the windshield was a flyer of Fischer. On another cop car that cruised down the main drag, Fischer's face stared out from the Missing Persons Bureau poster pasted to the cruiser's windows. Was Casares using the story of Gerardo Fischer's disappearance to tell the citizens of this fair country that those who dig up the past would end up reliving the past we would all prefer had never happened?

I wanted to tell my mother, my not-mother, Inmaculada Concepción, that it was okay, that it wasn't her fault. But – I'm sorry – it was her fault, too. She never fucking told me.

The sun burned into in my eyes.

I was outside my office on the steel platform at the top of the stairway.

Should I look for the grave of the people who were in the photographs in my pocket? Were there any graves to be found? Somewhere out there, maybe I had grandparents, maybe cousins, aunts, uncles. Who knew? I could look for them so my living relatives would know what had happened to me. Or I could remain unknown to them... a man without any family at all, a man without a past.

How had I got here? Where was I? Oh yes.

I grabbed the handrail for balance and walked down the steps to the street.

My car was parked in the shade of the alley.

I got in the black Ford and turned the key to start it.

The light was so bright on the street. I was looking for something but I didn't know what, like some kind of shadow at the periphery of my vision. Like the numbness inside me was now outside of me... but just out of sight. I had to go somewhere. I had to get out of this lakeside summer resort on the shores of the Lago Gran Paraíso.

I wished that I could talk to Ana but I couldn't face making a cell phone call and getting her voicemail again. I had a yen to go to the Temenos Artists Colony, up there, to Damien Kennedy's house.

Temenos – sacred space – fear us.

I had a yen to snoop around Damien Kennedy's personal belongings to see if there was any indication of why he might have lied to me about Francesca Damiani, other than the fact that their relationship was none of my fucking business; and about why they might have gone to Uruguay, and whether it had anything to do with the disappearance of Gerardo Fischer, the man who liked to strip away people's masks.

What a theater director! Orchestrating people's lives like God, or the Devil. What a fucking genius!

I drove out to the lakeside. I got caught in the traffic by the new flyover connection to the main highway to Córdoba. Three earth-moving machines pushed dry dirt into two-meter high piles, tall cranes swung nets full of concrete sacks and re-bar from one side of the site to the other, unseen jackhammers rattled from behind plywood walls that were topped with razor wire. The sun blazed down on the two lines of saloon cars and SUVs and pick-up trucks: one line inching single file through the orange and white striped barrels that marked the road through the construction zone.

I had a green light. The front end of the Ford Executive lifted and bucked over the dusty makeshift causeway. I eased between a cement-truck on my right whose mixer gently rotated and a row of I-shaped concrete beams some ten meters long. The traffic signal for the oncoming vehicles was about thirty meters away to my left. The lead vehicle for the stationary traffic was a yellow Dodge pick-up that seemed to belong to a construction company, the second car was a silver Hyundai saloon, the third a red Toyota Camry, and the fourth was a white GM truck with a closed cab and matching white box behind.

I slammed my palms onto the steering wheel.

'Hi, Pa!'

He couldn't hear me, of course. I was in my car with the air conditioning on and the construction noise drowned out the sound of the engines: he was in the driver's seat of the white cab with

Pablo Arenas beside him, still fifty meters away but the distance was closing. He saw me through his windshield. He looked to the right and left, said something to Arenas and now they were both looking at me. They weren't moving. They couldn't go back and they couldn't go forward. I slowed down and that meant the traffic behind me slowed down, too.

The signal for oncoming traffic was still red when I came to a stop.

Juan Manuel Senior and Pablo Arenas kept looking at each other, looking at me. I glanced in the rearview mirror. A young redheaded woman in the battered Ford behind me had a puzzled frown on her face. Her car stopped behind my rear bumper. Car horns started to blare from both lines of stalled traffic.

What had Isabel said?

'We believe that it will leave Ciudad Azul early tomorrow afternoon.'

I reached back under my jacket and pulled out the M1911 from the holster on my belt. It was pretty solid in my hand.

Juan Manuel Senior's eyes widened and his jaw fell a little. He was unshaven. His skin was a little grey. Arenas was at his shoulder. His face was still mottled by his bruises. I pointed at the driver's side window with the gun barrel and indicated that I wanted it lowered. Juan Manuel Senior lowered it.

'For fuck's sake, Juanma, what are you doing?'

We had an audience now. Construction workers with hardhats and some drivers of the cars behind mine who had got out to see why they were being held up. The blare of car horns was counterpoint to the jackhammer and the heavy diesel engines of the caterpillar-tracked earthmovers.

Juan Manuel Senior raised his hands palms toward me.

'Take it easy, Juanma.'

'That's not my fucking name.'

I had this heavy black gun in my hand that could stop this shipment here and now. I knew how to use it. I had been a policeman. I thought of Isabel: a woman who had been a pacifist in 1982 during the Israeli invasion of the Lebanon and who might yet be a pacifist now. She'd had enough information to stop this shipment and she wasn't going to.

Bigger fish.

With the M1911, I waved to Arenas and Juan Manuel Senior and tossed the unfired weapon onto the passenger seat. I put the car in gear and drove down the now empty road in front of me. I guess I was shaking a little. I didn't even look in the rearview mirror. I hoped that I'd made the right decision. I would never know.

I drove down Route 60. I passed the shrine to the Madonna... the Immaculate Conception. I turned off the main highway and onto the dirt road toward El Campanil. I let the big black Ford Executive buck over the washboard cambers and through the dry potholes and around the rocks that were exposed in the middle of the rutted road.

Inmaculada Concepción was not my mother. Had she really been in on this revelation by Casares and Juan Manuel Senior? Or had Casares just said that to twist a broken bottle in the wound he'd opened?

My real mother and father were dead and I had their pictures in my jacket pocket. I pulled in to the parking lot of the Temenos Artists Colony. It was empty.

No Dodge Ram.

No white Fiat van.

How come no van? I got out of the Ford.

I walked past Sara's house.

No sound of any dogs.

No wind to lift the branches of the eucalypts or the pines.

They'd all gone, the whole company.

I took out my cell phone and dialed.

'Hello, Ma.'

'Juanma, where are you? Are you okay?'

'I'm fine. And you?'

'Come and see me, Juanma.'

'Soon, Ma. I got a few things to do. I just wanted to make sure that you're okay.'

'I'm okay. Have you seen your father?'

'Don't worry, I've sorted everything out with him.'

'Oh, thank God, Juanma,' she said. 'I was so worried about you.'

'It's alright,' I said.

A long silence.

'He told you, didn't he?' she said.

'Yeah, he told me. But it doesn't matter, okay?'

That was a total lie and we both knew it.

'Come and see me, Juanma, please,' she said. 'Come now.'

'Don't do anything stupid, Ma, you understand? You don't need to get drunk, do anything... we can work this out, okay? I'll come and see you when... when I get back...'

'Where you going?'

'I have to go to Montevideo.'

She was crying now.

'Oh, Juanma... I'm so sorry...'

'Look after yourself, Ma, okay?'

'Come over, now, Juanma, I want to see you.'

'I can't right now. I'm in the middle of something.'

Silence.

'God bless you, Juanma,' she said.

'I'll see you soon.'

I hung up. I slipped the cell phone in my pocket.

I wish Ana had been around.

I took out the photographs from my jacket pocket. I looked into the terrified face of my mother, my real mother; the face of my real father was like a holiday snap.

What was I doing up here on this mountainside?

I heard a motor. The white Fiat van was coming up the hill.

Fischer?

No.

It was the American guy, Dean Mills, the old biker with the silvery hair, a bit jowly under the lenses of his shades, heavy body under his denim shirt. He pulled up, switched off the engine and got out of the van. He leaned on his cane.

'Everyone's gone to Buenos Aires,' he said. 'I'm meeting them there tomorrow morning.'

'I came to look around,' I said.

Mills shook his head.

'Still looking for Fischer?'

'Yeah.'

Mills limped to the edge of the parking lot and looked back across the valley to the ridgelines of the Sierras.

'You won't find him. Not unless he wants you to.'

My shoes ground against the dusty gravel; puffs of dust settled on the shiny leather.

'What do you mean by that?'

'Gerardo,' he said.

'You mean you know where he is?'

'I don't know where he is,' Mills said. 'You really think he's been kidnapped or killed?'

'That's why they hired me. To find out.'

'That's right.'

'So what do you think?'

'Look. Gerardo... what he does... what he's always done... Let's just say... well, what he likes to do... is to set in motion forces that are... unpredictable, volatile. He's always done that, hasn't he? In Argentina, in Italy, in New York, wherever...'

Mills took off his shades; he let them dangle beside his good leg. He squinted out into the sun's rays that slanted across the valley from the Sierras.

'Gerardo has a theory,' Mills said. 'You can read it in his book, *Los Delincuentes*, it's there in black and white since 1968: he wants to make theater that crosses into everyday life... that wakes people up. That's what he says. He likes to draw people into the theater, into the company even, and show them there's no distinction between theater and normal life; that so-called normal life is nothing but theater. Back then, he predicted that the extent to which we were all being conned all the time was going to escalate: newspapers, television... he couldn't know just how... but look... websites, businesses, banks and governments. He couldn't have known exactly how back then... but he saw it coming. He's a sharp guy.'

Fischer as prophet.

'I watched him operate up here,' Mills said. 'He creates situations where that becomes obvious. That's our theater. Maybe he's a fucking megalomaniac; or maybe he's one of the sweetest and most genuine guys on the planet... it depends on who you talk to.'

He put his shades back on.

The world as theater: I'd been acting all my life and I'd never known it. I'd even had a different name. My so-called father and my so-called mother had been knowingly acting all their lives to convince me I was someone I was not.

'I'm going to find him,' I said.

Mills tilted his head up. I couldn't see his eyes behind the shades but the smile was wry. He looked away again toward the sun.

'Look, just think,' Mills said. 'He got Carlos and Ramón going after Arenas... Gerardo just wanted them to act... real and present, you understand? And Gerardo knew that would have a ripple effect on all those people around them: on everyone at Temenos, for example, the theater company, and on Gerardo himself, of course. He always included himself. On whoever came into our orbit... like you, okay? Gerardo must have known that Arenas would have all kinds of criminal and political connections, but something made him do it; all these connections would all come to light...'

'Clara and Miriam told me that he wasn't political,' I said.

'Gerardo's not political,' Mills said. 'He just grew up in political times. Dangerous times. He made it part of his theater, that's all. The way I see it, Gerardo knew that if he just disappeared, all these criminal and political connections and our involvement in them would be given a far sharper focus; and people, like us, or like you, would wake up to something awesome, something special, something mysterious if we all started to look for him. He has an instinct for this. That's my theory, anyway. For what it's worth.'

'That's crazy,' I said.

This was Mills' vision of things. I didn't believe him. Was this what Dean Mills wanted to believe of Gerardo Fischer? That Fischer was some kind of mage, a seer of visions. There was a kernel of truth in it, of course. Fischer's disappearance had certainly stripped away the masks of my own life, of the people in my life. But that was pure chance, wasn't it? Mills' theory was just a way of coping with Gerardo's loss, wasn't it? Some crazy fantasy that Gerardo was always in control, always right, would show up when he wanted to.

Ana and Clara wouldn't believe the same as Mills, would they?

'I'm sorry,' I said. 'I think you're wrong. People care about him. Ana and Clara and Sara are terrified that something awful has happened to him.'

I stared across at the old biker's tanned face. The sun was behind his head. Its rays lit him up with a kind of saintly glow.

'He did it to Damien Kennedy in Italy,' Mills said. 'Seduced him into the company and abandoned him in Rome.'

'But he'd warned him beforehand. He didn't just disappear.'

Dean Mills shrugged.

Could Fischer have disappeared without telling anyone? I didn't think so. He must have known that the fallout could have been devastating. Especially when someone like Arenas was involved. I knew this. I knew this first hand.

'Fischer wouldn't do that,' I said. 'Nobody would.'

'Gerardo has never been afraid of any danger,' Mills said. 'Or upsetting people. You better know it.'

I better know it?

'You were close with Damien Kennedy.'

'Close as anyone,' Mills said.

'He went off with Francesca Damiani to Montevideo.'

'He always did have a shine for Francesca.'

'Do you think Gerardo might be in Montevideo?'

Mills shook his head.

'As good a place as any,' he said.

Mills didn't know where Fischer was. I left him staring into the bright rays of the sun. I walked back across the parking lot. Is it better to know? *Is it better to know?* Tell me. I don't know what to believe.

I climbed up the path to the ridge. If Fischer had deliberately disappeared, it was he who had done this to me. I'd certainly had my mask stripped away. Stripped away my name, my previous life. Where was Ana? Could Fischer have taken off for Uruguay, and Damien Kennedy and Francesca Damiani gone across to Montevideo with him? I couldn't believe that, could I?

Fischer couldn't have known that I would discover who my true parents were. He couldn't even have known that I'd be hired to look for him. But, according to Mills, that wouldn't have been the point: Fischer would know that whoever set out to look for him would discover something about himself: whoever that happened to be. And that's what I'd done, hadn't I? I was the living proof of Dean Mills' theory.

I had to stop thinking like this or I'd end up a paranoid basket case.

Why should I continue looking for Fischer now?

For the money? For Ana? To discover something more?

Could Ana have been in on Gerardo's disappearance? Could she have hired me to make it look like the theater company didn't know where he was in order to protect him from Matas and Arenas? I didn't know what to believe any more.

For over thirty years I'd believed I was the son of Juan Manuel Pérez and his wife, Inmaculada Concepción Guzmán Pérez. And now I wasn't.

Was that Fischer's gift to me? I'd been invited to take part in a game: a game without fixed rules, a role-playing game that led to the discovery of unknown truths.

Thanks, Gerardo.

Did I want to stay in it?

I could stay in if I continued to look for Gerardo Fischer.

Yes… I'd continue to look for Gerardo Fischer.

I was involved in a serious game. Whoever I was.

From the outside, Damien Kennedy's house was just as much of a construction site as the last time I was here, although now, I could see the skylight had been framed in. I tried the lock on the door. It was open. Just like Fischer's house had been open according to Ana. Had she been lying to me? Where was she now? Why didn't she call? I'd left a message on her voicemail.

The ground floor of Kennedy's house was just as much concrete and dust as the last time I'd been there, but the kitchen had been cleaned out: all the pots and pans were clean and upside down on the draining board of the sink. The *mate* gourd was empty and clean.

I climbed the concrete stairs.

The floor of Kennedy's bedroom-cum-living-room-cum-studio had been swept, although the dried paint drips hadn't been removed from the plywood panels. No paint tubes, no palette, no brushes. No sign of Kennedy's clothes or books or anything else. The mattress had been stripped and propped against the wall. The blackened empty pot with its hard membrane of dried rabbit-skin glue was still on the floor just in front of it. The bed-frame revealed bare floor below its wooden slats.

One thing rang true to me about what Mills had said.

I wasn't going to find Gerardo Fischer unless he wanted me to find him.

The black drape still hung over the scenery construction that Kennedy had said he'd been working on. I pulled the drape down off the top of it and the heavy cloth tumbled to the floor.

I was in front of a life-sized reproduction of the Porta Magica in Rome, just as it had appeared in Kennedy's illustrated diary. I laid my hand on the black surface between the painted pillars. The black surface, hinged on some slick castors, split and swung back. Latin and Hebrew letters, and planetary ciphers, danced in front of my eyes. I stepped through the open door and it slid shut behind me. I was inside a black cube, so dark that it was as if all light, all time, every memory could be absorbed by it. I couldn't see the hands in front of my face. I stepped forward in the pitch darkness and a tiny spotlight came on. It lit up a card that rested on Damien Kennedy's paint-spattered easel. I stepped back; the light went off: I stepped forward; it came on again. The card on the easel had a border of stylized artemisia flowers that framed the words for a simple sign that the theater company would probably set up on the stage, or in the foyer of a place where they might perform.

Crazy laughter bubbled up from somewhere down in the empty cavity of my chest. Had Gerardo Fischer set up this joke for me? Was he letting me know that I was one of them now? I was one of their own. I was in the game. I read the words on the card with the flowered border:

Welcome to the Real and Present
Theater Company

Editor's Epilogue
David Enrique Spellman

The Amtrak train from New York to Springfield was to leave Penn Station at 11:30 am. The PATH train from New Jersey into 33rd Street had been late: signal problems in the tunnel. I raced up the stairs onto Herald Square. The late-July damp heat wrapped me in its cloying blanket. Low cloud had clamped a dank and venomous lid on the city. The temperature must have been around forty degrees. I hustled west along 33rd Street, crossed 8th Avenue and ran down the steps into Penn Station to dodge through the crowd of travelers, beggars, shoe-shiners, cops, and late-morning tourists. Professor María Helena Molina was due to meet me at 3:12 pm in Springfield and take me on to Northampton. I was supposed to give a lecture on 'New Trends in Latin American Literature and Philosophy since the fall of the Dictatorships' to the Smith College Latin American Studies Department Summer School. If I missed the train, I'd miss the lecture. I made the escalator for Platform 13 and got down to train level just as the guard was about to seal all the doors.

I got to my seat. I slid my computer backpack onto the luggage rack.

Two passengers sat across the aisle from me: a woman I guessed was around thirty years old, with dark hair, slim, very attractive;

and a man, possibly slightly older, gaunt, with a shaved head and a goatee beard; both of them, I thought, Hispanic. I could read the title of the woman's book: *Orghast in Persepolis*. The title suggested orgy, or orgasm, or Gormenghast. But I could see from the cover that it was a book about Peter Brook, the theater director, close to a namesake. I'd seen three of Brook's movies and four of his plays but I'd never read that book, *Orghast*, and somehow I liked the look of it.

The train eased forward out of Penn Station. Electrical flashes lit up the tunnels and the odd black door in the general blackness, and banks of cables, and red lights that gleamed an instant and disappeared. The train picked up speed. It came out of the labyrinth and the city took shape beyond the window: the suburbs of Queens, row houses, detached two-stories with gardens, low apartment blocks, vacant lots, schoolyards, basketball cages. Across the East River, the clouds were bronze over Manhattan. The train ran north toward the Bronx.

'Excuse me,' I said. I said it in English because the book was in English. I assumed she was American. 'I hope you don't mind, but I'm curious about that book you're reading. I really like Peter Brook's theater work.'

The young woman looked up. Cool in a pale brown top and linen pants. She seemed quite relaxed about the interruption. The man, her partner I presumed, nodded to me, and resumed looking out the window. He didn't seem to be the talkative type.

'Oh... it's about a theater project,' the woman said. She had a slight Latin American accent. 'I can't imagine this ever happening now. Back in 1971, an Iranian woman organized an experimental theater festival in the ruins of Persepolis in Persia. This is before Khomeini, before the Islamic Revolution... I mean... the Shah was terrible but now... I can't imagine they'd have any grand scale experimental theater there any more, can you?'

It didn't take much thinking about. Since July 12th, Hizbullah in Lebanon had launched a series of cross-border rocket attacks against Israel, and had mounted a raid that resulted in the capture of two Israeli soldiers. Israel had been bombing Beirut and had invaded Southern Lebanon. Iran had been accused of supporting the Hizbullah fight. The Middle East had become a theater of war once more. The idea of an experimental theater festival anywhere in the region seemed absurd. The visions of carnage on TV news reports were appalling.

'No,' I said, 'I can't.'

But the young woman probably wasn't thinking about that. She was obviously excited about the book. Her dark eyes got so bright – maybe a reflection of the overhead carriage lights – as she looked straight at me. Something animated about her, charismatic, a wonderful dark and confident voice.

'A woman organized this festival,' she said. 'She invited Peter Brook's theater company. And the concepts here... A new language, *Orghast*... that English poet, Ted Hughes, invented it.'

She obviously loved language: a stunning and sharp intelligent woman. I found her fascinating right away.

'Would you mind if I take a look at the book?' I said.

She handed it to me with that intense gaze. I looked down at the cover, flipped the pages open at random: the pictures in the center. Even at that time, Peter Brook's theater group must have been a shock for the locals. Persia. Iran. The more I looked at the text and images, the more I wanted to read the book. I wanted to talk to her about it, what she made of the ideas in here.

'My name's Spellman,' I said. 'David Enrique Spellman.'

'Oh,' she said. 'A Spanish name.'

'Yes. I was born in New York but my mother's from Argentina.'

'Have you ever been to Argentina?' she said.

'Yes, of course. My grandmother still lives in Palermo.'

'Then you speak *Castellano?*'

'Quite well,' I said.

'My name's Clara Luz Weissman. And this is Javier Hernández.'

The man turned his gaze away from the window to look at me. I nodded to him.

'A pleasure,' Hernández said.

He said this in English. Despite the shadow of the stubble on Hernández's face, and the hollows below his cheekbones, I detected a kind of softness in him, a warmth in his dark eyes. It was the face of a man who had been through something traumatic perhaps, and who was coming out of it older and maybe a little wiser. All this on a few moments' observation, as if the intensity of these two people's presence and attention had drawn me into a kind of magnetic field across the aisle of the train to exclude the other passengers.

'Where are you from?' I said.

'I'm from Buenos Aires,' Clara said. 'And Javier's from Córdoba.'

'My mother's a *Porteña*,' I said.

Maybe because we'd begun speaking in English, Clara and I didn't switch to Spanish: even if I had the suspicion that Hernández didn't seem as comfortable as Clara with the language. And anyway, Hernández seemed content to let her do all the talking. Maybe they weren't a couple. He didn't seem to mind her talking to a strange man.

'What brought you to the United States?' I said.

'I work with a theater company. Javier, well, he's sort of looking for someone we know.'

He smiled again and nodded and turned back to looking out of the window. It wasn't that he was unfriendly; but rather it was as if he could sense the interaction that was going on between Clara and myself and was withdrawing to let it develop without his interference.

'Are you an actor?' I said to Clara.

Anyone with a voice like hers must be an actor, I thought.

'No, a producer,' she said. 'Our company is putting on a theater piece at La MaMa.'

'A theater piece?'

'It's called *Pablito's Milonga*. It's about an Argentine living in New York who has lost touch with his roots. He sees Buenos Aires like any other gringo: tango, Borges, labyrinths.'

I wondered if that was a friendly barb aimed at me. Is that the way she thought that I might see Buenos Aires because I was born in the US?

'A satire?'

'No, a tragedy really. Or a comedy...' She laughed. She was mocking me. I liked it. 'I mean... how can Pablito ever go back?' she said. 'The stability in the United States is so seductive, isn't it? The check at the end of the month, everything you need in the stores, you know what I mean?'

'Is it a new play?' I said.

'A few years old.'

'Who wrote it?'

'Gerardo Fischer.'

'I've never heard the name.'

'He's Uruguayan,' she said. 'But he worked a lot in Buenos Aires. Then in Europe during the late seventies, early eighties... here, too, in the nineties, but he's always been on the edge of things. Nothing mainstream.'

'Nothing mainstream, I like the sound of that,' I said. 'And this theater company has been going for forty years?'

'Not the same people, obviously; but yes, forty years.'

'How long have you been involved?'

She held my gaze even as she seemed to be calculating the time she'd been with this company. 'Oh... over ten years, now.'

'What's the name of the company?'

'*Compañia de Teatro Real y Presente*.'

'The Real and Present Theater Company.'

'Here, yes,' she said.

'Look,' I said, 'I teach up at Columbia...'

'You teach theater?' She reached over and touched me on the

forearm. I enjoyed the pressure of her fingers as they rested on my sleeve.

'No, Latin American Studies, but I'm interested in theater… especially Latin American theater…'

'I did my Masters in theater at Columbia,' she said.

'Really? What year?'

'1995–97.'

She leaned back again in her seat. So she was a little older than I'd thought, maybe late thirties.

'When's your next performance?' I said.

'Of *Pablito's Milonga?*'

'Yeah. At La MaMa.'

'Saturday.'

'I'll come.' I don't know if she believed me or not.

We sat in awkward silence for a while. At least, it was awkward from my side. She was a very attractive woman. I didn't know to what extent she was involved with the man by her side. Of course, I wanted to get to know her better.

I stood up and took my lecture notes from my computer backpack and started to look them over; but in my mind was the fact that this woman was part of a theater company that had been in existence since before I was born. I'd never heard of it. As far as I knew, nobody else in my field had ever written on it. She was too young to be part of the original group, so she must be part of a second or third generation, like the actors in Peter Brook's present company.

The train pulled into Stamford.

I was leafing through my notes when Clara leaned over again.

'When will you go to Argentina next?' she said.

So she wanted to engage with me, too. I had a small rush of elation.

'Well, I'm going to a conference in Montevideo in September: *Theater Arts in the New Democracies*. So I'll get to visit my grandmother then. I'll take the ferry.'

'What will you do at the conference?'

'I have to give a paper.'

'On what?'

'To be perfectly honest, I don't know. It's supposed to be about theater at the margins. We're academics, we like margins.'

She laughed.

'You can write about us,' she said.

Yes, I thought. I can. I probably can. And I'll get to meet you again.

And even then, while talking with this vivacious woman, the researcher in me was thinking, a theater group that's been in existence for over forty years, right through the dictatorship period and the restoration of democracy, and if they were still in existence, people must have continued to go to see them over all these years; and nobody had written a monograph or a book about them in the USA... at least as far as I knew. If they were any good, I'd write about them. They had to be good to have lasted forty years. I got that tingle, that avidity for something new.

'I'll come to see your show for sure,' I said.

'Yes. Yes, you must come.'

The train pulled into Bridgeport: dereliction to the left of the train, and marinas to the right of it.

'Does the company always develop its own work?' I asked.

'Until recently, yes.'

Now, for the first time in our conversation, she looked uncomfortable. One shoulder raised, she looked back over it, down toward the floor.

'Until recently?' I said.

'We'd like to keep going like that,' she said. 'Developing our own work.'

'Why wouldn't you? The company's been going for forty years. That's staying power... I don't imagine it was always that easy.'

'No, not always.'

She dragged her hair back with one hand, the warmth in her eyes replaced with a kind of ferocity. I was glad that the aggression wasn't being directed at me.

'Who writes for the company?' I asked.

'One writer,' she said.

'May I ask you for a name?'

'Gerardo Fischer.'

'Will he be at the La MaMa show?'

Hernández turned his head and exchanged a glance with her.

'Gerardo disappeared a few years ago,' she said. 'We're still looking for him. Javier is looking for him. We still hope he's alive.'

'Oh, I'm sorry,' I said.

'We've had no word of him since... a long time.'

'I'm sorry,' I said. 'I hope you find him soon. Alive and well.'

We sat in silence for a while. She reached into her purse and gave me her card.

'The more people who know about Gerardo the better,' she said.

I felt strange that we were talking about this in English; that the other passengers might be listening in to what we were saying, but Clara didn't seem to care. *Far South*. There was the address of a website.

'People have responded to Gerardo's disappearance,' Clara said. 'We've just launched this website in English to coincide with our tour of the United States. We have films there, images, sound files about Gerardo. But Javier wants to publish his case notes and transcripts of interviews in Spanish. We need English language versions. Javier thinks that Gerardo has found his way to the North. Up here. The USA. It's possible.'

Hernández turned to look at me again and the warmth that had been there was now a searching stare that made me uncomfortable. I had a sudden feeling of déjà vu. Maybe it was because I was sitting backwards on the train that I had a violent sense of losing my equilibrium. It was as if a vortex spiraled shut in front of me, cutting me off from the past, and a vacuum was sucking me backwards into the future. It was an altogether unpleasant sensation. It persisted for as long as the eyes of Javier Hernández were on me. I felt that I was looking at a man who could erase the past as much as uncover it, which is what his job must be – to uncover the past – if he was really looking for this Gerardo Fischer who had disappeared. I was glad when Hernández turned his gaze back to the window.

'Maybe Gerardo doesn't want to be found,' Clara said. 'But we're still searching for him. Do you understand? Perhaps you can help us find a good translator for Javier's casebook.'

I nodded. For all the warmth and attraction that I'd felt for Clara up to this moment, I sensed something darker about her and her theater company's history. It didn't make her and the company any less attractive to me. If anything, I really wanted to know more.

'Yes,' I said, 'perhaps I can help.'

I could. I might even do this translation myself. Why not?

'We like people to get involved with us as much as possible,' Clara said. 'We love interactions with new people. It's the beauty of live theater, isn't it? Don't you think?'

I was still recovering from the strange sense of vertigo that had overwhelmed me only a few minutes before. The warmth was back in her eyes, the smile on her face, but the darkness hadn't completely dissipated. It made her, if anything, more attractive.

'What would you say,' I asked, 'about your kind of dramaturgy?'

'It's about masks,' she said.

'Like classical Greek theater… that kind of mask?'

'Oh no, no, no. It's about stripping away masks.'

'*Pablito's Milonga*, too?'

'Yes, definitely.'

'How so?'

'You'd have to see the play,' she said. 'I can't explain.'

'I'm intrigued,' I said.

She laughed. It was a sound that was to echo in my skull for days.

'We're getting close to New Haven,' Clara said. 'We'd better get our things.'

I didn't want her to get off the train.

'I wish we had more time to talk about this,' I said. 'Perhaps I could give you my card, too.'

'Yes, yes, of course.' Clara stood up in the aisle and so did Hernández.

I already had a tremendous sense of loss. I didn't want to lose contact with her.

Hernández pulled two small overnight bags from the overhead rack. I took a card from my wallet and handed it to Clara. She tucked it into the side pocket of her overnight bag. I hoped she wasn't going to misplace it.

I would go the performance at La MaMa. No need to panic, was there?

The train pulled into New Haven. The train always stops here for a while to change engines. I couldn't help but follow Clara and Javier out onto the platform.

'I'll come and see your play for sure,' I said.

'Yes, okay,' Clara said. 'I'll call you. I promise.'

Clara stepped toward me. She surprised me with a single Latin-American-style kiss on the cheek. Javier Hernández shook my hand. He leaned forward and kissed my cheek, too. It felt as if they really would stay in touch with me, and that I wasn't just a passing encounter on a journey that they'd forget as soon as they'd left the station. The subway stairs were near the middle of the platform. All the other passengers had gone down them. Hernández and Clara turned and waved once.

The train guard called, 'All aboard.'

I raised a hand and stepped into the open doorway of the train carriage. They didn't look back again. His right hand and her left drifted towards each other. Clara took his fingers in a momentary collusive squeeze and let go again. That small action caused me a quiver of anxiety, a sensation of profound envy.

The door to the train carriage slid shut.

Hernández and Clara disappeared down the exit steps.

I went back to my seat, and I sat down and stared at the card that she'd put in my hand.

www.far-south.org

Explore the files of the Far South Collective at
http://far-south.org

David Enrique Spellman is the voice for the Far South Project. The Far South Collective is a loosely affiliated group of artists, writers, actors, filmmakers, musicians and dancers. He works in close collaboration with Esko Tikanmäki Portogales, a Uruguayan web designer.

'*Far South* is like a lucid dream, a book that fuses acts of creativity with matters of absolute seriousness' Álvaro de Campos

'The spirit of collective endeavour is alive and vibrant in the Far South Collective. I wish them all good fortune in their search for Gerardo Fischer' Ramón Benítez